"I want you..."

"Words I've be... quipped, smilin... blue-eyed brunette standing before his desk. He had no idea who she was, but he certainly intended to find out. The fact that she had just said she wanted him sounded promising.

"Well, you can continue waiting," she informed him coldly, "because I didn't mean them that way."

Luke leaned back in his chair. His eyes slowly passed over her, taking careful measure of every attractive inch. No doubt about it. She was the best looking woman he had seen in a long time. The annoyed expression on her face just made her that much more of a challenge as far as he was concerned.

"And just what way did you mean them?" he asked her. His smile only grew wider.

* * *

Be sure to check out the next books in this exciting miniseries:

Cavanaugh Justice—Where Aurora's finest are always in action

* * *

If you're on Twitter, tell us what you think of Harlequin Romantic Suspense! #harlequinromsuspense

Dear Reader,

Every time I start one of these books, I never know if I can pull it off. All I can do is pray that I will muddle my way through to finding that even balance of two sparring protagonists set against a backdrop of solving a mystery. I always worry that the mystery might not be interesting enough, or that the main characters won't seem real and will fall flat right before your eyes. Each and every story is important to me because I have an obligation to you, dear reader. You've plunked your money down (or run your credit card through the card reader) and in exchange you deserve to be entertained. To be pulled out of your world and into the one you're holding in your hand. My obligation to you is to make you laugh a little and, hopefully, to intrigue you as we both go on this journey together.

In the thirty-fifth Cavanaugh Justice series book, Detective Lukkas Cavanaugh O'Bannon of the Homicide Department is out to catch a serial killer who preys on lonely young women. Detective Francesca DeMarco of the Major Crimes Division, on the other hand, just wants to catch the man who murdered her cousin. Forming a wary alliance, they wind up catching more than the killer. Come along on their journey and see how they do it—and hopefully you'll be entertained in the bargain.

As always, I thank you for taking the time to read one of my stories, and from the bottom of my heart, I wish you someone to love who loves you back.

All the best,

Marie

CAVANAUGH ENCOUNTER

Marie Ferrarella

HARLEQUIN® ROMANTIC SUSPENSE

Recycling programs
for this product may
not exist in your area.

ISBN-13: 978-0-373-40222-9

Cavanaugh Encounter

Copyright © 2017 by Marie Rydzynski-Ferrarella

Printed in U.S.A.

www.Harlequin.com

USA TODAY bestselling and RITA® Award–winning author **Marie Ferrarella** has written more than two hundred and fifty books for Harlequin, some under the name Marie Nicole. Her romances are beloved by fans worldwide. Visit her website, marieferrarella.com.

Books by Marie Ferrarella

Harlequin Romantic Suspense

Cavanaugh Justice

Mission: Cavanaugh Baby
Cavanaugh on Duty
A Widow's Guilty Secret
Cavanaugh's Surrender
Cavanaugh Rules
Cavanaugh's Bodyguard
Cavanaugh Fortune
How to Seduce a Cavanaugh
Cavanaugh or Death
Cavanaugh Cold Case
Cavanaugh in the Rough
Cavanaugh on Call
Cavanaugh Encounter

The Coltons of Shadow Creek

Colton Undercover

Coltons of Texas

Colton Copycat Killer
The Pregnant Colton Bride

Coltons of Oklahoma

Second Chance Colton

Visit the Author Profile page at Harlequin.com for more titles.

To
The memory of
My Mother,
Who got me hooked on Agatha Christie,
And always said that there was nothing
She liked better
Than a good, clean murder.
This one's for you, Mama.

Prologue

"Oh, thank goodness you're here. I didn't know who else to call."

Twenty-five-year-old Amanda Culpepper was shaking as she threw open the front door of the apartment she shared with her roommate. The same roommate who was facedown and sprawled out on the living room floor. The young woman appeared to be unconscious and was totally unresponsive.

Detective Francesca DeMarco hardly spared the tall blonde by the door more than a quick glance. Her attention was entirely focused on Kristin Andrews, the young woman on the floor with the syringe in her arm.

Her cousin.

Years ago, she would have anticipated this call.

But not now. Not when Kristin had been clean for so long. This didn't make any sense to her.

"How long has she been like this?" Frankie asked her cousin's roommate. Amanda was hovering nervously behind her.

"I don't know," Amanda cried breathlessly, wringing her hands. "I was away for three days with my boyfriend. I just walked in the door and found her like this." Amanda was struggling not to break down in tears. "I tried to rouse her, but when Kris wouldn't wake up, I called you immediately." Amanda was shifting from foot to foot, as if unable to put any weight down. "Kris is going to be all right, right?" she asked, growing more and more distraught and agitated.

Frankie hardly heard the other woman. She was looking for Kris's pulse. She pressed her fingers against the side of her cousin's neck, then on her wrist. Unable to find a pulse, she put her head against Kristin's chest, praying she would detect at least a faint heartbeat.

There was none.

Adrenaline surging through her body, Frankie began applying CPR. "Call 911," she ordered Amanda.

Amanda looked confused. "But you *are* 911," the young woman protested.

"But I can't pull a damn ambulance out of my pocket," Frankie snapped. She was silently counting off numbers in her head as she applied compressions to Kristin's chest. Despite her efforts, her cousin still wasn't coming around. "Call 911 and tell them to send an ambulance to this address!" she ordered. "Now!"

Snapping to attention, Amanda hurried to make the call.

"C'mon, Kris, open your eyes!" Frankie begged as she continued pushing against her cousin's chest. "Do it for me. Please!"

All sorts of thoughts charged in and out of her head. The last words she and Kris had exchanged. The time she had bullied her cousin into rehab. Teaching her cousin how to ride a bike. All that and more whisked through her brain with the speed of a bullet, all while she worked over her cousin's prone body.

She was still pushing down on Kristin's chest when the high-pitched whining sound of an approaching siren registered.

The ambulance was here!

Frankie realized that there were tears in her eyes. Maybe the paramedic would be able to save Kris.

Would be able to bring her around.

Drained and wired at the same time, Frankie moved out of the way as the paramedics took over for her. The taller of the two attendants did compressions.

After several moments, he turned to look at her.

Frankie knew why he had stopped the compressions and why her cousin wasn't being placed on the gurney in order to be taken to the ambulance.

Frankie could feel her heart constricting. There wasn't going to be an ambulance ride to the hospital. "She's gone, isn't she?" Frankie asked in a low, hoarse voice.

"Yes." The attendant was kind. "You're going to need to get the coroner out here," he told her. Taking out his cellphone, the attendant offered, "I can call him for you."

Frankie put up her hand to stop the man from placing the call. "That's all right. I'm a detective with the Aurora Police Department. I'll call the coroner and tell him it's a homicide," she told him.

"Homicide?" the second attendant echoed. "This looks like a drug overdose to me," the man said. He pointed over to the side. The syringe had come out and was lying near the body.

This just wasn't right, Frankie thought. Yes, Kristin had had a drug problem, but that was years ago. She'd sustained an injury, dislocating her shoulder while playing soccer in high school. Prescription drugs had helped her put up with the shooting pain. Gradually that had led to her becoming dependent on other ways to numb the misery, but all that had been years ago. Kristin had dealt with her demons and finally vanquished them.

It hadn't been easy for her, but she did it.

Frankie refused to believe that after fighting her way back to the point where she could finally enjoy a normal lifestyle, Kristin would have just thrown it all away for a weekend binge.

"No," Frankie said fiercely, addressing the attendant. "This was *not* a drug overdose, accidental or otherwise. It was staged to look that way. This is a homicide," she declared in no uncertain terms, her sweeping gaze taking in the attendants and her cousin's sobbing roommate. The way the syringe was positioned would have indicated that Kristin had used her right hand. Kristin was left-handed. "And I intend to prove it."

Even to her own ears, it sounded more like a vow than a statement.

And maybe it was, but she still intended to do it.

Chapter 1

"I want you, O'Bannon."

Lukkas Cavanaugh O'Bannon looked up from the report on his desk. It was an autopsy, and it made for grim reading. It was the information on the latest victim who had been discovered only a day ago. A young kindergarten teacher was found dead by her mother in the house they shared.

The autopsy was one of six and only confirmed Luke's suspicions. Someone was out there, preying on young, intelligent professional women, capitalizing on their apparent loneliness and cutting their lives short before they ever had a chance to really experience life to the fullest.

It was only ten o'clock in the morning, but Luke already felt as if he could use a break. He just hadn't thought that his break would materialize in such a shapely form.

"Words I've been waiting a lifetime to hear," he quipped, smiling at the petite blue-eyed brunette standing before his desk. He had no idea who she was, but he certainly intended to find out. The fact that she had just said she wanted him certainly sounded promising.

"Well, you can continue waiting," she informed him coldly, "because I didn't mean them that way." She was going to have to learn to pick her words better, Frankie admonished herself. It was just that right now, she was extremely agitated and she felt as if she was walking across a tightrope.

One misstep on her part and she wasn't going to be allowed to work this case.

O'Bannon was flashing a wide, brilliant grin aimed right at her, and she did her best to ignore it.

Detective Lukkas Cavanaugh O'Bannon had a reputation for being a ladies' man. The reputation reached all corners of the police department, even Major Crimes, which was where she worked. The problem was that O'Bannon had the looks and the charm to back up his bravado.

But none of that mattered to her. What did matter was that O'Bannon was also a damn good detective. And, most important of all, he was lead detective on a case that involved homicides that were eerily similar to her cousin's.

"And just what way did you mean them?" he asked her. His smile only grew wider.

Luke leaned back in his chair and his eyes slowly passed over her, taking careful measure of every attractive inch. No doubt about it. She was the best-looking woman he had seen in a long time. The annoyed expression on her face just made her that much more of a challenge as far as he was concerned.

"Word has it that you're working on a case that might involve a serial killer killing young, dark-haired women." Frankie kept her voice neutral, professional. She couldn't afford to have O'Bannon suspect just how important this case was to her.

Luke shrugged. "You know how rumors fly around the precinct..."

Although his voice trailed off, his eyes never left her face. It wasn't difficult to see that this case was important to her. Why? She didn't remind him of a reporter, searching for an in. And she definitely wasn't part of Sean Cavanaugh's CSI unit. He knew every face in his uncle's department, both the day and the night shift.

"Don't toy with me, O'Bannon."

The corners of his mouth curved deeper as he leaned slightly forward. "Is that a dare?"

This was getting her absolutely nowhere and it was just wasting time. Given the man's reputation, she should have known better than to approach O'Bannon directly with anything.

"Maybe I'd be better off going to Lt. Handel with this," Frankie said, already turning on her heel. Handel's office was in the back.

"Wait," Luke called after her.

Frankie spared the detective a cold glance over her shoulder. "Why?"

"Well, for one thing, you'll wind up talking to

yourself," he pointed out. "The lieutenant's not in his office."

Was he playing her? She was tempted to look in the general direction of the lieutenant's glass-paneled office, but she refrained. For now, she gave O'Bannon the benefit of the doubt. She actually did need the man on her side, which meant that she had to build up some sort of rapport.

"Where is he?" she asked him, trying to control her impatience.

"At a meeting with the new chief of police," Luke replied, referring to his cousin, Shaw Cavanaugh, who had recently assumed the position after the previous chief had suffered a heart attack in his sleep and died. "No telling when he'll be back." He watched the woman when she reluctantly turned around again to face him. "So you might as well finish filling me in on why you're asking questions about my case."

"Because I think I might have…stumbled across another victim," Frankie said.

She could see that she had gotten O'Bannon's attention. His whole countenance grew more alert.

"And by 'stumbled across,' you mean…?" He waited for her to fill in the blank.

Frankie knew she needed to keep this as close to the truth as possible. It was a trick she had learned a long time ago. The closer to the truth something was, the easier it was to keep track of the things she said about it.

Ordinarily, she wouldn't have felt the need to play games like this. However, if it became known that she was Kristin's cousin, then it went without saying that she wouldn't be allowed to work on the case.

And she intended to work the case, no matter what. Even if it wound up costing her her job. With luck, it wouldn't come to that.

Frankie framed her answer carefully. O'Bannon's reputation as a ladies' man wasn't the only reputation he had. The man was sharp. "The victim's roommate called me when she found the body."

"And why would she do that?" he asked, his voice low, probing.

Frankie took a small, unobtrusive breath. "Because I was the first one she thought of when she came home to find the victim on the floor, unresponsive. I met her in an adult education course," she threw in, hoping that would answer any stray questions O'Bannon might have about her association with the roommate.

It didn't.

"What kind of a course?" he asked, appearing to be mildly interested.

"A boring one," Frankie answered crisply. "Can we please get on with this?" she pressed.

"All right," he obliged. "What makes you think this dead woman you 'stumbled across,'" he said, using her own words, "is one of my serial killer's victims? Was she stabbed? Or shot at close range?" Luke fired the questions at her in staccato fashion.

Frankie's eyes narrowed. "Your serial killer's victims are all women in their twenties, not men. And your serial killer doesn't stab or shoot his victims," she concluded.

Luke leaned back in his chair, never taking his

eyes off her. "I'm impressed. You've done your homework on me."

"Correction," she retorted. "I've done my homework on your case. And since I think the woman I found is another one of your killer's victims, I thought we could work together to find this piece of filth before he kills anyone else."

"So you *are* with the police department." Until this moment, he hadn't been sure about that.

"Major Crimes," she informed him.

"And why would Major Crimes be interested in having one of their own work with me on this case?" he asked.

"Turns out that Debra Evans, one of the victims, is the niece of one of the state's senators," she replied.

"You really have done your homework on this case," he said, duly impressed. "Well, I have no objections to you throwing your lot in with mine, but just to play by the rules, we're going to have to clear it with Lt. Handel when he gets back."

From what she'd learned, O'Bannon wasn't one who really cared about playing by the rules unless it suited him. But she wasn't about to say that and risk getting on the man's bad side. She really needed to work this case. She owed it to Kristin.

"I assumed as much," Frankie replied.

He flashed another broad grin at her. "That's what I like. Someone who's on their toes. I take it that you have the victim's name."

"Kristin Andrews," she replied. "She is—was—" Frankie corrected herself, doing her best not to let O'Bannon see that having to refer to her cousin in the past tense really bothered her "—twenty-five and she was a nurse working at Aurora General."

"You *are* thorough," Luke said. He was beginning to see past her good looks and was taking stock of her as a detective. "Any theory about her cause of death?" he asked, curious to see if there were similarities to his killer's victims and the one that this knockout on two shapely legs was bringing him.

"There was a syringe in her arm," Frankie replied, every word burning on her tongue.

"So you think it was a drug overdose," Luke concluded.

"No, I think it was made to *look* like a drug overdose," Frankie replied tersely, correcting him.

"And you know this how?" he asked.

He was leaning back in his chair again, studying the brunette with the piled-up, impossibly sexy hair that seemed to be falling every which way and yet somehow remained in place. Whenever possible, Luke was always open to accommodating pretty women, but not at the expense of his job. That always came first, as did the victims he had sworn an oath to do right by.

"Her roommate told me that Kristin, the victim, had had a painkiller problem dating years back to a knee injury she'd sustained in high school, playing soccer." Frankie answered him slowly, careful not to allow her emotions to get the better of her. She needed to lay this out for him carefully so that she didn't trip herself up and allow her actual involvement in the case to slip out. "Her roommate also assured me that Kristin had kicked that habit years ago and hadn't taken any drugs since then. Kris had been clean for years," Frankie emphasized.

The detective she was talking to nodded slowly and appeared to be listening. Frankie couldn't escape the feeling that he was examining every single word that was coming out of her mouth—as well as studying her as if she were a slide mounted under a microscope.

"When did all this happen?" he finally asked, after a prolonged pause that admittedly made her uneasy.

He didn't believe her, Frankie thought. Determined, she pushed on. "The roommate came back from a three-day weekend and found the victim, unresponsive, on the living room floor this morning. After trying to revive her for several minutes, the roommate began to panic, at which time she called me."

Frankie noted the skeptical expression on O'Bannon's face. "If you're friends with this woman," he asked, "why do you keep calling her *the roommate*?"

Frankie never missed a beat. "I'm just trying to keep the details simple for you. And, for the record, we're not friends." She corrected the detective. "We're acquaintances. I already told you that."

Luke pretended to glance down at his notes. "So you did." He raised his eyes to meet her magnetic blue ones. "Where's the body now?"

The body.

It was hard for her to think of Kristin that way. She had always been so full of life, so ready to always laugh. Kris had a very infectious laugh that left no one untouched.

"Detective?" Luke prodded when he thought the woman had drifted off.

Frankie roused herself and flushed for the momentary lapse on her part. "Sorry. I called the ME. He told me he'd be doing her autopsy right away, which, with any luck, means today."

"You know the ME?" Luke asked her, curious.

"Some of them," she answered, wondering if he was trying to trip her up. The department had three medical examiners, one of whom they tended to share with several of the other, smaller cities in the county.

"Well, you've covered all the bases," Luke told her. "Tell you what, pending the lieutenant's approval of all this, we'll call your find victim number seven."

Frankie frowned. "She has a name," she told O'Bannon stiffly.

"They all have names," he replied mildly. "What they no longer have are lives. Those were stolen from them and it's up to us to make that up to them by catching the bastard who's responsible for cutting those lives short."

She couldn't make up her mind whether he was being a crusader or a wiseguy. Either way, she nodded and quietly told him, "Sounds good to me."

"Oh, there's just one more thing," Luke said as she began to walk out of the squad room. She had yet to clear this temporary move with her own lieutenant, wanting to make sure that she could convince O'Bannon to take on this case first.

Frankie braced herself and slowly turned back to face him. Deep in her soul, she felt she was going to regret coming to this man. She knew all about him. Lukkas Cavanaugh O'Bannon was oil and she was water and there was no way that they were ever going to find a way to mix.

But for Kristin's sake, she would do her damnedest to try to work with this man until such time as the scum who was robbing all these young women of their lives could be found and put down.

Taking a deep breath, Frankie kept her expression unreadable as she said, "Yes?"

Luke's lethal smile unfurled slowly. He knew the kind of effect it had on women. This one, though, seemed to be immune to it. She would definitely be a challenge, he thought. The idea spurred him on. "You didn't tell me your name."

Ignoring the smile that had been the undoing of more than a score of women—or so the legend went—Frankie kept her eyes on his. "I thought you knew everything," she said crisply.

"Close," Luke agreed, not rising to the bait she'd cast. "But in this case, close isn't good enough. So, what is it?" he asked. "Your name," Luke prodded when the brunette with the attitude didn't volunteer the information immediately. "Unless you want me to refer to you as 'Hey You' while we're working together," he said, giving her a less than desirable option.

If she had her way, Frankie wouldn't have wanted O'Bannon to refer to her as anything at all, but that wasn't being reasonable. The man was smug and annoying from the get-go, but at bottom, she knew that her prickly attitude was because she was still devastated over her cousin's death. Not only had she been close to Kristin, but Kristin was also the last family that she had. With her cousin murdered, she had no one left. Both her parents were gone, as were Kristin's.

She was alone.

Stop it, damn it. Stop feeling sorry for yourself. That isn't going to bring Kris back and it sure as hell isn't going to help you solve her murder. Get a grip.

She saw that O'Bannon was still waiting for an answer. If they were going to work together, she had to attempt to be civil to the detective—no matter how annoying she found him.

"My name is Detective Francesca DeMarco," Frankie informed him. "And, as I told you, I'm from Major Crimes."

The major crime here, Luke thought, was that he had never noticed her before. The building wasn't *that* big. He made up his mind to make up for lost time when the opportunity arose.

"The detective part was a given," he acknowledged. "Francesca, huh?" Luke rolled the name over on his tongue as if he was tasting the first slice of a rich, homemade chocolate cream pie—his favorite. "Pretty," he commented, and she couldn't tell if he was referring to her name—or, given his reputation, to her. "You don't seem like a Francesca."

Her eyes narrowed. "What is that supposed to mean?" she demanded.

"Just an observation," he responded mildly. "*Francesca* belongs to a lady in some ivory tower. You look more like you're a go-getter. A Frannie or a Fran or—"

She winced at both names, names she'd been taunted with as a child.

"Frankie," she told him, unwilling to listen to a further litany of possible nicknames he could come up with carving up her formal name. "People call me Frankie."

The moment she said it, bells went off in his head. He'd heard some of the detectives referring to a Frankie—except that he'd thought the name belonged to one of the guys. This, he thought, regarding her again, was *not* one of the guys.

"That wouldn't have been my third guess," Luke admitted glibly, and then he shrugged, "But if you like that name—"

"I like it better than Fran or Frannie," she informed him coolly.

Luke nodded. The first rule of working with another detective, as far as he was concerned, was getting along with them, and if that meant calling an out-and-out knockout by the unlikely name of Frankie, then so be it. He wasn't about to argue the point and create tension. It wasn't worth it.

"You're right. You don't look like a Frannie. Okay, Frankie it is," he told her agreeably, with a smile that definitely lit up his entire chiseled face.

Looking at him, Frankie experienced a sinking sensation in the pit of her stomach. She couldn't help thinking that by asking to work on this case with O'Bannon, she had just voluntarily sold her soul to the devil.

Chapter 2

"Looks like you get to talk to the head guy himself after all," Luke said to her the next moment.

Frankie looked at him, confused and not sure where he was going with this. "I thought you were the head guy."

A tall, imposing man with straight blue-black hair gave the chair he was sitting in a swift push with his boot, sending it closer to Luke's desk. Rick White Hawk, Luke's partner, had been listening to the exchange in silence for several minutes now.

"Don't flatter him. His head's already too big to fit into the elevator car when it's crowded," he told the detective from the Major Crimes division.

Luke ignored his partner's crack. "I was just telling Major Crimes here that the lieutenant walked in through the door," he pointed out.

Frankie turned to see the man O'Bannon was referring to. Lt. Mike Handel, a tall, gaunt-looking man with a perpetual two days' growth of beard was just entering the squad room. Because Frankie was five-one, everyone had a tendency to look tall to her.

Handel, a twenty-one-year veteran of the Aurora Police Department, looked neither to the left nor to the right as he crossed the room. He appeared focused on reaching his office, preferably without being engaged in conversation.

His scowl was meant to put people off and to guarantee swift passage across the room. To a great extent, it worked. But his ploy failed as O'Bannon rose to his feet.

"Lieutenant," O'Bannon called out. "You got a minute?"

"No," Handel answered curtly as he continued crossing to his office.

Not one to be brushed off, Luke told him, "You might want to hear this."

Handel's scowl looked as if it went clear down to the bone. He stopped, retraced the last five steps and glared at Luke as he retorted, "Fine," then barked, "What?"

Luke gestured toward the rather petite detective who had approached him about another victim. "This is Detective DeMarco from Major Crimes," he told his lieutenant by way of an introduction.

Handel bobbed his head in quick, dismissive acknowledgement. The scowl never lifted. "And?" he asked impatiently.

O'Bannon played out the line. "And she's brought us something."

Handel still seemed annoyed at being delayed. He glanced impatiently toward his office. "Like what?" he demanded. "Homemade cookies she baked?" Then, sparing the young woman under discussion a quick, appraising glance, he told her, "No offense meant."

Frankie highly doubted that, but she needed to be part of this investigation, so, against her will she replied, "None taken. And I'm not bringing cookies, I'm bringing you another homicide."

If possible, Handel's scowl deepened, all but etched into his bones. "Just what I needed." He glared at the woman. "Why is Major Crimes bringing me another homicide?"

"They're not," Frankie corrected. "I am. I believe that this victim was murdered by your serial killer."

Handel looked at O'Bannon, seeking a contradiction. "Is this true?"

"I haven't had a chance to check it out yet," Luke answered, "but on the surface, it sounds like it might be one of his."

"Then what are you waiting for?" Handel asked. "Go! Check it out. And then get back to me."

"You got it," Luke said. He pulled his jacket off the back of his chair and shrugged into it. "White Hawk, you're with me," he said to the imposing man he'd been partnered with for the last three years.

Frankie blinked. It felt as if everything was suddenly whirling around her and she was being left behind. That wasn't why she had come to them with the case, and if O'Bannon and his superior thought that, then they were sadly mistaken. She had no intention of being left behind.

"Lieutenant," she called out to the man's back as he was walking away. "There's one more thing."

Exasperation etched lines into Handel's sallow complexion as he turned to her. "What?" He all but bit off the question.

"I come with the case," she informed him in a no-nonsense voice.

It was obvious by the look on Handel's face that this was not something he had expected to hear. He wasn't accustomed to being given conditions. "How's that, again?"

Out of the corner of her eye, she saw that O'Bannon and his partner had stopped moving and were listening, as well. And they appeared to be amused.

They were probably curious to see if Handel was going to have her for lunch was her guess.

Not likely.

"Major Crimes wants me to follow through on this. I was the first responder on the scene," she told the scowling lieutenant.

Frankie braced herself for an argument and she was ready to hold her own if it came to that. Instead, Handel waved her on her way.

"Sure, fine. The more the merrier. Knock yourself out," he told the woman invading his squad room. "Whatever gets this case off my plate."

Moving again and picking up his pace, Handel hurried across the now-short distance to his office. He quickly closed the door before anyone else had a chance to further annoy him.

"Nicely done," Luke commented as he walked over to her side. "You do realize that we have to take

you with us because you're the one who knows where
the body was found, right?" he asked her, clearly
amused.

They were walking now. Frankie hurried to keep
up as they entered the hallway. She had gotten so
caught up in trying to convince the lieutenant to
allow her to take part in the case, she'd forgotten
about that small, practical matter.

"I know that," she lied, her mind working fast.
"But I thought Handel would appreciate being asked
for permission."

A glimmer of appreciation entered Luke's green
eyes. "So I take it that you're not a newbie," he said
with an approving nod.

"No, I'm not." Frankie answered him in no uncertain terms, insulted by the mere suggestion that she
could be seen as a novice.

The elevator arrived and all three of them got in.
They had the car to themselves. White Hawk took
the opportunity to lean forward and whisper to her,
"Don't mind O'Bannon. He likes getting under people's skin, but he's not nearly as bad as he pretends
to come off." Extending his hand to her, he went on
to introduce himself. "Rick White Hawk."

"Nice to meet you, Detective White Hawk." She
shook his hand. "I'm—"

"Frankie DeMarco, yes, I heard," White Hawk
said, smiling at her.

"Okay, now that we're all acquainted, let's get
back to the business at hand—checking out the crime
scene and catching a serial killer—unless anyone has
some objections," Luke prodded just as they reached
the ground floor.

"You're the lead detective," White Hawk told him agreeably.

Frankie suppressed the sigh that seemed to automatically rise to her lips. For the most part, she worked cases in Major Crimes on her own.

"What he said," she murmured as agreeably as she could.

When they walked out of the rear of the building and headed for the parking lot, Frankie began to go in a different direction than the other two detectives.

Looking over his shoulder, Luke called to her, "Hey, DeMarco, where are you going?"

She assumed that the answer to that was self-explanatory. "To get my car."

"Since we're all going to the same place, why don't we all go there in one car?" O'Bannon suggested.

She couldn't shake the feeling that he was speaking to her as if he was addressing a child. Doing her best not to lose her temper, she said, "Okay, we'll use my car since I'm the one who knows where we're going."

Luke gave this temporary addition to his team a tolerant look. "I'm assuming this isn't some secret location where we'll have to be blindfolded before we can go there."

"Of course not."

"Good," Luke declared. "Then we'll go in my car and you can give me directions," he told her. "You do know how to give directions, right, DeMarco?"

Frankie gave the man a withering look. She might have to mind her Ps and Qs while talking to him, but he had no control over the thoughts going through her head.

"Yes. I'm giving you some right now," she told O'Bannon.

White Hawk nearly choked, trying not to laugh out loud.

"Good thing I'm not a mind reader," he responded. Hitting a button that opened all four of the car doors, he said, "Okay, let's go."

Frankie got in on the passenger side. "The crime scene investigators have already been there," she told him.

Luke opened the driver's side door and got in. "I kind of figured that out when you said that your victim was in autopsy," he told her. "But I like looking around the crime scene for myself. Humor me," he added.

"You're the lead," she replied tersely, just before giving him the address where her cousin's body had been found.

Luke heard the less-than-happy note in her voice and assumed it referred to the fact that he had taken over the case.

"Any time you want to jump off the merry-go-round, go right ahead. You're more than welcome to do so," he told her. He glanced in his rearview mirror to see if White Hawk had gotten in and buckled up yet.

"Understood," she told O'Bannon in the same tone of voice.

Having secured his seatbelt, White Hawk took a moment to lean forward in his seat. "Don't worry. He'll grow on you," he promised the sexy detective.

"Maybe that's why I'm worried," she responded, then explained, "so does fungus."

"Luckily, they've got medications for that," O'Bannon told her as he adjusted his side mirrors before putting his key in the ignition.

Shifting ever so slightly in her seat, Frankie looked at the lead detective pointedly and said, "I sincerely hope so."

White Hawk sighed quietly. It was obvious that he felt called upon to act as a referee in this verbal sparring match. He spoke up, trying to distract the new member of the team by asking her a simple question.

"How did you happen to catch this case? I missed that part."

Frankie knew the other detective was just asking her that in order to try to keep the peace. But she found him rather easygoing and likeable, so she answered his question.

"I know the woman who was the victim's roommate, Amanda Culpepper." She recited the story that she had memorized for O'Bannon's benefit—and in order to be allowed to work this case. "When Amanda found Kristin unconscious on the floor and couldn't revive her, she panicked and called me."

"Found her how?" White Hawk asked. "Did she wake up in the morning and walk in to find the victim just lying there like that?"

"No, Amanda had gone away for the weekend. She told me that she had gone to Las Vegas with her boyfriend and spent three full days there."

As Frankie recited the details for what felt like the umpteenth time, she could literally *feel* O'Bannon listening to her every word despite the fact that she had already told him all of this. She had a feeling that the lead detective was paying such close attention to what she was saying because he expected her to trip herself up and confuse the details.

Frankie couldn't help wondering if she had suddenly become a suspect by bringing her cousin's murder to the department's fair-haired boy. She found herself wishing that the detective in the backseat was the lead on this multiple murder case instead of O'Bannon.

White Hawk didn't make her feel uneasy. O'Bannon did. She felt as if, despite his laidback manner, O'Bannon was scrutinizing every word out of her mouth and comparing them to every other word she'd already said.

"When did this happen?" White Hawk asked.

"I got the call early this morning."

"So the crime scene's not that fresh," O'Bannon said, whether for her benefit or for his partner's, she wasn't sure. In either case, she did her best to take the remark in stride and not view it as a criticism that she'd been remiss in not bringing the matter to Homicide's attention immediately.

It left her wondering if O'Bannon actually wanted the case and had just been yanking her chain earlier about her reasons for bringing the case to him.

"It was fresh when the CSI Unit arrived to go over it a couple of hours ago," she replied coldly.

"We'll talk to them after we have a look around," O'Bannon said, and it was clear to Frankie that he was addressing his partner and not her.

Even so, she was determined to work with this man. It was the only way she would find Kristin's killer.

Frankie nodded in response to what he had just said and murmured, "Fine."

"Glad we have your permission," Luke replied.

"Turn right at the corner," she directed coldly.

He spared her a glance before doing as she had prompted. Luke was deliberately trying to rattle her, to get her to squirm and lose her cool. It was his way of seeing just what she was made of and who he was actually dealing with.

Had Francesca DeMarco been just another beautiful woman who crossed his path, his approach to her would have been entirely different. But he wasn't trying to date her—that was on the back burner for now—he was attempting to find out just what sort of a person was trying to be part of his team, no matter how temporarily.

The team was only as good as its weakest link, and he needed to evaluate just what kind of detective DeMarco was.

He was fairly sure he could ascertain this from her record on the force. There were reports on file that could be accessed, if not by him, then by his cousin, Valri, who worked in the police department's computer lab.

A tour of social media would get him additional personal information.

He doubted if DeMarco would believe him if he told her, but he was actually rooting for her.

Still, he had to be sure before he let her sign on for this. If she messed up the investigation for whatever reason, that would be on him, and his lieutenant would be the first one to say it, despite Handel's blasé attitude about DeMarco's joining the investigation.

"Where's this roommate staying?" Luke asked out of the blue.

She knew why he was asking. Amanda couldn't stay in her apartment until the yellow tape went down. "She's crashing on a friend's couch until the crime scene's been cleared."

"Yours?" Luke asked bluntly.

"Someone else's," she answered, bracing herself for a barrage of questions as to why she wasn't taking in the victim's roommate. She decided to jump ahead of him and answer the main question before it was asked. "Wouldn't seem right if I had her staying at my place while I'm investigating her roommate's murder. That would look like a conflict of interest."

Silently he congratulated her for being one step ahead of this pantomime even as he asked, "Do you always play by the rules?"

Her eyes met his as she quietly told him, "That's all we've got, are the rules."

A hint of a smile curved his lips. "Huh. You didn't answer my question, DeMarco."

"Why are you badgering her, O'Bannon?" White Hawk asked his partner. "She's on our team, remember?" he pointed out.

Rick White Hawk smiled his support at the petite brunette when she turned around in her seat to look at him.

Frankie returned his smile.

"Yeah, so she is," was all Luke said in response to his partner's observation.

He didn't trust her, Frankie thought, looking at O'Bannon.

Well, she didn't need O'Bannon to trust her. She

just needed him to work with her and help her find her cousin's killer. After that, they never had to see each other again.

As a matter of fact, she preferred it that way.

Chapter 3

The yellow crime tape was still fastened across the door of the apartment where Kristin's body had been found. Frankie silently drew in a breath as she watched O'Bannon pull aside the tape that announced to the world at large that a crime had taken place here and that no headway had been made because the investigation was obviously still ongoing.

O'Bannon unlocked the door and pushed it open, then entered the apartment. White Hawk was right behind him, but to Frankie's surprise, the tall detective stepped back and instead waved her in ahead of him.

"Ladies first," White Hawk said.

A small hint of a smile fleetingly graced her lips as Frankie murmured, "Thank you," just before walking into the apartment.

It felt as if she was moving in slow motion along the bottom of a lake filled with Jell-O. She'd been to her share of homicides when she'd worked as a detective in Los Angeles before transferring to Aurora, but everything seemed eerie and unreal to her within the apartment.

Doing her best to appear unaffected, Frankie slanted a glance toward the living room floor where she'd last seen her cousin lying facedown right in front of the entrance at the rear of the apartment.

Damn it, snap out of it and get a grip on yourself. You're a detective working a case, not a cousin mourning the loss of the last of her family.

"Something wrong?" Luke asked her, his deep voice disrupting her thoughts.

Rousing herself, she shook off her mood and made eye contact with O'Bannon. She would have to watch herself around him.

"No, just reviewing the crime scene, that's all," she answered.

He'd been watching her face since they had walked in. Something was off, Luke thought. "Something look out of place to you?" Luke questioned.

Yes. Kris shouldn't have been killed, here or anywhere else.

"No," Frankie said out loud. "Everything is just the way I saw it when the EMTs arrived to try to revive Kristin."

An alert look came into his eyes. "You said she was dead."

"She was, but Amanda called 911 and requested an ambulance before I was sure that Kristin was already dead," she told him. Why was he trying to trip her up? "The ME was called in right after that."

"And who called for the CSI unit?" Luke asked.

Frankie couldn't shake the feeling that she was being grilled, but she knew it was important to keep her cool, answering his questions. There was nothing to be gained by losing her temper and telling O'Bannon to back off. "I did," she told him.

"And you remained here while they canvassed the apartment." It was more of a statement on his part than a question.

"Yes."

Luke nodded his head. All the while his eyes swept over the immediate area. "Very thorough of you."

Despite everything, Frankie could feel her temper flaring. She struggled to keep it in check.

"It's not my first rodeo, O'Bannon. You needn't patronize me," she told him.

"Sorry," he told her, raising his hands. "I wasn't aware that I was doing that."

"Yes, you were." Her eyes met his. If she was going to be tossed out, she might as well speak her mind and be dismissed for a reason. "I work in Major Crimes, not the neighborhood sandbox," she told him. "I don't deserve to be talked down to like some kind of wet-behind-the ears novice."

She heard White Hawk laugh, something she assumed would further anger O'Bannon.

"She's got a point, O'Bannon," he told his partner when Luke shot him a reproving glance for laughing at the woman's retort.

Rather than contest the words, or give them both

a piece of his mind the way that Frankie expected, O'Bannon merely shrugged.

"Sorry," he said to her. "I didn't mean to insult you. Just trying to be thorough on my end." He paused for a moment, then asked her, "Do you know which is the victim's room?"

"The second one right off the bathroom. Your uncle's unit has already gone over the entire apartment," she pointed out again. Not to mention that she had, as well. Exactly what did he hope to find?

"I know," Luke replied. "But it never hurts to have another set of eyes going over the apartment—or, in this case, a fourth set," he said, recalling that his uncle usually took at least two other members of the unit with him to go over any crime scene he was investigating. Luke turned his attention toward his partner. "Why don't you look around and see if you notice anything out of place. Anything that might help us with the case," he emphasized.

"What do you want me to do?" she asked O'Bannon when he didn't give her any instructions.

"The same," he answered. "Unless you'd rather sit in the car," he added. Seeing the insulted look Frankie shot him, he dug into his pocket and took out a set of rubber gloves. He held them out to her. "Here."

"I have my own, thanks," she replied, taking a set of clear plastic gloves from the inside pocket of her jacket.

Luke smiled. "Brownie points for the new kid on the block," he said with approval. "Okay, get busy, people. We've still got another crime scene waiting for us after we deal with this one."

"Another crime scene?" Frankie questioned.

"When you came in this morning, we'd just caught another murder. Body's with the medical examiner," he said matter-of-factly. "Your victim's apartment was on our way so I decided to stop here first."

This was staggering. "How many victims did you say that this guy has killed?" she asked.

"Seven," Luke answered. "And you're jumping to conclusions that the killer is a man."

She looked at O'Bannon, puzzled. "Then the serial killer's not a man?"

"Most likely it is. But what I'm saying is that, in this modern age, nothing's a given anymore," Luke informed her. "There was a time when no one believed that a woman could be capable of doing something so heinous as killing one person, much less enough people to qualify being regarded as a serial killer.

"But the times, they are a-changing and there have been a number of documented female serial killers. It doesn't happen very often—but it *does* happen. So, bottom line, rule out no one because of their gender," he advised. "Keep an open mind at all times."

"Sorry, just a figure of speech," Frankie told the lead detective.

Luke nodded, accepting her explanation. "I'll consider this as part of your learning curve," he replied. He began to head toward the victim's bedroom only to realize that Frankie was going in the same direction. "Why don't you take a look around your friend's bedroom? Sorry," he caught himself before she could correct him. "I mean your acquaintance's bedroom. I got the victim's bedroom," he said pointedly. Turning to the other member of the team, he said, "White Hawk, you've got everything else."

White Hawk sighed. "I figured as much," the tall detective acknowledged.

"Then let's get to it," Luke instructed, walking into the victim's bedroom.

It was small, compact and orderly. The victim had been a great deal neater than he was, Luke noted, thinking of his own living quarters.

He reviewed everything methodically. If Kristin Andrews had done any entertaining in this bedroom the night she was killed, there didn't seem to be any evidence of that fact at first glance.

But if she had been murdered by the serial killer he was currently hunting down, Luke had already learned that the man was methodical, not sloppy.

If it was a man, he added silently with a slight ironic smile.

En route here, Luke had had his uncle send him a list of things that the CSI unit had taken from the apartment to examine for possible clues as to why Kristen been chosen by the killer. Scrolling through that list now on his smartphone, he found no indication that a cell phone or a computer of any sort— laptop or tower—had been found on the premises and taken to the lab.

Luke stared at the list and frowned. That didn't seem right. In this day and age, everyone had electronic gadgets. They were all but hermetically sealed to them. Why weren't there any in Kristin's room?

His first guess was that this meant whoever had killed Kristin had made off with her cell phone and whatever laptop, tablet or other electronic device she used to surf the net and entrust with her personal data.

Still, he went through her closet and her bureau drawers, just in case he was wrong. After all, the killer got his kicks terminating the lives of young women, not making off with their electronic gadgets.

The killer also didn't sexually attack his victims, which only added to the mystery. Just why were these women killed?

Coming up empty in his search, Luke decided to check one last place—under the victim's mattress. Lifting it as far up as he could, he reached in and felt around along the entire perimeter of the box spring.

The tips of his fingers came in contact with something hard and smooth.

"Eureka," he declared a little louder than he had intended.

The next moment, White Hawk peered into the bedroom. "What's up? Did you just discover buoyancy?"

After putting down the mattress, he pulled out what he had found. "What the hell are you talking about?"

"You know, that Greek guy, Archimedes," White Hawk said. "He yelled 'Eureka' when he realized that water caused his legs to be buoyant."

Luke snorted. "You are one strange guy."

"No," White Hawk corrected, coming farther into the bedroom. "Unlike you, I read."

Luke regarded the laptop he had uncovered. "If you ask me, White Hawk, you need to get out more. You definitely need a life."

"I'll tell Linda you said so," White Hawk said, referring to his wife.

Drawn by the commotion, Frankie walked into her cousin's bedroom, joining the other two detectives. A shiver went down her back. She did her best not to show it.

"Is this a private party, or can anyone join in?" she asked sarcastically. And then she saw the laptop O'Bannon was holding. Her heart froze for a moment. "You found something."

Luke laughed dryly as he turned toward White Hawk. "Nothing gets past her."

Could that possibly contain the identity of the person who had killed Kris? How had she missed that? She'd been in this room, looking for a clue. But, she recalled, Sean Cavanaugh had been with her, working the scene at the time.

"What is that?" she asked in a quiet voice.

"On second thought, maybe some things do get past her," Luke couldn't resist commenting.

Annoyed, Frankie asked, "Is that the victim's laptop?"

Luke had noticed that she paled slightly when she first looked at the computer. What was up with that? Was this woman somehow involved in this latest homicide? He found that hard to believe, but there was no denying that her complexion resembled the hue of a melted marshmallow.

"I haven't gotten on it yet, but considering where I found it, I'd say that's a pretty good guess." Luke turned his piercing green eyes to meet hers. "Is that a problem?"

She was careful not to blow out a breath or appear

to be anything but blasé. "No, no problem," Frankie lied. "Why should there be?"

To the best of her knowledge, Kris didn't have any photographs of the two of them on her laptop. If her cousin did, then she'd find a way to explain it away, Frankie told herself.

Luke continued eying her. "I don't know," he answered. "You tell me. You're the one who looks pale enough to have seven little men following you wherever you go."

Frankie stared at him, confused.

"O'Bannon's talking about Snow White," the other detective explained. "That's his clever way of telling you that you look ghostly pale."

Her eyes momentarily shifted toward O'Bannon, then back to White Hawk. "Not all that good at communicating, is he?"

"Oh, I don't know. I got my point across, didn't I?" Luke asked cavalierly. And then the smile on his lips disappeared. "Seriously, is there anything on here you don't want me to see?"

She lifted her shoulders and let them drop in an exaggerated shrug of indifference.

"I haven't got the faintest idea what she might have had on her laptop," Frankie told him, "so off the top of my head, I'd have to say that the answer to your question is no."

"Good," Luke pronounced—not that anything she could have said would have stopped him from putting the laptop into evidence. "Then I'll hand this over to Valri and have her take a look at it after we get back from the second crime scene."

The second crime scene. She'd forgotten about

that. "You want me to come along to that?" Frankie asked as they walked out of the apartment.

Luke paused as he locked up the apartment again, then proceeded to replace the yellow crime scene tape across the door.

"Well, unless you want to walk back to the station on your own, yes, you're invited to come along," he told her as they walked back to his vehicle. He'd left it parked at the curb. "Why wouldn't we want you to come with us?" he asked, curious to hear what her answer would be.

She had no solid answer for that. She'd assumed that he had brought her along only to work Kris's crime scene, not anyone else's.

"I thought you just took me along because I brought the crime to your attention," she told him.

"I've decided to keep you on because of your keen insight," Luke told her as he hit the key fob to open the car's locks.

Frankie didn't trust herself to answer the comment civilly. Instead, she looked at White Hawk. "Do you want to ride shotgun this time?"

The other detective laughed.

"You'll find that O'Bannon is an acquired taste."

She tried to find a graceful way out of the situation. "No, it's just that I figured that I needed to ride up front before because I was giving O'Bannon directions. But now that he knows where he's going, I thought maybe you'd want to trade seats."

"That's okay," White Hawk demurred, opening the rear door and climbing into the backseat. "I've ridden shotgun with this guy for three years. You can keep him for today."

"Shotgun for three years?" Frankie repeated, opening the passenger door and getting into the passenger seat. "Doesn't he let you drive?"

White Hawk thought for a moment. "The one time he was wounded, he did. Although, as I recall, I had to bully him into that. He can be a real ornery son of a gun when he wants to be."

Key in the ignition, Luke cleared his throat. "In case it escaped both of your keen detectives' eyes, I'm right here," he pointed out.

"I bet his disposition gets even worse when he's been shot," Frankie guessed, turning in her seat to look at White Hawk.

The other detective rolled his dark eyes. "You have no idea."

"Still here," Luke reminded them tersely. He started up the engine. "And if *both* of you don't plan on walking to the next crime scene, I'd suggest tabling this little discussion right now."

White Hawk smiled. "Sorry, O'Bannon, I keep forgetting how touchy you can get before your fourteenth cup of coffee."

"Don't give away all my secrets," he told his partner with a straight face.

"No chance of that happening," White Hawk said cheerfully. "That would take me longer than either one of us have left on this earth."

Leaning back in her seat, Frankie continued listening to the two men bantering and exchanging quips. Very slowly, she found herself beginning to relax just a little.

Chapter 4

It was immediately obvious that the distraught-looking older woman who answered the front door had been crying. Holding on to the door almost for support, she appeared to be struggling to keep from falling apart.

Standing on the other side of the threshold, Luke politely asked, "Mrs. O'Keefe?"

"Yes?" the woman responded hoarsely.

Luke held up his credentials for the woman's benefit. "I'm Detective O'Bannon. This is Detective DeMarco." He nodded toward the woman on his left. "And that's Detective White Hawk."

Both Frankie and the other detective quietly displayed their IDs as well as their shields.

Mrs. O'Keefe's red-rimmed eyes barely turned in their direction.

She addressed her words to Luke. "If you're here

to tell me about Ellen, I already know," she told him, her voice breaking at the end of her sentence.

Frankie's heart ached. She felt for the woman. More than that, she could easily relate to what Mrs. O'Keefe was going through. Without thinking, she stepped forward and took the grieving woman's hands in hers.

"We're *very* sorry for your loss, ma'am," Frankie told her with genuine feeling. "Detectives O'Bannon, White Hawk and I are here to ask you a few questions so that we can find whoever did this to your daughter and make him pay for it."

Mrs. O'Keefe pressed her lips together to suppress the sob that rose to her lips and threatened to burst out. When she spoke, her voice was hardly above a whisper.

"Please come in."

Turning, the woman, bent with grief, led the way into her small, two-bedroom house.

Deferring to the lead detective, Frankie waited for Luke to follow the woman, but he surprised her by waving her in first.

"Not bad," he mouthed to her as she passed him.

Frankie assumed he was referring to the fact that she had managed to get a sliver of the woman's trust.

Mrs. O'Keefe brought them into her living room. Despite the fact that it was a little past noon, the room was shrouded in darkness. The house's orientation kept the sun from coming in.

The victim's mother turned on a lamp as an afterthought.

"Please sit," she said, gesturing toward the sofa.

And then, as if suddenly remembering the rules of etiquette, she asked, "Can I get any of you anything?"

"No, we're fine, ma'am," Luke assured her. There was a kind expression on his face as he asked, "Can you tell us about your daughter?"

Clutching a worn handkerchief, Mrs. O'Keefe knotted her long, thin fingers together in her lap. "Ellen was a wonderful girl. She was smart, kind, thoughtful. She was a kindergarten teacher, you know," she told them with pride. "The children all loved her. She just graduated from college last year." A small sigh escaped her lips. "She'd had a setback a while ago, but my daughter had finally gotten her life on track."

"What do you mean by a setback?" Luke asked the woman gently.

Mrs. O'Keefe's shoulders stiffened, as if she was bracing herself for an ordeal. "Ellen had an addiction problem, but she conquered that. It was all behind her," she told them with finality. "Everything was fine. Everything was fine," she repeated, her voice coming very close to cracking again.

Luke noticed the way DeMarco looked up, alert, when Ellen O'Keefe's mother mentioned that the victim had been an addict.

Pulling herself together, Mrs. O'Keefe told them, "She was even beginning to date again."

"Was that unusual for her?" Luke asked.

Mrs. O'Keefe offered them a small smile. "Ellen was very shy. She always had been. Getting addicted to painkillers had only added to her sense of being worthless. It made her feel that she had nothing to bring to a relationship. But getting her teaching degree and working with all those children changed all that." Mrs. O'Keefe's eyes shone briefly. And then she clutched the handkerchief she was holding. "I was so hopeful…"

"Would you happen to know the name of the person your daughter was dating?" Luke asked. He knew that this was too much of a break to hope for, but he still had to ask.

Mrs. O'Keefe shook her head. "Ellen wouldn't tell me. She was afraid that she'd wind up jinxing it if she said his name out loud."

Luke tried another approach. "Did your daughter happen to say if she met this man at school? Was he another teacher?"

Mrs. O'Keefe shook her head. "I'm sorry, I really don't know. Wait," she said suddenly, as a memory returned to her. "I think she met him on one of those online dating services."

These days, there was no end to dating sites, Luke thought. He had a friend who was extolling the benefits of online sites for anonymity. Luke preferred finding his dates the old-fashioned way—face-to-face.

"Would you mind if we took a look at Ellen's computer?" White Hawk asked the woman.

Mrs. O'Keefe nodded numbly. "She had a laptop. Do what you want with it. It's in her room," she told the detective. "Ellen moved back here after rehab. She said living at home would help her keep from relapsing—and she couldn't afford to rent a place of her own because she needed the money to finish up and get her college degree. She dropped out when she was taking drugs." Mrs. O'Keefe's eyes filled with tears. "How could anyone do something so horrible to her?" she asked all three of the people in her house.

Frankie was the one to step forward again. "I'm afraid that there are terrible people in the world that do unspeakable things that we can't begin to understand. Is there anyone who we can call to come stay with you?" she asked.

The older woman took a shaky breath. "My sister said she would be here as soon as she could."

"Does she live around here?" Luke asked. "We could send someone to bring her."

Mrs. O'Keefe shook her head. "No, my sister wouldn't like that. She's very independent, but thank you," she said, doing her best to smile. She placed a hand on Frankie's arm. "When I found my little girl lying on the floor, there was a syringe in her arm. I don't care what it looked like, or what your fancy medical examiner says he found in Ellen's—Ellen's autopsy." Mrs. O'Keefe nearly choked on the word. It took her a moment to pull herself together so that she could continue. "My Ellen was clean. She was very proud of that fact. Proud that she had managed to kick her drug addiction," Mrs. O'Keefe told them with the fierceness of a mother lion protecting her cub. "And she had," the woman insisted. "I would bet my life on that." Again, her eyes filled with tears that spilled out onto her cheeks.

White Hawk was about to tell the woman that it wasn't uncommon for an addict to relapse. Drugs were far more available these days than they used to be. There was no end to temptation for a former addict.

Frankie could see by the look in White Hawk's

eyes that he was about to say something and she shook her head, mouthing *don't*.

Out loud, she managed to waylay him by asking, "Got a minute, Detective White Hawk?"

Puzzled, he said, "Sure," and followed Frankie outside. "What's up?" he asked.

"I know your heart's in the right place, White Hawk," she told him, starting out diplomatically. "But that woman inside the house doesn't need another dose of harsh reality. She's just had way too much of it. If she believes that her daughter was drug free, let her believe it."

White Hawk studied her for a long moment, then asked, "What if it's not true?"

"What if it is?" Frankie countered in the same tone of voice.

He inclined his head, going along with Frankie for the time being. "Why don't we hold off on any speculation until we get the lab results back?" White Hawk suggested philosophically.

"And maybe even longer than that," Frankie tactfully suggested.

"You do know that you're a softie, Detective De-Marco, right?" White Hawk asked her with a wide smile.

"Not really," Frankie denied. She preferred to think of herself as being tough as nails. But in this instance, she wanted to go easy on Mrs. O'Keefe. The woman had been through enough. "But I just don't see the advantage of robbing a mother of her last illusion about her daughter. If Ellen's relapse helps to crack the case, then we'll push forward with it. But until then, there's no harm in letting Mrs. O'Keefe remember her daughter the way she wants to."

"White Hawk's right," Luke said, coming out to join them. He had a laptop tucked under his arm. The victim's mother had handed it over to him in the young woman's bedroom. "You are a softie."

She didn't mind White Hawk calling her that. But hearing the words coming out of O'Bannon's mouth just put her back up.

Frowning, she pointed toward what he was carrying. "Is that Ellen's laptop?"

"It is," he confirmed. Looking down at it for a moment, he smiled. "My guess is that Valri's going to be very busy for the next couple of days," he commented.

He was talking about Kris's laptop, Frankie thought. She was uneasy about anyone poking around her cousin's computer until she got a look at it herself.

"I'm pretty good with computers," she told Luke. "Why don't I take a crack at Kristin's and you can bring the one you're holding to your cousin? That way, the work'll get done twice as fast."

Luke looked at her for a long moment. She felt as if he could literally see every thought in her head.

"Any particular reason you're volunteering to take that one instead of this one right here?" he asked, holding up Ellen's laptop.

Frankie spread her hands in exaggerated innocence. "None whatsoever. The other one was just the first one that came to mind since it was initially *my* crime scene."

"Don't worry," Luke told her. "Valri likes a challenge. She can handle both of them. Besides—"

he unlocked all four doors of his vehicle and then popped the trunk "—she likes having people owe her." He placed the second laptop in the trunk of his car beside the first one. Since they were made by different manufacturers, there was no chance of getting them mixed up.

His stomach was making rumbling noises in loud protest. A rueful smile curved his mouth. "Now, unless either one of you have any objections, I vote we stop for lunch before driving back to the station." He looked at the other two for an answer.

"Hey, fine by me," White Hawk said. "I'm always hungry."

Both detectives turned to look at Frankie, waiting for her answer. She shrugged. "You're the one with the car keys."

"I guess then it's settled," Luke said. "Lunch it is."

But as the other two detectives began opening their doors to get into the vehicle, Frankie held up her hand. "One minute, please," she said, ignoring the impatient look on O'Bannon's handsome face. "I just want to check on Mrs. O'Keefe one more time before we leave."

"Why?" Luke asked, but she had already hurried back to the front door.

"She really does seem to be pretty compassionate," White Hawk commented, watching the detective disappear into Mrs. O'Keefe's house.

"Either that," Luke replied thoughtfully, "or she relates to the woman's grief."

Curious, White Hawk asked his partner, "What are you thinking?"

"I'm not really sure yet," Luke answered truthfully. "But you'll be the first to know if something occurs to me."

White Hawk snorted as he gave Luke a pointed look. "I'll hold you to that."

Inside the house, Frankie found Mrs. O'Keefe in the living room, exactly where they had left her. She handed the woman her card.

Accepting it, Mrs. O'Keefe gazed at her.

"It's my card," Frankie explained. Turning the card over for the woman, she pointed out, "That's my cell phone number on the back. If you need anything— anything at all—give me a call. Any time," Frankie emphasized. "Day or night."

Holding the card in her hand, Mrs. O'Keefe made a dismissive motion. "Thank you, but I already told you, my sister's coming to stay with me."

"I know. But sometimes, you need someone to listen who isn't family." Frankie smiled sympathetically at the woman. "Who won't bring up old flaws. And," she added, "you can use that number in case you think of anything that might be useful to our investigation."

Folding her hand over the card, Mrs. O'Keefe tucked it into her pocket.

Just as Frankie was about to say goodbye and leave, Mrs. O'Keefe took her hands in hers and held them fast. When Frankie looked at her quizzically, the woman said fiercely, "Promise me. Promise me you'll catch the miserable bastard who did this to my little girl. I'm counting on you," she said with feeling, then, looking into her eyes, the woman added with a knowing expression, "You understand."

There was a bond between the two of them, she

could feel it. Somehow, the woman knew. Frankie nodded her head.

"I promise, Mrs. O'Keefe," she told her with sincerity.

Taking a breath, the woman released her hands. "Thank you," she whispered.

The simple words continued to echo in her head as Frankie hurried back to the two men she'd left outside, standing by O'Bannon's vehicle.

"Hey, everything okay?" Luke asked her when she rejoined them.

Frankie opened the rear passenger door and took the seat behind the front passenger one. "As okay as they can be for that poor woman," she said evasively.

"No, I mean with you," Luke said deliberately, getting in behind the car's steering wheel. The fact that she had taken a seat in the back of the car wasn't lost on him.

Was she afraid of being scrutinized? Or was there something more?

"Just dandy," she told O'Bannon with a false cheerful note. The next second, she changed the subject. "You two decide where we're going for lunch?"

Luke blew out a breath. For now, he let the other matter drop, even though he knew something was definitely bothering the newest member of the team. Instead, he went on to answer her question.

Sort of.

"Well, White Hawk here says he wants burgers. I like Thai food. We thought we'd leave it up to you," Luke told her. "You can be the tiebreaker."

"Well, I vote for pizza," she told them.

"So much for a tiebreaker." White Hawk laughed.

"Great, a stalemate," Luke said with a huff. And then he shrugged, exhibiting what his uncle Andrew referred to as grace under fire.

"Okay, since you're the newbie," he told her, "we'll let you pick the place. Pizza it is."

He turned left at the next corner, heading toward a restaurant that, in his opinion, served the best pizza in the area.

"What did you have to say to Mrs. O'Keefe?" he asked casually.

"Nothing, really." She met his eyes in the rearview mirror and knew that the man wasn't about to let the matter go at that. "I just gave her my card and told her to call me in case she thought of anything she might have forgotten." She debated adding the next part, then decided to do it in case O'Bannon thought she was holding something back. "And then she asked me to promise that we would catch the bastard responsible for her daughter's murder."

"And did you?" Luke asked.

She paused, anticipating a lecture. But she wasn't about to lie, either. "Yes, I did. But I said that *I* promised. I didn't include either one of you in the promise."

"Want to hog all the glory yourself, is that it?" Luke deadpanned.

"No," she protested. "I just didn't think that you'd appreciate my making any promises in your name," she told him.

"He's just yanking your chain, DeMarco," White Hawk told her. "And as for making promises, I've heard him say the same thing to the grieving relatives of other victims. It's hard to walk away, indifferent, in the face of that kind of gut-wrenching grief. You did what you had to, newbie. It's not just *protect and serve*," he told her. "Sometimes that includes comfort, too. Consider it all part of the job description."

"Is that what *he* believes?" she asked White Hawk, nodding at O'Bannon.

"Yeah," the detective assured her. "Even if he doesn't say it. Trust me," he added.

"And me without my violin," Luke murmured sarcastically.

Frankie merely shook her head. The sooner they found the killer, the sooner she'd be able to get back to her own department.

Chapter 5

"Hey," Luke said suddenly, directing the question to the woman sitting directly behind him as a thought occurred to him. "You're not one of those people who insist on having vegetables on their pizza instead of cheese, are you?"

The idea was abhorrent to her, but the tone of O'Bannon's voice was challenging and she wasn't one to just submissively allow a challenge to go unanswered. "And if I was?"

His answered surprised her. "Then we'd have to go someplace else, because the place I'm taking us to doesn't serve that kind of pizza."

Since he was being so nice about it, Frankie decided to let the matter drop rather than drag it out a little longer.

"Well, luckily for all of us," she said, "I like my

pizza the traditional way—lots of cheese, pepperoni and super-thin crust."

"Wow," Luke responded. "Finally something we can agree on."

"Probably the only thing we can agree on," she murmured under her breath. She didn't think he heard her, but he did.

Luke stopped at the light and glanced over his shoulder at her for a moment. "Oh, I don't know. Maybe we'll find something else eventually."

She had no idea why the way he looked at her—even though it was only for a split second—sent such a hot shiver zigzagging up her spin.

Almost in self defense, she told him, "I wouldn't hold my breath if I were you."

She expected a sarcastic retort from O'Bannon. Instead, he made no response whatsoever—which wound up unsettling her even more.

The pizzeria he was taking them to was just around the corner on the next block. It was in the middle of what had once been a thriving strip mall but the stores on either side of Gino's had changed hands several times and the stores on either side of *those* stores stood empty, with For Lease signs prominently displayed in their windows.

Frankie noticed that the sign in the window that they passed by first appeared dusty, a testimony that the property had been vacant for a while now. She wondered if people in the area were just losing interest in supporting their neighborhood stores, or if this was now an ongoing trend because people preferred doing their shopping online instead of in actual buildings of brick and mortar. She'd read that somewhere, and the thought of that happening made her sad. She could remember hanging out at the mall all day with Kristin.

Everything was changing, and not always in a good way.

It felt about ten degrees warmer inside Gino's when they walked in. It was also dimmer. The sun was bright outside, but it seemed as if someone had flipped a switch the moment they came in and the front door closed behind them.

In contrast, the person behind the counter seemed to light up when he saw them. He also appeared to be standing just a little taller by the time O'Bannon approached him.

"Why don't you two find a table?" Luke suggested to her and his partner.

Frankie scanned the small restaurant. Finding a table wasn't going to be a problem. Every other table in the place appeared to be empty. Was it always like this or had they come in at a bad time?

"After you," White Hawk told her.

"Is this place always this empty?" she asked White Hawk as she sat down at the closest table.

"You've never been here before?" Luke asked, joining them and taking a seat. "This place makes the best pizza in town. I thought since you liked pizza so much, you would have found this place yourself."

Frankie noticed that he hadn't answered her question, just asked one of his own, possibly to throw her off. She shrugged. "I live in the other direction," she said simply. "There're a couple of decent pizza parlors between the station and my place."

"Pizza parlors," Luke repeated, the corners of his mouth curving.

She had no idea why that would amuse him but she braced herself for some kind of a cutting comment. "That's what I said," she replied crisply.

His smile only seemed to widen. "You're not from around here, are you?"

She wasn't, but she wasn't ready to admit anything until she knew why he was asking and what he would do with the information once he got it.

"And just what makes you say that?" she asked.

"They're not called pizza parlors out here," he told her. "That's something people say back East. Are you from back East, DeMarco?" he asked, looking at her. "You don't sound like you are."

Frankie didn't really feel like sharing any personal information with O'Bannon, no matter how harmless it was, but she knew that he wasn't going to back off until she satisfied his curiosity.

One glance at White Hawk told her that she was right on that score.

"I was four when my family moved out here. My mother loved pizza and she called them pizza parlors. I guess I picked that up from her." She was not about to elaborate any further on either of her parents. And when she asked, "Any more questions?" it sounded almost defensively waspish to her own ear.

"I'll let you know when I think of them," Luke told her mildly.

Frankie had no doubts that he would do exactly that, no matter what those questions involved. And she was just as determined not to answer them. The next moment, she saw him standing up next to his chair.

"Here comes our pizza," Luke said, waving at the teenager in the stained half apron who had emerged from behind the counter. He was carrying a large, banged-up silver-colored pizza tray in his hands and had a lost look on his tanned face.

"What do I owe you?" she asked O'Bannon when the teenager placed the extra-large pizza on the table before them. She reached into her pocket to extract her wallet, but it turned out not to be necessary.

"Your undivided attention when I need some work done," Luke replied.

Her eyes narrowed. He was playing games with her. "I meant for the pizza."

Luke's smile was wide and innocent—and didn't fool her for a moment. "So did I."

"Look—" Frankie tried again, not willing to be in anyone's debt, least of all O'Bannon's. "I asked for a pizza, you got the pizza, now I want to pay my share of the pizza—"

"Just accept it, DeMarco," White Hawk advised, helping himself to a slice. "Nobody's ever won an argument with this guy. You might as well not let your pizza get cold," he told her. "Or your blood pressure go up."

She thought of O'Bannon's response when she asked what she owed him. She didn't like owing someone something that sounded so vague, but she supposed she had no choice—at least, for now.

"I'll pick up the next one," she told O'Bannon.

She expected the lead detective to offer an argument of some sort over that, too, but all O'Bannon said was, "Okay."

Frankie picked up a slice and began eating, not trusting herself to say anything further to the man. Having her mouth full was a way to curtail that.

"You're right," she grudgingly admitted several moments later. Much as she hated to do it, she had to give the man his due. "This *is* good pizza."

"I'm always right," Luke replied. And then, because of the look that she had just shot him, he added, "At least, usually."

Less than forty-five minutes later, all three of them were pulling into the rear parking lot of the police station.

Once back in his parking space, Luke popped open his trunk and carefully removed the two laptops he had placed there. Each was securely wrapped within a large plastic envelope to preserve possible prints, although the odds of getting a set of useful ones were small.

"Are you sure I can't help out by taking one of the laptops to work on?" she asked, giving it one last try. "The search'll go twice as fast if each of us takes one laptop."

"Not that Valri wouldn't appreciate you volunteering," Luke told her, "but she has a certain way of doing things." Ways he knew that she didn't want interfered with, he thought. In her own unassuming way, Valri was a tyrant when it came to operating her area of the computer lab. "And as for the search going twice as fast, you've never seen Valri work. That woman's fingers fly over those keys almost faster than the speed of light—or, at least, it seems that way," he said, deep admiration resonating in his voice as all three of them walked to the back entrance of the building.

"She'd appreciate hearing you say that once in a while, you know," White Hawk told him.

Luke looked at him as if his partner was talking nonsense. "Valri knows how good I think she is. How good *everyone* thinks she is."

Frankie laughed shortly. She agreed with White Hawk. "Knowing is not the same thing as hearing," she told him. She couldn't help thinking that O'Bannon was just being thick.

"Speaking from personal experience?" Luke asked her, his expression unreadable.

"As a human being, yes," Frankie retorted, opening the door to the stairwell. "But, hey, you do whatever you want to."

He was about to press for the elevator, but stopped as he looked at her. "Where are you going?" he asked.

"Well, since you don't want me working on one of those laptops," she reminded him, "I'm going up to the squad room."

He'd figured that was where she was going, until he saw her opening the stairwell door. "Why are you taking the stairs?" he asked.

She assumed that the answer was self-explanatory. "That was a filling lunch. I thought I'd walk off a little of the pizza."

If she was looking to burn off the calories, she needed to do a lot more than that. "It's only five flights up to the homicide squad room, not fifty."

Frankie shrugged. "Gotta start somewhere," she told him philosophically.

He didn't want to take a chance that she was up to something. "White Hawk, you go with her," he told his partner.

Instead, White Hawk pressed the Up button for the elevator.

"Why?" he asked. "She's not a suspect. What do you expect she's going to do?"

"I don't know her well enough to know what she's capable of doing," Luke told him. He looked pointedly at the stairwell.

White Hawk blew out a breath. "If I keel over from a heart attack, it's on you," he told his partner, walking over to the stairwell.

"I'll deal with it," Luke said.

As far as he was concerned, the man was in a hell of a lot better shape than most of the men currently in the precinct. White Hawk just liked being melodramatic.

Waiting until his partner was inside the stairwell, Luke took the elevator down to the basement to take his cousin the two laptops. In addition to sealing them, he had also labeled them.

He sincerely hoped that at least one of the laptops would yield some sort of information that would finally lead them to a break in the case. They needed to find out just who was responsible for killing all these young women.

Walking out of the elevator, Luke made one quick stop at the breakroom, then turned right instead of left. Left led to where his uncle worked in the crime scene investigations lab. Turning right took him to the computer lab where the chief of detectives' daughter-in-law, Brenda, and his cousin Valri, as well as several other gifted people, worked their magic uncovering secrets that were embedded within the hard drives of completely innocent-looking computers.

Stopping before the glass-enclosed office, Luke knocked lightly on the door frame. Since the door was already open, he peered in.

"How's my favorite person?" Luke asked cheerfully.

"Not here," the petite blue-eyed blonde replied, never looking up from her monitor.

"Yes, you are," Luke said. "You know that I mean you, Val."

Valri went on working. "What I know is that you mean trouble every time you turn up, Luke. You're just like your brother Christian."

After setting down the laptops he'd brought in, Luke dramatically placed his hand over his heart. He was holding a covered container in his free hand that he'd gotten from the breakroom's vending machine.

"You wound me, Valri," he told her. "Chris and I are nothing alike."

This time she looked up, even though she didn't stop typing. "You're right. He doesn't try to sugarcoat things the way that you do."

"That's just because he's not as charming as I am," Luke said, pretending to defend himself. "I brought you a big container of your favorite tea. Chai—with that creamer you really like." He set it down to her right.

Still, she told him, "Bribery is not going to get you anywhere."

"It's not bribery, Val," he protested, wounded. "It's thoughtfulness. Take a sip," he urged. "It's still warm."

She looked at the container and then back at him. "You got this from the vending machine," she accused.

He didn't bother denying it. Instead, he argued, "But it's still warm."

Valri sighed. "You are incorrigible." After removing the lid, she took a deep sip. "This is very good." Still, she teased, "I pity the woman who's going to wind up with you."

"Never going to happen," Luke told her. "I would never be able to find a woman who could come anywhere close to measuring up to you, Valri—even though we are cousins."

Valri shook her head. "You lay it on any thicker and I'll have to get a shovel to make my way to the door." She sighed, giving him her full attention. "All right, Lukkas, what kind of a puzzle did you bring me this time?" she asked.

"I come bearing laptops," he told her, indicating the two sealed envelopes he'd placed on her desk. "They belonged to two women who were recently murdered. In each case, the murderer made it look like it was a drug overdose."

"But you think it wasn't?"

"Questioning one victim's mother and going by information from someone who knew the other woman—" for now, he was deliberately keeping De-Marco's name out of it, although he did mean to get back to that "—they swear that both women had conquered their drug problems and were leading normal, productive lives."

She made the logical leap. "You think the two cases are connected?" Valri asked him.

"I'm pretty sure, but that's what I'm hoping you and your magical ways are going to find out and prove for me. And, just for the record, there aren't two cases, there are seven."

Valri eyed him. "Seven?"

He nodded. "Seven. All were dark-haired young women in their twenties, all were found dead from a drug overdose with a syringe either in their arm or lying near them. The scenes were all staged," he said, telling his cousin what his gut had led him to believe.

"It could all just be a terrible coincidence," Valri commented.

He gave her a patient, if somewhat patronizing, look. "And what was it that we all learned when we were growing up?"

She glanced at the container of chai tea on her desk. "Beware of good-looking men bearing gifts?"

"No," he corrected. "There are no such things as coincidences." Luke paused as he played back her words in his head. "You think I'm good-looking?" he asked, amused.

"In a motley sort of way," Valri told him. "Now go," she ordered. "Leave me to my work before I find a way to bury these laptops under a pile of paperwork," Valri warned.

Luke was already out the door. "You'll call if you find something?"

"I'll call if I find something," she told him. It was a given. "Now go!"

She found herself talking to empty space. Luke had left.

"I should have said that in the first place," she murmured under her breath as she got back to work.

Chapter 6

When Luke walked back into the squad room, he found the newest member of his team standing in front of the bulletin board. The board was periodically hauled out of storage whenever one of the homicide detectives were dealing with a killer who had multiple victims, or they had one murder with multiple suspects.

Currently, Luke had been the one to press the bulletin board into service.

There were seven photographs mounted at the top of the board, one for each victim who had died at the hands of the serial killer they were hunting. The latest victim's photograph had just been put up.

He really hoped that it was the last one.

DeMarco had her fisted hands on her hips as she moved from one column to the next, reading the highlights listed beneath each photograph. She appeared to be committing everything she read to memory.

"Come up with anything?" he asked the woman, coming up behind her.

Frankie congratulated herself for not jumping. O'Bannon hadn't made any noise when he had come up behind her.

Still studying the board, she answered, "Yes, that the milk of human kindness is in very short supply when it comes to some people." She had certainly dealt with homicides before, but she'd never dealt with any one single person who had been guilty of committing so many murders. "How can anyone do this?" she asked Luke, turning around to face him. "How can he—or she—kill all these people and still look at themselves in the mirror every morning? I don't understand that kind of behavior," she confessed.

"We don't have to understand it," White Hawk told her kindly, coming up to join them. "We just have to stop the killer before they can kill anyone else."

Frankie didn't agree. She turned to look at the tall detective. "But if we don't understand," she pointed out, "then how do we stop the next one from starting a killing spree?" she asked. "Or the one who comes after that?"

"Good point," Luke commented, nodding his head. "Understanding why the killer kills helps us to prevent other sprees—or so the theory goes," he allowed. He'd been at this too long to feel that anything was foolproof. "Maybe someday we'll be able to get the jump on a would-be serial killer in the making, but right now, I'll settle for stopping this one," he told both of the other two detectives.

"That's our Detective O'Bannon," White Hawk said as an aside to Frankie. "A man of few requirements."

She hardly heard White Hawk. Her mind was on another matter. "The laptops yield anything?" Frankie asked.

The expression on Luke's face all but shouted *You've got to be kidding.* "Hey, hold your horses, DeMarco. Valri barely has had time to log them into the system. She certainly hasn't even booted one of them, much less both."

"What did the other laptops yield?" Frankie asked.

His eyebrows drew together in a puzzled line as he looked at her. "What other laptops?"

"The ones belonging to the five other victims." She saw the blank expression on O'Bannon's face. She didn't think she was asking anything particularly confusing. "You did pick those up so that Valri could make a comparison, didn't you?"

He could have lied, but he didn't see the point. Lies always had a way of tripping you up at the worst possible time. "I didn't. The CSI unit picked those up. I'm assuming that they were handed over to the computer lab once the unit had finished going over them for any useful prints."

"So then Valri has seven laptops and computers to review?" she asked, surprised. "Maybe I should go down there and volunteer my services," Frankie said, already turning away from the bulletin board.

"If you're thinking of running down to the lab— *don't*." Luke advised. "Val's got enough people to turn to if she needs help. Trained people," he emphasized, "not just eager people."

Frankie took that to be a put-down, but she maintained her temper. "Nothing wrong with an extra set of helping hands," she told him crisply.

He wasn't about to drop the matter—or to let her go down to the lab. While she was part of his team, he was responsible for her.

Something didn't feel quite right to him. "Just why is it that you're so eager to get your hands on the laptops?"

"What I'm so eager about is getting the slime bucket who killed my friend's roommate and that poor woman's daughter—not to mention all those other young women," Frankie informed him angrily.

"Tell you what," Luke suggested, taking several files and dropping them on her desk, "why don't you review what's inside these files and see if we've accidentally overlooked or missed something," he told her. "Take your pick. White Hawk and I will split and go over whatever files you leave."

She gave him a look and picked up not just the files he'd put on her desk, but the ones he'd left on his desk, as well.

"Okay, DeMarco, what do you think you're doing?" he asked her. He gestured pointedly at the files in her arms. "Those are all the files."

"Yes, I know," she replied, uttering the words slowly, as if she was talking to someone who was having trouble processing her words. "In order to get a complete picture of the killer, I think I need to go over all of the files that were put together on the victims."

That was obviously a tall order. "You'll be here all night," he said.

"That's okay," she told him glibly. "I didn't have any plans."

"Maybe you didn't," he responded, "but maybe your body did."

She looked at him as if he was talking nonsense. "What's that supposed to mean?"

"It means that you're not any good to me if you don't get any sleep," he said.

She didn't particularly like being dictated to or talked down to, but because O'Bannon was the lead, she did her best to try to placate him—in her own fashion. "I'll take catnaps."

"Not too many cats get issued gun permits," he told her. "You go home end of day, same as the rest of us, DeMarco. End of story," he told her with finality.

She was already busy reading one of the files. "Whatever you say," she murmured, without bothering to look up.

"Yeah, right," he muttered under his breath. The woman wasn't about to listen to him any more than she was about to take wing and fly.

He was just going to have to make her, Luke thought.

But before he could say anything further, his cell phone rang. Digging it out of his pocket, he swiped it open.

"O'Bannon," he declared once he heard something on the other end of his line.

"Luke, I think you might want to come down and see this."

It was Valri. He hadn't expected to hear from her for a while. Definitely not so soon.

"You found something already?" he asked. He noticed that both White Hawk and DeMarco were looking at him. There was curiosity in the former's eyes and something he couldn't quite place in the latter's. The woman sparked a lot of questions in his mind.

"Just come down here," Valri told him before ending the connection.

"Valri find something?" White Hawk asked him.

Luke slipped his phone back into his pocket. "Your guess is as good as mine," he answered. "She just said to come down. She didn't say why."

"I could go in your place if you're busy," Frankie volunteered.

I just bet you would. What is it you're hoping to find on that one laptop?

DeMarco sounded far too eager and she really had his curiosity ramped up.

"Thanks, but you've already got enough to do," Luke reminded her pointedly. "I think I'll just go see why Valri called for myself," he told her. Glancing at White Hawk over his shoulder, he told his partner, "Hold down the fort."

White Hawk laughed. "Now there's something my people never thought they'd hear your people say."

Pausing, Luke looked at his partner. "Haven't you heard? There's no more *your* people or *my* people, there's just one great big *us.*"

White Hawk's smile widened. His friendship with Luke went back to their academy days.

"I must have missed that memo," White Hawk

said dryly before he went back to looking at the file he'd been reviewing.

"Must have," Luke agreed, walking out of the squad room.

He was very aware of the fact that DeMarco was watching every step he took as he left the room. Why was she so concerned?

And about what?

Luke made a decision. After the day was over, he intended to ask DeMarco to Malone's for a drink. The relaxed social scene had a way of removing inhibitions and allowing reserved people to talk.

"What's so important that you couldn't tell me over the phone and had to see me in person?" Luke asked his cousin when he walked into the computer lab. "I know it can't be because you missed me— can it?" he teased.

"I am not that hard up for company," she informed Luke, then she proceeded to answer his question in earnest. "Look."

Turning the laptop in his direction so he had a better view, Valri pulled up a photograph she'd found on the hard drive.

"Okay," he said gamely, "I'm looking." And then he glanced at her. "What is it that I'm supposed to be seeing?"

Valri frowned. How was Luke missing this? She tapped the smaller of the two women in the photo. "Isn't that the detective who's working with you and White Hawk on the serial killer case?"

Luke nodded. "Yeah, so?"

"So, what is she doing in a picture with the victim?" she asked her cousin.

That seemed simple enough to explain. "Her friend was the victim's roommate."

"Why wasn't DeMarco in a picture with the roommate?"

He had no answer for that. "I don't pretend to understand women," he said with a sigh. "What bothers you about this?"

She shook her head. "This doesn't take understanding, Luke—at least, not deep understanding. Here, let me blow this up for you," she suggested. "Maybe you can see my point then."

The next moment, Valri had made the photograph of the victim and DeMarco large enough to fill the entire computer monitor.

But she wasn't finished yet.

"This is obviously a regular photograph taken by a camera, not a cellphone," she told Luke. "It was probably scanned into the computer in order to save it." Pressing a few keys, she made the photograph even larger for him. "Take a look at the lower right-hand corner," she told her cousin.

He obliged by lowering his head, focusing on the area that she'd indicated. "Okay, I'm looking."

"There's a date there," Valri prompted.

"Make it larger," he told her. When she did, he still found it to be a bit blurry. "Damn, I think I'm going to need glasses," Luke complained. "All that close reading I've been doing. I—" He was beginning to make some of the numbers out. "Hold it," he cautioned. "Can you make that any bigger?" he asked.

"I can, but it's going to get even more blurry," she warned him. Even so, she did as he asked.

He could make out the year. "That's five years ago. That means that DeMarco knew the victim five years ago," he said, talking to himself, not Valri. And then he looked at Valri. "According to my notes, the victim and DeMarco's friend have only been renting that apartment for less than two years."

"Maybe they were friends before that?" Valri suggested.

"No, DeMarco told me that the victim had answered an ad looking for a roommate almost two years ago. They didn't know each other five years ago," he said, frowning at the date on the photograph on the monitor. "Any chance that date could have been faked?"

"For what reason?" Valri asked.

Luke smiled at her. She was right. There was no reason to fake the date.

"You know, you're getting to be a damn good little detective, Valri," he told her. "Your brothers and sisters would be really proud of you."

"They already are," she answered.

"You're right."

Saying that, Luke turned on his heel and started to leave the lab.

He was leaving her with more questions than before. "So, what are you going to do?" Valri called out, addressing his back.

Luke sighed and just kept walking. "I don't know yet."

But by the time Luke was in the hall, he knew what he was going to do.

Instead of going upstairs to the squad room, he looked in on his uncle in the CSI lab.

The broad-shouldered, distinguished-looking man with a full head of grey hair spoke in his customary quiet voice. "To what do I owe the pleasure?" Sean Cavanaugh asked his nephew as the latter walked into the darkened lab.

"I need a DNA workup on the serial killer's latest victim that was just brought in."

"I thought we had an ID on her." Sean looked a little puzzled. "Why do you want a workup? We didn't do one on the others," Sean pointed out.

"I know."

"What makes this victim so special?" Sean asked.

"That's exactly what I'm trying to find out," he told his uncle. "Can you do it?" he asked,

Sean smiled at him. "I can do almost anything when it comes to identifying a victim. Whose DNA will we be comparing the sample to?"

"I'll get that for you," Luke promised. "For now, just do the initial workup."

Sean couldn't resist asking, "Exactly what is it that you're looking for?"

"A possible familial match," Luke told him.

"To?" Sean asked.

For now, Luke didn't feel comfortable naming names. "Let's just take it one step at a time, if that's all right with you."

Sean looked at him thoughtfully, but as the head of the CSI day unit, he was accustomed to the "need to know" axiom and apparently, in this set of circumstances, he didn't have a need to know.

At least, for now.

Nodding, Sean told his nephew, "It's your call to make, Detective."

Luke smiled at his uncle. He appreciated the man's restraint. He was well aware that there were some heads of departments who felt that they knew best and would insist on being in the loop at all times.

"Thanks for that," he told his uncle humbly.

"Don't mention it," Sean replied. Putting his arm around the younger man's shoulders, he gently guided him toward the door. "Now, if you don't mind, I've got to get back to processing the rest of the evidence from this sick son of a gun's latest crime scene."

Luke paused in the doorway just long enough to ask the question. "So, you do feel that this is the work of the same killer who murdered the other women?"

"There's no doubt about it, Luke," Sean confirmed for his nephew.

"That's what I thought." Nodding his head grimly, Luke made his way back up to the squad room. He had a sample of his own to collect.

Chapter 7

Frankie looked up when she heard O'Bannon walk in and return to his desk. When she spoke, she tried not to sound as anxious as she felt. But she felt there was a strong possibility that Valri Cavanaugh had found the connection between her and Kristin.

"Anything?" she asked.

Luke dropped into his chair, his mind elsewhere. Belatedly, her single word replayed itself in his head. "Come again?"

Was he toying with her, or was there nothing to say? "Your cousin called you and you went down to the computer lab," she said, going over the chain of events. "Did she find out something of interest?"

"Oh, that. Not yet," he lied. He wanted to work this out in his head first and then pick his time before questioning DeMarco. "It was just family business," he told her, anticipating the detective's next question.

She didn't look as if she believed him and made no effort to explain anything any further. They all had their secrets, Luke mused. "How about you?" he asked, glancing from her to his partner. "Either one of you find anything new in those files?"

"All of the victims were in their twenties," White Hawk said. He was saying it for Frankie's benefit.

"And the killer definitely has a type," Frankie added, trying to keep the bitterness out of her voice. "All the victims were dark-haired, intelligent, professional women—" She rose from her desk and crossed back to the bulletin board. She indicated the women one by one. "Ellen O'Keefe was a kindergarten teacher, Kris Andrews was a nurse, as was Elena Vegas. Jane Gorman was an accountant. Kelly McClusky was interning at a law firm. Penny James was a resident in a hospital, while the first one, Debra Evans, the senator's niece, worked at an advertising firm." She frowned as she studied the board again. "Did any of them know any of the others?" Nothing she'd found in her files indicated that they did, but there was always a possibility.

Luke shook his head. "As far as I can tell, they weren't even remotely connected."

"Did they have anything else in common besides their looks and their ages?" she asked. It almost sounded as if she was posing the question to herself. Since she had just been brought into the case and the other two detectives were more familiar with the details, she asked them, "Did any of the victims have a record?"

"No," White Hawk answered. "Not even a parking ticket. From all indications, they were all exemplary citizens."

There was only one other factor she was aware of. "What about addiction?" she asked. "Mrs. O'Keefe said her daughter had beaten her addiction to painkillers and so did Kristin—according to what Amanda had said," she added as an afterthought, referring to her cousin's roommate to cover up her slip. "Did any of the other victims have either stints in rehab or drug addictions they had conquered?" Even as she asked the question, another thought occurred to her. "Maybe they all attended the same rehab center?" she suggested, looking from Luke to White Hawk.

Luke considered the question. "I don't know, but it's worth looking into. If there's nothing in the files, maybe talking to their friends and families could shed some light on the subject," he said to the other two detectives.

"Maybe we're going to need a bigger team," White Hawk said. When Luke looked at him quizzically, the other detective added, "You know, like when that guy in *Jaws* said, 'We're going to need a bigger boat.'"

Frankie nodded. "That's an apt comparison. They were hunting a predator in the movie and so are we, only ours is human."

"For the time being, let's just see what we can accomplish before we go to Handel, begging for help," Luke said. It was obvious from his tone that the idea didn't exactly appeal to him.

White Hawk inclined his head, ready to go along with whatever Luke wanted to do. "You're the lead on this," he said. "If you think that the three of us can handle it, then we can."

"Let's put it to the test," was all Luke said.

For once, Frankie agreed with him.

For the remainder of the day, they carefully went over all the information in the files, each of them taking turns reviewing all the folders.

Finally, Luke leaned back in his chair and scrubbed his hands over his face. It felt as if he had been reading for hours and his eyes were just about ready to cross, not to mention that his head was about to explode. As part of his review, he'd made notes on all the files, listing short, descriptive phrases for each of the victims and then comparing them.

Beyond what had already been mentioned, there appeared to be no other similarities between the victims. He looked over toward White Hawk who seemed as mentally worn out as he was.

DeMarco had been placed at a desk near his. The former occupant was currently out on medical leave. Luke sincerely hoped that by the time the detective was cleared for duty and had returned, the case they were working on would be solved, which meant that there would no longer be a need to make use of the detective from Major Crimes.

Although, Luke caught himself thinking, as annoying as the woman could be, at the same time there was something extremely appealing about Detective Francesca DeMarco.

She was very easy on the eye if not on the ear, he thought with a smile.

That was when Frankie looked up and her eyes

met his. "Find something?" she asked, responding to the obvious smile that was curving his mouth.

Much as he hated to admit it, even to himself, De-Marco had caught him completely off guard.

"What?"

"You've got a smug look on your face," she told him. "Like you just came across something. I was just curious what it was."

"No smug look," he denied, thinking that would put an end to her speculation and questions. "I was just thinking of calling it a day and stopping to get a beer at Malone's."

The words were no sooner out of his mouth than White Hawk closed his folder and pushed it away on the desk.

"That gets my vote," he told his partner. Turning toward Frankie, he asked, "How about you?"

She had absolutely no interest—or desire—to go out to get a drink. "I think I'll keep at this a little longer."

"No need to impress anyone," Luke told her, powering down his computer.

"I'm not trying to impress anyone," she responded indignantly, rather insulted that he thought so little of her. Besides, she had no plans to remain with this branch of the department, so there was no point in trying to impress anyone here. "All I want to do is just catch this bastard."

"So do the rest of us," Luke assured her. "But there's nothing in any of these files that won't keep until morning."

"What if he's somewhere in here?" she asked, gesturing at the scattered files. It was possible that all three of them had missed something, some glaring fact that would lead them to the serial killer's identity. "What if putting in that extra hour helps us locate this fiend and stop him—or her," she added as an afterthought, recalling what O'Bannon had said about gender, "from killing the next victim?"

"That argument can be extrapolated to include the next day—or the next five. At some point, a person needs to step back and unwind, if only to get a clearer perspective," Luke told her. When he saw the stubborn expression come over her face, Luke quietly added, "That's an order."

"You can't order me around," she protested.

"While you're working my case I can," he informed Frankie in no uncertain terms, even though he kept his voice low.

Following Luke's example, White Hawk was shutting down his own computer.

"The man has a point," he told Frankie. "He isn't right often, so when he is, I say we just give him his due and all head down to Malone's for that drink." He looked at Frankie. "C'mon, how about it?" he coaxed. "One drink isn't going to hurt," he said, guessing at the source of her reluctance.

For a moment, Frankie debated just turning them down flatly and going home. She had the names of the victims and she could do a little investigating after hours on her own time.

But then it occurred to her that if she got O'Bannon on what he probably regarded as his home turf, he might be more relaxed and pliable, which meant that she stood a possibility of getting more information out of him. She couldn't shake the idea that there had been more to his return visit to see his cousin in the computer lab than he was letting on.

"Okay," she agreed, forcing a smile. "I guess that one beer isn't going to impair my drive home."

"And if it does," Luke said, more or less tongue-in-cheek, "Malone's has got a room in the back of the bar. You can sleep it off there. Half the people who frequent Malone's have made use of that room at one time or another."

He was pulling her leg, she thought, although she wasn't a hundred percent totally confident of that. "Have you?" she asked, studying him closely, looking for an indication that he was putting her on.

"Actually, no," Luke admitted. "I can hold my liquor—and if I couldn't, there's always someone from the family there to drive me home."

In an odd way, his words got to her. "Must be nice," she commented, more to herself than to him as she closed down her computer.

"To have a family member drive you home?" Luke asked, not quite sure if he got her meaning.

"To have a family," she answered before she could censor herself and keep the words from emerging.

White Hawk looked at her in surprise. "You don't have any family?"

"I'll just follow you guys over," Frankie said, abruptly changing the subject. Out of the blue, she added, "I don't have a lot of time tonight." She was paving the way for her exit.

"I thought you were planning on staying here all night, working," Luke reminded her.

"I just remembered something I was supposed to take care of," Frankie replied evasively. Aware that

White Hawk was taking all this in and grinning, she looked at the detective and nodded toward O'Bannon, asking, "Does he always require an excuse to be submitted in writing before he accepts it?"

Amused, White Hawk replied, "Like I said, the man takes some time to get used to."

Leaving the squad room, they walked down the hall to the elevator.

"I don't intend to spend enough time here for that to happen," Frankie told him—as well as indirectly putting O'Bannon on notice. "The minute this killer is arrested, it's back to Major Crimes for me."

"Someone would think that you don't like being around us," Luke quipped.

"That's not true," Frankie said as they got into the elevator. She pressed the button for the first floor. "At least, not about both of you."

White Hawk laughed. "I think she has your number, O'Bannon."

She expected Luke to be annoyed. Instead, she found that the man's grin was nothing short of wicked. Sexy and wicked.

Her reaction unsettled her.

"Then I hope she remembers to use it," Luke said, looking directly at her.

Frankie was doing her best to mentally keep her distance, but it really didn't seem to be working.

Stepping out of the elevator on the ground floor, Frankie looked at the two men. "Just one drink," she emphasized.

"Nobody's going to hold you down and pour liquor down your throat, DeMarco," Luke told her, wondering why she felt the need to put them on notice like this. "The idea behind going to Malone's is just to unwind, not to get falling-down drunk. You can do that with a cheap bottle of whisky in the privacy of your own home," he added. "You do know how to get to Malone's, right?" he asked, just to be sure.

"I've been there before," Frankie answered.

She hadn't gone there often, but she was telling them the truth. She'd gone with the rest of her class the day they all graduated from the academy for a celebratory drink. She'd also gone to Malone's one other time, although she didn't remember the circumstances that had prompted that visit.

Frankie had nothing against sharing a sociable drink, it was just that she always found she was too busy to indulge in that sort of behavior. Working in Major Crimes, she was always the first one in and the last one out—by a long shot. That left her precious little time for any socializing outside of the office.

"Okay, then we'll see you there," Luke said, looking at her expectantly.

"I said you would," she answered with a touch of impatience. Why did it matter so much to him if she went out for a drink with them or not?

"And you are a woman of your word," he replied.

Frankie was all set to accuse him of ridiculing her—except that he looked as if he believed what he had just said.

Maybe, just for the duration of this investigation, O'Bannon and she would find a way to get along.

But most likely not.

"Yes, I am," she said with finality.

With that, she walked over to where she had parked her vehicle that morning.

Getting in, she buckled up and started her car. After a moment, not seeing either of the other two detectives, she blew out a breath of relief and pulled out of her parking space.

With an eye on the rearview mirror—just in case—Frankie left the lot. She didn't like the idea of being followed and it looked as if she wasn't.

Frankie drove down the block in the general direction of the establishment where so many of the men and women from the Aurora police station tended to gather.

She was still not a hundred percent sold on this idea of socializing with the two men she had spent the day working with. If Malone's parking lot was crowded, she told herself, she would circle it once. If she didn't readily find a parking space, then she intended to just go home and see how far she could take the investigation on her own.

If she was being completely honest with herself, Frankie had to admit that she was rooting for there being no available parking spaces when she pulled into the lot in front of Malone's.

But she could see that there were several spaces available. One was even right up front, a few feet from the entrance. With a sigh, she pulled in and turned off her ignition. She sat there for a moment, debating whether or not to get out. By the time she did get out of her car, she saw that both Luke and White Hawk had already walked up and were on either side of her vehicle.

She looked at them in surprise. "Were you right behind me?" she asked. How else could they have appeared so quickly? But she hadn't seen either of their vehicles, she thought.

"If you have to ask that," Luke told her, "we're going to have to work on you being able to spot a tail. White Hawk's car was right behind yours. And I was right behind his."

That almost sounded like a mini-convoy—or an escort. "Why?"

"Because we were all going in the same direction to the same place," Luke answered matter-of-factly. "I guess maybe we'll have to work on your paranoia, as well."

"Maybe what we have to work on is you not *making* me feel that way," she told him. She had half a mind to get back into her car and drive away.

Luke nodded his head as if considering her words. Going up the front steps to Malone's, he opened the front door and held it for her, waiting.

"Fair enough," he told her. "But right now, what we have to work on is unwinding," Luke said. "Agreed?" he asked, his eyes meeting hers.

The word came out grudgingly and under duress. "Agreed."

With that, she walked in—counting the minutes until she would walk out again.

Chapter 8

"You know," Luke said as he set down the mugs of ale he'd brought over to the table for himself and for her, "you might enjoy yourself more if you didn't look as if you were bracing yourself to face a really eager firing squad."

If anything, Frankie sat up even straighter. "I'm just exhibiting good posture," she told him.

"Compared to you, a wooden ruler has the rigidity of a strand of overcooked spaghetti," he informed Frankie with a good-natured laugh, taking a seat opposite her at the small table.

Frankie frowned. She had no intention of sitting here, having to endure insults. She looked around. "Where's White Hawk?"

Luke nodded back toward the bar. "He ran into someone he hadn't seen for a while, so they're catching up. Why?" His smile widened. "Are you nervous being alone with me without a chaperone?"

She was not about to have him think that she was afraid of him—because she wasn't. She was just a little…uncomfortable, she finally admitted. "I wouldn't exactly call a bar full of cops being alone."

"Good," Luke commented, looking pleased. "Then relax."

Frankie looked at the drink he had put in front of her. "Isn't this a lot of beer?"

Luke shrugged. "Standard-size mug," he told her innocently.

The hell it was. If she were any shorter, she could go for a swim in the mug. "I thought we were just getting a glass of beer," she said.

He hadn't specified either way, but he had his reason for getting mugs. "Getting a mug is actually more economical," he told her.

"And finishing it takes longer," she said. She was onto O'Bannon, Frankie thought, and saving money had nothing to do with it.

Luke made no effort to deny what he took to be her accusation. Instead, he grinned as if she'd caught him. "There's that, too," Luke agreed. "C'mon, De-Marco, kick back. Relax. We're all friends here."

"We're coworkers," she corrected him pointedly. "We're not friends."

"We can be," he countered. And then he became serious. "What's so wrong with having friends, Frankie?" he asked.

She looked at O'Bannon sharply. This had to be the first time he'd used her first name. She wasn't altogether sure how she felt about that, despite the warm ripple that had just corkscrewed through her stomach.

Because she could see that O'Bannon was still waiting for an answer, she came up with one for him.

"In order to be friends, you have to talk to someone, exchange personal information with them, get close to them." None of which was acceptable to her, she added silently. "And then get hurt if something happens to that person."

"Speaking from experience?" he asked her. He'd been intently listening to her, studying every movement as Frankie spoke. Her body language said far more than she did.

"Just conjecturing."

Luke knew he should just let this slide, but she had inadvertently given him the perfect opening he'd been looking for. He needed to get this matter out in the open and sooner was always better than later—for both their sakes.

"The serial killer's latest victim," he began slowly, "The one you brought to us."

Her eyes narrowed. Frankie was instantly on her guard. "What about her?"

"What's the story behind that?"

"I already told you," Frankie reminded him impatiently. "I know the—the victim's roommate casually and she called me when she saw her friend on the floor and panicked."

"So you said," Luke recalled. And he wasn't buying it. "Now, what's the real story?"

"That *is* the real story."

"Okay." Luke was willing to buy that she had given him some of the details—just not the ones that mattered. "What's the *rest* of the story? And before you sink deeper into this lie, Valri found photos on Kristin Andrews's laptop. Photos of the two of you."

Frankie shrugged, looking away. "Kris was always taking pictures. She must have taken those when I dropped by to see Amanda," she said, trying to sound uninterested.

"I thought you and Amanda weren't close," Luke reminded her.

She felt as if he was tightening a noose around her. The man was really beginning to annoy her. "Well, we weren't complete strangers. Kristin was always snapping selfies. She must have snapped that picture you saw when I was at the apartment."

His expression was unreadable. "How long did you say they were roommates?"

At least here she didn't have to lie, Frankie thought, feeling relieved. "Two years."

He nodded, taking the information in. "Then why is the photo dated five years ago?"

Damn! Frankie thought. "Probably a glitch in the software." She shrugged off his words.

"You're quick on your feet," Luke noted with a touch of admiration. "You've got an answer for everything."

Not trusting herself to meet his gaze, Frankie deliberately looked away. "Just answering your questions," she told him. Setting down the mug, she began to get up from the table. "Look, I really should be going home—"

His next words stopped her cold. "She's your cousin, isn't she?"

Frankie struggled to compose herself before turning to look at him. "Amanda?"

"Kristin."

Frankie's mouth went dry, but she did what she could to try to brazen the moment out. "I think you've made a mistake," she informed him coldly.

"I'm capable of mistakes from time to time," he admitted. "But not this time. I did a little digging after Valri found the photos—there was more than one, by the way." The wary expression entering her eyes told him that he was on the right path. "Your mother and Kristin's mother were sisters," he told her. "I believe that makes you her cousin."

There was a sinking feeling in her stomach even as she narrowed her eyes, giving him a steely look. Denying what he'd just said was futile. She had no doubt that O'Bannon was thorough and had the proof he needed to back up what he was saying.

"So, now what?" Frankie demanded, not bothering to hide her annoyance. "You're going to tell Handel? Or have you already told him and you thought you'd buy me a beer before giving me the bum's rush?" she asked.

Instead of answering her, he asked Frankie a question. "Why did you lie? Why didn't you just tell me that you were the victim's cousin when you first came to me?"

Frankie glared at him. He knew the answer to that. Why was he torturing her like this?

"Because I wouldn't be allowed anywhere near the case if I said that and you know it. My being related to the victim would be considered a conflict of interest or some such bull," she retorted.

He was well aware of that rule. He was also aware of other factors. "And you didn't think it was worth the effort to try to convince me to let you work the case with us?"

What was he trying to prove with all this? "I wasn't about to grovel if I knew all along what the answer would be."

"You're that sure?" Luke asked pointedly as he continued probing.

O'Bannon was just messing with her mind, trying to create doubt. "You don't know me from Adam," she began, but got no further.

He laughed at that. "Oh, trust me, I know a few Adams and *none* of them look a thing like you," he guaranteed, allowing a note of appreciation to slip into his voice.

Impatience was making her very short-tempered. "What I meant," she tried again—he was forcing her to jump through hoops and this wasn't going to lead anywhere, she fumed, "was that I didn't think I stood a chance of convincing you to let me in on the case. There are rules on the books against this kind of thing."

The expression on his face was completely unreadable. "I know."

"So why are you playing this elaborate game of cat and mouse with me?" she asked angrily.

Frankie began to get up from the table again, but this time he caught her by the wrist, keeping her in place.

She yanked, trying to get her wrist free, but he continued holding it fast.

"Sit down, DeMarco," he ordered her in an even

voice. "The last thing you want to do is to make a scene."

Still fuming and biting back a few choice words, she sat down.

"You don't know what I want," she informed him heatedly.

"Oh, don't be so sure of that," he told her. "You want in on this case. You want to catch whoever cut your cousin's life short. You don't want to be a spectator or stay on the sidelines, you want to be right there in the thick of the investigation and eventually take the bastard down."

"Yes," she answered between gritted teeth. "But I'm not about to sleep with you to get you to keep my secret," she told him, guessing at the price he was about to exact from her in exchange for allowing her to remain on the case.

Luke surprised her by laughing as he released her wrist.

"If I wanted to sleep with you, I wouldn't need to use your secret as leverage," he assured her. Before she could make any sort of a retort, Luke became serious and continued. "She was your cousin and someone killed her. In your place I would want exactly what you want—to catch the bastard who did this to one of my own.

"I've got a really big family," he told her, "and I'd go to hell and back for each and every one of them. If someone hurt—or killed—one of them, I wouldn't let protocol shackle me."

He made it sound like a vow.

Frankie stared at him. She was afraid to allow her

hopes to be raised. Hopes that were raised could be dashed, hard.

But at this point, Frankie realized that hope was all she had left.

"So, what are you telling me?" Frankie asked, lowering her voice to a steely whisper. "That you'll let me stay on the team?"

"We need the extra help," he told her matter-of-factly. "And you need the closure. From where I'm standing, it's a win-win situation."

"And what happens if Handel winds up finding out that Kristin was my cousin?" Frankie asked him. "And that you knew all along and didn't tell him or bar me from the case?"

"Why should he?" Luke challenged seriously. "It's not as if you're planning on taking out a front-page ad in the local paper proclaiming your connection to the latest victim."

"And you're not going to tell anyone?"

He looked at her incredulously. She really was paranoid. He did what he could to reassure her. "Why would I? Your relationship to her doesn't have any bearing on the case. It certainly doesn't bring us one step closer to the serial killer's identity," Luke pointed out.

Frankie relaxed by degrees as relief slowly slid through her veins, taking root. And then suspicion suddenly raised its head again. "Why are you being so nice to me?"

"Haven't you heard?" Luke asked her innocently. "I'm a really nice guy."

Frankie blew out a breath. She didn't know if she would go that far, but for all intents and purposes,

O'Bannon was being extremely nice to her. And understanding. She was beginning to believe him when he told her how he felt about his own family.

In a way, she supposed that gave them a connection and allowed him to understand how she felt about Kristin's murder, about her need to bring the person who killed her to justice.

She owed him.

"I guess I should say thank you," Frankie said in a low voice.

"Only if you want to," he responded with a careless shrug.

She just couldn't figure him out. But then, she supposed that she didn't have to. All she needed was to have him let her remain as an active member on the team.

Frankie raised her beer mug—which was still three-quarters full—in a silent salute to the man sitting opposite her. Looking directly into his eyes, she said, "Thank you."

"Don't mention it," Luke responded. "Hey—" he sounded pleased "—you're starting to relax. Knew coming to Malone's was a good idea for you."

It wasn't the beer or the establishment that had gotten her to relax. It was being allowed to share the burden that she was carrying around with someone who understood.

But if O'Bannon chose to believe what he had just said about Malone's, who was she to dispute it? "I guess you were right," she conceded, with just the smallest hint of a smile.

Her admission pleased him.

"Yeah," he replied with an understanding expression. "I was."

"You were right about what?" White Hawk asked, finally coming over to join them.

Turning to look at the taller man, Frankie couldn't help wondering if it was just a coincidence that the detective had been absent while she and O'Bannon had had it out. She had never believed in coincidences, but White Hawk had a completely innocent expression on his face as he asked the question and looked from her to O'Bannon and back again.

"Most everything," Luke answered with a glib smile on his lips.

"Well, I'd love to stay and listen to some more of this ego fest of yours, O'Bannon, but Linda just texted me." White Hawk patted the pocket where he kept his cellphone. "She wanted to know if I was ever coming home again."

"Linda?" Frankie asked, looking at White Hawk. It wasn't like her to ask even remotely personal questions. But evidently the rules were changing.

"His better half," Luke told her, and then he grinned. "His *way* better half," he emphasized.

"I'll tell her you said so. Might make her overlook that you dragged me to Malone's and that I'm coming home smelling of beer."

"Probably not," Luke predicted. "Give her my love anyway."

White Hawk laughed dryly. "The hell I will. You've got enough women without poaching mine." He turned toward Frankie and nodded at her. "See you tomorrow, DeMarco. Really glad you're on the team."

He sounded as if he genuinely meant what he'd just said, Frankie thought. She smiled back at him, pleased about the way the day had gone, despite all her initial concerns.

"Between the two of us," White Hawk continued, "maybe we can keep O'Bannon on an even keel."

"You're going to need more than a feisty Major Crimes detective to do that," Luke told his partner.

"A man can dream," White Hawk responded, winking at the new member of their team.

With that, both Frankie and O'Bannon looked on as White Hawk walked out of Malone's.

Chapter 9

"How close were you to your cousin?" Luke asked.

Frankie stared at him. The question had come out of the blue and caught her totally off guard. She'd just turned away from the entrance and wasn't sure why O'Bannon was asking her that or how she should respond.

"Close," she finally answered stoically. "She was my only family and I was her only family. That kind of thing tends to make you closer. Why?" she asked. She saw no reason for Luke to be poking around in her private life.

Luke toyed with his beer. "Would you know if there was a jealous boyfriend in the picture? Or maybe an ex-boyfriend who didn't like her dating anyone else?"

"No," she answered.

"There wasn't, or you don't know?" he asked.

"There wasn't," she told him.

"You sound pretty sure of that," he observed. The noise level was rising at Malone's and he was forced to lean in so that she could hear him without his having to raise his voice.

Frankie's first reaction was to pull away, but she didn't want to make it look as if she was causing a scene. So she remained where she was, trying to ignore the fact that she could feel his breath on her face when he spoke.

"I am," she told him. "Kristin didn't date. She was too busy with her career. She had just gone to work for Aurora General Hospital six months ago, and she was working really hard to make a good impression. She intended to become a head nurse some day and she wanted to make up for lost time."

He looked at Frankie skeptically. "I saw your cousin's picture. She was way too pretty not to be dating."

Frankie shook her head. Typical male reaction. "Looks don't mean anything. Dating is a mind-set. I don't date."

"You're putting me on."

"Why would I do that?" Frankie asked.

Luke stared at her, trying to wrap his head around what she was telling him. If she'd said that she was going out every night, that she was beating off men with a stick, *that* he would have readily believed. But this? It just didn't make any sense to him.

"You don't date?" he asked incredulously.

Frankie took another sip of her ale before answering. "I don't have the time. I'm a detective. I get wrapped up in my work." She shrugged as if the fact was commonplace in her job and no big deal. "You know how it is."

"Actually," he told her, "I don't. You know that old saying, all work and no play makes Jack a dull boy? Well, it applies to guys named Luke, too." He was allowing himself to stray off the topic, Luke admonished himself. "Anyway, the reason I asked you about your cousin's dating habits is because I thought if she had some unreasonable boyfriend in the background, he might turn out to be a person of interest."

Things were rarely that simple or easy, she thought. "Well, there was no one like that in the picture as far as I know. I mean, Kris talked about wanting to date. She wanted to have kids someday." Frankie stopped for a moment, struggling to get control over her emotions. The last thing she wanted to do was cry in public, especially in front of O'Bannon. Taking a breath, she said, "But Kris was shy, and despite her looks, she really didn't have much confidence in herself."

He could see that Frankie was having a hard time with the subject and he didn't want to press, but these were questions that needed answering and she would be in the best position to provide those answers.

"How about enemies?" he asked. "Did your cousin have any enemies?"

She looked at him, stunned. The idea was totally ludicrous. "Kris? She was the sweetest person you'd ever want to meet. Everyone loved her."

And I'm going to miss her like crazy. She was still having a really hard time dealing with this. It just didn't seem real to her, even though she had seen Kris's body.

Luke frowned as he looked down at what was left in the bottom of his mug. "Obviously not everyone," he said, more or less to himself.

From the way Frankie straightened rigidly, he knew she had overheard him despite the din in the bar.

"Maybe she was just a random choice," she suggested. "Kris opened the door to the wrong person."

"It wasn't random," he told her. Luke took the last sip of ale and put his mug down on the table. "This had to be someone your cousin knew, at least, to some degree."

"Why would you say that?" she asked.

He drew even closer, knowing she wouldn't want this fact advertised. "You mentioned that your cousin had a drug problem."

She looked at him sharply. Kris had a great many attributes and good qualities. She didn't want her cousin's former drug addiction to be the first thing that came up when her name was mentioned.

"Emphasis on *had*," Frankie reminded him crisply. "Kristin beat her addiction. She was clean. I would swear to that on a dozen bibles, if you like."

"My point is that the person who killed her knew that about your cousin. Knew that she'd been involved with drugs," he emphasized. "That's why the killer made it look like a drug overdose."

She recalled the photos of the other women on the bulletin board. "Just like he did with the other women he murdered."

"Exactly," Luke agreed.

"That means he had to have gotten that information from somewhere." She started reviewing the various ways that sort of information could be obtained. "Maybe they went to the same Narcotics Anonymous meetings." It was the first thing that came to her mind.

It seemed unlikely to him that all the victims had attended the same meetings, but he wasn't about to discount that possibility yet.

"That's a long shot, but it's worth looking into," he agreed.

He could see what Frankie was thinking. She appeared ready to go back to the squad room and do another search through the files and online records.

"Tomorrow," he told her in no uncertain terms.

Preoccupied, she heard his voice only belatedly. Looking up, she forced herself to focus. He'd just said something to her, but she couldn't summon up what it was.

"What?"

For her benefit, Luke put it into a whole sentence. "We'll look into that angle tomorrow."

"Tomorrow might be too late," she protested, going back to her old argument. "What if the killer's out there, killing someone right now and we could have stopped him if we'd only found his name sooner?"

It was the what-ifs that could undermine and destroy a detective, Luke thought. He'd seen it happen more than once.

"You think like that, you'll make yourself crazy," he told her. "Even if we did burn the midnight oil, there's no guarantee we're going to find this guy tonight. Odds are against it," he told her calmly. "And burning the candle at both ends means that whatever's left is no good to anyone. The only place you're going from here is home," he said with finality. "And that's a direct order."

Frankie felt her back going up. "I think you should know that I'm not very good at taking orders."

Leaning in even closer, he had one word for her. "Learn."

The hell she would. This was *her* cousin they were talking about, not one of his. "Yeah, okay, fine," she told him, standing up.

"Hold on," he instructed, the sheer force of his voice stopping her. "I don't trust you to go home," Luke told her.

She fisted her hands on her waist and glared at him—but she didn't move. "So, what do you plan to do, strap me to the roof of your car and take me home yourself?" she challenged.

"Tempting, but I left my rope at home. What I plan to do is follow you, DeMarco, and make sure that you get home."

Frankie stared at him. Was he serious? He was treating her like a child.

"You're kidding," she said in disbelief, unable to imagine O'Bannon actually carrying out his threat and going out of his way like this.

"I've been known to kid," he agreed. "But not this time. I'm serious." He pulled on her elbow, bringing her back down to her seat so he could issue his warning without having anyone else overhear. "You want me to keep your secret, you play by my rules—and don't say *you're kidding* again, because at this point, you know damn well I'm not." His eyes held hers. "Have I made myself clear?"

"Perfectly," she ground out between clenched

teeth. Frankie pulled her elbow away. "And here I thought you were actually a nice guy."

He rose to his feet. "I am a nice guy," Luke told her. He gestured for her to walk out of the bar with him. "I want you to go on living." He watched Frankie grudgingly walk out of the bar ahead of him. "Sleepy people get sloppy. Sloppy people run the risk of getting themselves killed—or getting their partners killed."

They walked over to her car. "I am not your partner," she reminded him. That honor belonged to White Hawk.

"Let's just say that you've got the role of sub-partner," Luke quipped. He nodded at her vehicle. "Now get into your car and wait until I pull up near you."

She frowned at him, doing her best to banish the feel of his breath on her face. He was too close again. "You are really bossy, you know that?"

"Comes with the territory" he answered. "And I wouldn't have to be if you knew how to take orders," he pointed out.

Getting into her vehicle, Frankie fumed as she waited until she saw his car pull up parallel to the one next to her.

She'd been tempted, just for a moment, to just take off the moment she was behind the wheel, just like the cars in one of the *Fast and Furious* movies that Kris had loved to watch. But she had no doubt that O'Bannon would make good on his threat to talk to his lieutenant, thereby getting her kicked off the case.

So she waited until she saw Luke's car in her rear-view mirror and then she pulled out of her parking space. She made her way out of the lot more slowly than she was happy about.

He kept up with her, shadowing her every move and never more than approximately three feet behind her car.

The more she was aware of O'Bannon, the more annoyed she grew.

But not annoyed enough to test him and peel out away from him.

True to his word, Luke followed her all the way home. She expected him to pull away once she'd pulled in to her apartment complex, but he didn't. Instead, he parked his sedan two spaces away from hers.

Getting out, she crossed to him and looked at Luke reprovingly. "That space belongs to the apartment above me," she told him. "Guest parking is all the way over there," she said, pointing toward it.

He made no effort to get back into his car and move it.

"Don't worry. I'm not going to be here long enough to cause a problem—unless your neighbor comes home in the next ten minutes or less."

That seemed like an odd choice. Why would he need ten minutes to watch her? She wasn't that far from her apartment.

"Why ten minutes?" she asked.

He had an answer all ready for her. "Because that's approximately how long I need to make sure you're safe inside your apartment."

"Are you worried about my safety?" she questioned.

She might be the serial killer's type, but there was no history of a substance abuse problem in her past so she definitely didn't qualify as someone the killer would want for his next victim.

"No, I'm worried about you living up to your word," he said simply.

Her eyes narrowed. "You'd rat me out, wouldn't you?" Even as she asked the question, she knew the answer.

"In a heartbeat," he said without hesitation. "If I can't trust you to keep your word, I can't work with you."

A few choice words rose to Frankie's lips, but she didn't utter them. She supposed she could see his side of it. Not the part about her being too tired to be of any use if she didn't get her sleep, just the part about not trusting her if she went back on her word.

"You can trust me, O'Bannon," she told him grudgingly. With that, she went to her door and unlocked it.

"Good," Luke said, coming right up behind her. "Because I'd really hate to have to have you kicked off the case."

She turned the doorknob and opened her door, then turned around to face him. Again, he was standing closer than she felt comfortable about. The man just kept invading her space.

"You can go home now," she told him. "You have officially delivered me to my doorstep."

"You delivered yourself," he corrected. "I just wanted to make sure you got in," he told her.

He was stalling and he knew it. There was no reason for him to still be here in front of her apartment like this, no reason not to turn on his heel and go back to his car.

And definitely no reason to linger, watching the way the moon seemed to play off her skin, making it a gold hue. Caressing it.

The way he was sorely tempted to do.

Her eyes met his and Frankie felt that odd pull again. The one that made no sense to her, given the circumstances—and the person it involved.

There was also no reason her breath suddenly caught in her throat, she thought, then decided that it was undoubtedly the result of her anger over being treated just like a five-year-old who had to be herded to her room.

Loosen up, Frankie. He's letting you stay on the case. There's no one making him do that. You're the one behaving like a little brat, she told herself.

Frankie squared her shoulders.

"O'Bannon," she said, just as he was about to walk away.

He looked at her. "Yes?"

There was just the slightest hint of a smile beginning to curve the corners of her mouth. "Thanks."

Confusion entered his eyes. "For what?"

"For the…beer," Frankie said haltingly, then forced herself to add, "and for letting me stay on."

He laughed shortly. "Yeah. Don't mention it," he muttered. "The beer or the other stuff," he added.

If he didn't leave now, he was in danger of doing something stupid. Something that would really compromise everything.

With effort, Luke shut down the attraction that

had suddenly washed over him, drawing him to this detective with the fiery tongue.

"I'll see you in the morning," he told her.

For one sliver of a moment, Frankie had the feeling that he was going to lean in and kiss her—which was ridiculous, because he'd given no indication that he was the least bit drawn to her.

Maybe it was all that talk about dating that was responsible for making her think like this. Or maybe he saw her as some kind of a challenge because she said she didn't date. Despite what she'd said in Malone's, she was well aware of O'Bannon's reputation. He went through women like most men went through clean socks.

Other than the fact that he seemed to be close to his family, they had nothing in common.

This was all probably just her imagination, anyway.

"Yeah, see you in the morning," she echoed, then slipped inside her apartment and closed the door.

"Don't forget the lock," he told her, still standing on her doorstep.

Luke smiled to himself. He could almost *hear* her scowling.

"I'm not a child, O'Bannon," she retorted.

He raised his voice just a little bit. "If you were a child, DeMarco, you wouldn't be living in an apartment by yourself and I wouldn't need to tell you to lock the door."

He heard her utter a muffled scream, followed by the sound of a lock being flipped. Smiling to himself, he walked away from her door and back to where he had parked his vehicle.

Frankie went to the window that faced the parking area and cracked the blinds just enough to watch O'Bannon head back to his car. She supposed that part of her didn't really believe he was actually going to drive away. But he did get into his car.

After a moment, he started it up and slowly pulled out of the spot. As he drove past her apartment on his way out, he waved at her.

She pulled her fingers away from the blinds, letting them close quickly.

Damn him, he'd known she was watching him. O'Bannon seemed to be one step ahead of her no matter what she did, Frankie thought, irritated.

So what? All that matters here is that you're still part of the investigation. Focus on that—and not those hypnotic green eyes!

Easier said than done, she thought grudgingly as she went into her bedroom.

Chapter 10

Luke turned down the radio in his vehicle as he approached the cul-de-sac in the development where he lived. Focusing, he could make out a gleaming red sports car that was parked in his driveway. Since it was the middle of the week, he wasn't sure exactly who to expect.

Certainly not the only person he knew who drove a red sports car.

But as he drew closer, he saw that he was right. He knew who it belonged to. Parking next to it, he got out and circled around to the driver's side. The window was rolled down.

Peering into the car, Luke asked, "What are you doing in my driveway, Mom?" just before he opened her car door for her.

He would have helped her out, but he knew that

would irritate her. She was exceedingly independent, and even now Maeve Cavanaugh O'Bannon had more spring to her step than any of her five children. She maintained that it was because she refused to retire and still, on occasion, drove one of the ambulances that she was now in charge of at the fire station if they turned out to be shorthanded.

"I'm waiting for you, Lukkas," Maeve answered, getting out. She paused to lock her car. "Are you sure that you're a detective, dear?" the lively woman with the expressive green eyes deadpanned.

Luke smiled tolerantly at his mother as he led the way to his front door. For as long as he could remember, the petite woman who looked years younger than her age had always struck him as being a dynamo. "You could have waited for me inside, you know. You would have been a lot more comfortable. Did you forget your key?" he asked.

He, like the rest of his siblings, had given his mother a key to his house to use in case of any emergencies.

Maeve shook her head. "I don't feel right just letting myself in like that."

They'd gone over this before. Maeve had instilled a keen sense of privacy within each of her children, and he appreciated her toeing the line herself, but she did have a habit of carrying things too far. He had nothing to hide from her and had said as much more than once.

Luke shook his head as he unlocked his door. "I guess you can't teach an old dog new tricks."

"Hey, watch that *old* stuff," Maeve warned him,

following her son into his house. "I can still take you over my knee."

"I'll keep that in mind," he told her. Closing his door again, he flipped the lock then turned around to face her. "So, to what do I owe this surprise visit?"

She cleared her throat as if she didn't know how to start. "Well, I won't keep you—" she began.

"That's not what I asked, Mom." He looked at her more closely, searching her face. She wasn't in the habit of just turning up on any of their doorsteps. "Something wrong?"

Rather than meet his gaze head-on, Maeve looked away. "Not exactly…"

That just made him more concerned. This wasn't like her. "Mom," he said, a touch more sternly. "Level with me. What's going on?"

Maeve pulled back her shoulders, making her stand a shade taller—which brought her all the way up to five foot three—as she searched for the right words. Still not sure if she had them, she forged ahead anyway.

"I need some advice."

That really surprised him. In all the years that he had known her, his mother was always the decisive one. Widowed shortly after she had given birth to her fifth child, rather than turn to her three brothers for help, she had shouldered the responsibility of providing for her children right from the very beginning.

She was their rock, the one everyone else turned to—including, on occasion, his uncles.

For his mother to show up now, asking for advice, was completely out of character. He wasn't sure just how he was supposed to respond.

"I'm flattered," he told her.

"Don't be flattered, just be thoughtful," Maeve requested.

"Okay." He gestured toward the sofa. "Why don't we sit down and you can tell me what's going on? Take your time," he told her, thinking that this thing—whatever it was—was undoubtedly difficult for her to talk about.

Maeve folded her hands gracefully in her lap and looked into her son's eyes. "Craig Carlyle just asked me out."

For the second time that evening, Luke was completely stunned. To his knowledge, the only time his mother went out was to attend one of the many family get-togethers that Andrew Cavanaugh, the former chief of police, had a fondness for throwing. She never took anyone with her who wasn't directly related to her.

Looking at his mother now, he couldn't gauge whether or not she was happy about being asked out by the fire chief, or if she was searching for a way to let him down easily.

Still watching his mother's face, he asked, "What did you tell him?"

He noticed that her fingers seemed to tighten around one another before she answered. The topic definitely made her uncomfortable.

"I didn't tell him anything," Maeve said. "I said that I'd get back to him."

Luke laughed softly. "You romantic little vixen, you know just how to get to a man's heart, don't you?"

She frowned at him, not sharing his sense of

humor about this. "Lukkas, I'm serious," Maeve stressed. "What do I tell him?"

"Isn't this something that you should be asking Ronan?" Luke told her, referring to his oldest brother. "Or better yet, his fiancée, Sierra. I mean, she does just happen to be Chief Carlyle's daughter," he pointed out. "She's got more at stake in this."

"Exactly," Maeve agreed. "I came to you because you have no skin in the game," she told him.

"You do know how to turn a phrase, Mom," Luke marveled. He slid forward on the sofa, getting closer to his mother as he looked into her eyes. "What do *you* want to do?"

She sighed and shook her head, lost. "I don't know…"

He wasn't buying that. "Yes, you do, Mom. You're the most organized person I know. You've always had an answer for everything. What's your answer to this? *Do* you want to go out with Chief Carlyle?"

Maeve took a deep breath, as if she was preparing herself to jump off the high board and dive straight into the pool. "Yes."

"Problem solved," he told her. "Now you need to *tell* him that," Luke urged. "And do it quick, before his ego gets really bruised with all this waiting."

"His ego isn't bruised," Maeve scoffed, waving away the very suggestion.

But Luke had a very different viewpoint of the situation. "Trust me, Mom. He's a guy. All guys' egos get bruised—and it doesn't matter how old they are," he underscored.

Maeve looked a little concerned. "Maybe you're right," she conceded. "I'll call him as soon as I get home," she said, making the decision right on the spot. Smiling, she reached up and patted Luke's cheek. "This is why I came to you instead of one of the others. You cut through all the layers and got to the heart of the matter, even better than your twin sister," she remarked, referring to Brianna.

He slipped his arm around Maeve's small, slender shoulders then gently guided his mother toward the front door. Now that she had what she came for—his input—Luke knew she was anxious to get home and put her plan into motion.

"I just said what you wanted to hear, Mom," he told her.

Maeve laughed softly. "There's that, too. See? Like I said, you cut through all the layers. No flattery, no unnecessary rhetoric."

Reaching around his mother, Luke opened the door for her. "Mom?"

About to walk out, she looked up at him. "Yes, Lukkas?"

He grinned at her. "Just don't do anything I wouldn't do."

Maeve laughed in response. "That leaves me a great deal of territory to cover."

"And tell Chief Carlyle," Luke added as he walked her back to her car, "that if he does *anything* at all to hurt you, I will end him."

Maeve opened the driver's-side door. "I'm sure that'll have him shaking in his boots, dear," she replied. Getting in, she buckled her seatbelt and then gazed up at her son. "What's wrong, Lukkas?"

Rousing himself, he smiled at her. "I was just thinking about that old adage."

"What old adage, dear?"

"They grow up so fast," he told her, struggling to keep a straight face.

His mother's hazel eyes crinkled at the corners as they met his. "Yes," she told him with a touch of seriousness. "I know."

Luke stepped back from the sports car as she started it up. "Be sure to let me know how it goes, Mom," he requested.

"I might have to censor some things," she told him. "But you'll be the first one I call."

Then, with a deep laugh that was so familiar to him, his mother drove away.

Luke stood in his driveway for a while, watching as the red sports car made it down the block and turned left, disappearing from view.

Who would have ever thought that his mother would be out there, dating? he mused. This was an entirely new side of her, and it was definitely going to take some getting used to, even though he was happy for her.

He just hoped she wouldn't wind up getting hurt.

Damn, he thought as he went back into the house, something new to worry about.

"You're in early," he commented to Frankie the next morning shortly before eight as he walked into the squad room. "But then," he reflected, "I suppose that doesn't really surprise me. I half expected you to sneak out of your apartment last night and come back to the squad room after I drove away."

"How did you know I didn't?" Frankie challenged,

wondering if he'd actually parked on the outskirts of her complex for a while, out of view.

"You're wearing different clothes," he answered, nodding at her outfit. The two-piece suit she'd had on yesterday had given way to jeans and a short jacket over an emerald-green pullover.

"I could have had a change of clothing in my car," Frankie pointed out.

"I guess you could have," he acknowledged. Luke put the container of coffee he'd brought in for her on her desk, then sat down at his own desk. Leaning forward, he took the lid off his coffee. "You like to keep me guessing, don't you, DeMarco?"

She gave him an innocent look. "Complacency slows your reflexes."

He pretended to look impressed. "You just come up with that?" he asked.

"Seems like the appropriate response," she answered, then asked, "What do I owe you for the coffee?"

"Well, for starters, how does your undying loyalty sound?" he quipped.

Frankie slid the unopened container over toward his desk. "Too high a price."

He put up his hand, keeping the coffee from coming any closer. "Then how about truthful answers?"

Frankie inclined her head and drew the container back over to her side. "That I can do, seeing as how you ferreted out my one secret."

"That's not ferreting," he told her with a self-satisfied smile. "That's just plain old good detective work."

"No, that's having a cousin in the computer lab," Frankie corrected.

"That's all part of the good detective work," he responded. Changing the subject, Luke nodded at the back of her monitor. "So, did you find out anything new about our victims?"

"Not new," Frankie qualified. "But I'm compiling a list of all of their friends and coworkers that we can question. I thought that might lead us to some sort of an overlap, which just might ultimately bring us to the killer."

He looked at her, pleased. "See how much you can accomplish when you get a good night's sleep?" Luke asked her.

"Aren't you afraid that you'll wind up pulling a muscle, patting yourself on the back like that?" she asked.

"Nope," he answered, grinning. "My mother thought it was a good idea for all of us to take yoga classes when we were kids. Turns out that I'm still pretty flexible," he said, his eyes meeting hers as he grinned.

Frankie felt herself growing warmer.

Why did she feel as if he was putting her on some kind of notice?

Maybe you didn't get as much sleep as you thought you did.

With effort, she shifted the conversation to what he'd just said about his mother. "Your mother sounds like a very progressive woman."

A fond look came into his eyes. It wasn't lost on Frankie.

"Oh, that she is," he told her. "She raised the five

of us all by herself—or as *by yourself* as you can be if you're a Cavanaugh," he added. "Mom drove an ambulance for years, then branched out and wound up buying the company, adding a couple more ambulances to the number along the way." He thought of last night's unexpected visit. "And, apparently, she's still up for new challenges."

Frankie raised her eyes from the monitor. Something in the other detective's voice made her think he wanted to speak but was holding back.

She didn't exactly know O'Bannon all that well, but he didn't strike her as the type who ordinarily withheld information.

"What sort of new challenges?" she asked.

Luke took a breath, as if to fortify himself before answering. At the last second, he stopped before he told her. It was as if the words couldn't make it all the way out.

"What sort of challenges?" she repeated, telling herself that if he didn't answer her this time, she was letting the matter drop.

And, in actuality, it was probably better that way, since she really didn't think that sharing things with this man was a good idea. As far as she was concerned, his knowing about Kris was sharing more than enough.

"My mother's thinking about dating again," Luke told her without any preamble.

"And you disapprove?" she heard herself asking. Why was she asking him that? She didn't care how he felt about this.

Right?

The awful thing was that she really didn't know

how she felt about O'Bannon sharing something so personal as his mother's unorthodox behavior—or, at least, unorthodox in his eyes.

"No, I'm happy for her," he told her. "I really am," he added after a moment.

"Then what's the problem? Because there's obviously a problem from that expression on your face."

"It just—feels odd," he finally said. That was the best word for it, he thought. Odd.

Frankie laughed, more at the perplexed expression on his face than what he'd just said. "She probably felt the same way when you started dating."

"You expect your kids to date," Luke answered. "You don't expect your parents to suddenly do that after a thirty-year dry spell."

"It hasn't been that long between dates for you, has it, O'Bannon?" White Hawk asked, walking in on the tail end of his partner's conversation. He draped his jacket over the back of his chair, still looking at Luke. "Because if you want, I can have Linda fix you up with someone—"

"I was just talking about my mother. She's suddenly decided that she's going out on a date," Luke clarified.

Just then, his cellphone rang.

As did White Hawk's.

They exchanged looks. That only meant one thing. Another victim had turned up.

Chapter 11

Frankie braced herself just before she walked into the apartment where Vanessa Jackson's lifeless body had been found. As ready as she would ever be, she followed O'Bannon in through the open door. White Hawk remained outside, canvassing the neighbors to see if anyone had heard or seen anything that might be useful in the investigation.

The scene inside the apartment was similar to the one she'd seen when she found her cousin. An attractive, dark-haired young woman was lying on the floor, dead. There was a syringe on the floor not far from her body. A rubber cord was still tied to her left arm, as if the last thing she had done was to administer the fatal overdose to herself.

Mechanically slipping on a pair of rubber gloves, Frankie crouched down beside the body. She touched the victim's neck. Vanessa Jackson's body had already grown cold.

"Best guess," Sean Cavanaugh told them as he came up to his nephew and the detective working with him, "she was killed sometime last night."

"You sound very sure that she was killed," Luke commented. "No chance that this case was just an overdose?"

"No," Sean replied, shaking his head. "This one tried to fight back." He raised one of the dead woman's hands so that he could prove his point. "She just had a manicure," he told them. "Look at the nail polish. It's fresh—and expensive-looking. Yet all her nails are broken. It looks to me as if she tried to fight off her killer."

Had they finally caught a break? "That means that the killer's skin should be under her nails, right?" Luke asked.

Again, Sean shook his head. "In a perfect world, yes," he agreed. "But the killer has obviously watched his share of crime procedurals. The area under all her nails was thoroughly scrubbed with some sort of brush. Maybe the victim's toothbrush. I noticed that there wasn't one in the bathroom," he told them.

"All her nails?" Frankie repeated, feeling a wave of disappointment. "Are you sure?"

"Well, there still might be some hope left. The ME has to perform the autopsy," he told her. "There's an outside chance that there might be something the killer missed and left behind."

"Who called the police?" Luke asked.

"The victim's mother," his uncle answered. "That very broken-looking woman sitting in the corner over there. She told the police that she called her daughter this morning to find out how her date had gone last night. When she received no answer, she said she had a bad feeling and came over. Her daughter didn't answer the door. That's when Mrs. Jackson had the building manager unlock the door."

"Wait, back up," Luke said. "A date? Does the mother know who her daughter was dating?"

Sean shook his head. "I didn't have the heart to interrogate her. She's been crying the entire time I've been here. She only stopped just now. I thought I'd leave the questions up to you," he told Luke. "I knew you'd want to talk to her, and this way, the poor woman only has to go through the process once."

Luke nodded. And then, rather than go question Mrs. Jackson, he surprised Frankie by turning toward her. "You want to take the lead on this, DeMarco?"

Frankie stared at him, confused. "Me?"

He nodded. "I figure you'd have a lighter touch. You know, woman to woman," he said pointedly, deliberately leaving out the part that she could relate to the woman because she had suffered her own loss recently.

But she knew what he meant.

Still, Frankie hesitated for a moment. She wasn't really a people person. "Are you sure about this?"

"I'm sure," he told her. "I'll just hang back and let you do the talking."

She knew that O'Bannon thought she was in a better position to relate to the woman, but all things considered, she was going to have a hard time handling the woman's grief.

However, she couldn't say that to O'Bannon because she wasn't about to appear as if she was shirking an assignment he was giving her.

Steeling herself, Frankie made her way over to the victim's mother.

Mrs. Ada Jackson gave the appearance of someone who had had her insides hollowed out with the edge of a jagged spoon. She didn't look up at first when Frankie said her name. It took her three attempts to get the woman's attention.

Finally, Mrs. Jackson lifted her head and looked at her, confused and at a complete loss.

"I'm sorry," the victim's mother said in a shaky voice. "I didn't hear you. Were you talking to me?"

Frankie smiled at her kindly.

Her expression wasn't lost on Luke. He noted that Frankie's face had softened.

"Yes," Frankie replied. "I'm very sorry to have to bother you at a time like this, Mrs. Jackson, but I wanted to ask you some questions while the events were all still fresh in your mind."

"Still fresh in my mind?" the woman repeated, her throat raspy from the crying she'd done. "It will *always* be fresh in my mind." Mrs. Jackson shivered. "The image of my daughter, lying there, dead, will haunt me for the rest of my life." Fresh tears rose to fill her eyes. "I should have done something," she sobbed. "I should have told her not to go. But she was so eager, so hopeful. She just wanted her life to be normal again."

"Normal? Why hadn't her life been normal prior to this?" she asked the woman gently, watching Mrs. Jackson very carefully as the woman responded.

Mrs. Jackson took in a long breath, as if that would

somehow help her get the words out. "Vanessa had had her nose to the grindstone for years now, trying to make a name for herself. She was a set designer— a really *good* set designer," the woman emphasized with pride. "But it's such a competitive business and she felt that she had to make up for the precious time she'd lost."

"How, Mrs. Jackson?" Frankie pressed. "How did she lose precious time?"

The woman looked away, as if she couldn't bear the shame of what she was about to say. "Vanessa took on too much. She started to feel that she was falling behind so she turned to amphetamines to keep going. She became addicted to them before she knew it. When I finally realized what was happening, I made her go to rehab. She resisted at first, but she knew I was right and she finally agreed to go."

Mrs. Jackson's voice broke as she said, "She kicked it. Vanessa kicked her addiction," the woman repeated. "It was the hardest thing she ever did and I was so proud of her." She raised her eyes up to look at the woman she was talking to. "Why did this happen to Vanessa?" Mrs. Jackson demanded tearfully. "She was doing so well."

"You said that you should have stopped her," Frankie prodded gently. "Stopped her from doing what?"

Mrs. Jackson drew in a shaky breath before she answered. "I should have stopped her from going out on that date."

Frankie exchanged looks with Luke. Another attractive young woman found dead right after she'd gone out on a date. "Would you happen to know who your daughter was seeing?"

But Ada shook her head. "It was someone she met online. She'd never met him before. This was going to be her first date. She was so excited," the woman sobbed. "Why didn't I try to stop her?" she lamented again.

Going on instinct, Frankie took the woman's hand in hers. Mrs. Jackson's fingers were icy.

"Because you wanted her to be happy," Frankie told her. "And you were being a good mother. Do you know the name of the online site?"

The victim's mother pressed her lips together, struggling to keep from sobbing again. "The Perfect Date. It was called The Perfect Date," she told Frankie. "One of the people she worked with told her about it. She said she met her fiancé through that site." Mrs. Jackson raised her tear-stained face. "Why did he have to kill her?" she asked. "Why did that animal have to kill my baby?"

Frankie felt as if the woman was shredding her heart. "I don't know, Mrs. Jackson. But I promise you, we're going to find out who did this and we will make him pay for killing your daughter."

Ada Jackson nodded numbly.

Frankie beckoned the policeman who had been first to respond to the woman's frantic 911 call. She turned Mrs. Jackson over to the patrolman. "Please see that Mrs. Jackson gets home all right," she requested.

Feeling somewhat drained, Frankie stepped away from the woman.

Luke came over to her. "You did good, DeMarco," he told her, finally speaking up.

"I didn't get the guy's name," Frankie complained.

"But you got the name of the dating site," Luke reminded her. "That's something to go on."

Frankie didn't seem to hear him. She was dealing with her own thoughts. "He killed her last night, O'Bannon," she said in a hollow voice.

Luke looked at her sharply. "I know what you're thinking. Even if you'd stayed in the squad room and worked on this case all night, you wouldn't have come up with a name, a lead to follow," he insisted. "There's no way you could have prevented this, De-Marco. Take the pluses and we'll work with that."

"Another woman is dead, O'Bannon," Frankie said through clenched teeth.

"I know that," he responded calmly. "And maybe, if we use her dating profile and look into the hits she had, we'll find out the name of the guy who did this."

She wasn't nearly so hopeful. "He probably used an alias."

Luke sighed. "Didn't anyone hug you as a child?" he asked, feeling for her and feeling exasperated at the same time.

Frankie looked at him, confused. "What does that have to do with it?"

Luke just shook his head. "Think positive, De-Marco. Just think positive."

"That's not easy for me to do," Frankie quietly confessed.

He laughed dryly. "Yeah, I noticed. *Try*," Luke urged. He saw that she was staring intently at something in the vicinity of the coffee table. "You think of something?" he asked.

"Vanessa had a vase with orchids," Frankie replied.

He wasn't following her. "So?"

"Orchids aren't exactly your run-of-the-mill flowers."

"Still not following," he confessed.

"Ellen O'Keefe had a vase of yellow orchids in her living room. The vase was identical to this one." She looked at Luke, excitement beginning to enter her voice. "Now that I think of it, Kristin had the exact same orchids and vase in her living room, too."

"You think a florist is our killer?" Luke asked, trying to follow her line of thinking.

Frankie shrugged, frustrated. This was as far as she had gotten.

"I don't know," she admitted. "Maybe. Or maybe the killer leaves this behind as his calling card." She came closer to the vase. "Yellow orchids symbolize new beginnings and friendship."

It was his turn to look at her, a little mystified. "And you know this how?"

She supposed that did seem to just come out of the blue. "I worked part-time for a florist when I was in high school," she told him. The next second, she was annoyed with herself for telling him that. She was letting O'Bannon into her life a lot further than she'd intended. It was as if she'd lost the ability to censor herself when she was around him.

He read her body language and put two and two together. It wasn't all that difficult. "Don't worry, that secret's safe with me, too," he told her. Then, turning toward his uncle, he raised his voice and said, "De-Marco and I are going to join White Hawk and finish canvassing the neighbors, then we're going back to the squad room. Let me know when the victim's autopsy and the tox screen are done," he requested.

"Hold on a minute," Frankie requested as he started to leave the apartment. "I want to give Mrs. Jackson my card." She saw him raise his eyebrow. "Just in case she thinks of anything else that might help," she explained to O'Bannon.

Luke nodded. "I'll be outside," he told her. "Maybe White Hawk's finished canvassing and we can just get back to the squad room." It was wishful thinking, but he was nothing if not optimistic.

Frankie went over to the victim's mother. She was still trying to pull herself together so that she was able to have the patrolman take her home.

"I forgot to give you my card, Mrs. Jackson," Frankie told the woman, placing it in her hand. "If you think of anything else that might be helpful to the investigation, please don't hesitate to call."

The woman nodded, not trusting herself to speak.

"And if you need someone to talk to," Frankie added, looking at the distraught woman, "that's my cell number on the back."

Mrs. Jackson nodded numbly. She folded her fingers around the card.

Feeling incredibly helpless, Frankie walked out of the garden apartment.

She stood in front of the door, scanning the area for Luke. He was across the way, just outside of the development's fenced-in pool. He was talking to a woman dressed in clothes that seemed to be just a little too young and too tight for her. The woman had a very hyperactive toy poodle on a leash.

White Hawk was standing right next to him.

Seeing her, White Hawk waved her over.

Maybe they'd found a witness, Frankie thought, hurrying over.

My Lord, now I'm being optimistic, like O'Bannon.

She couldn't wait for this investigation to be over. Not just because that would mean they had found Kristin's killer, but because she wanted to be back on her own, able to think dark thoughts without having O'Bannon's cheerful platitudes invading her mind.

She worked better alone, anyway.

"This is Gloria Hernandez," Luke told her as soon as she drew closer. "Ms. Hernandez says she saw our victim and her date returning around nine-thirty last night."

Gloria had a mass of bright blond curls that bobbed up and down as she nodded her head. "I was out walking Clancy. It feels like I'm always walking Clancy. Poor baby has a bladder the size of a pea," she confided, bending over for a moment to pet the dog's head affectionately. "Anyway," she continued, standing up again, "I saw this big, fancy car pulling up in guest parking and this girl and guy get out. I'd seen her around, so I knew he had to be the one who was the guest."

They were obviously in the presence of an Einstein, Frankie couldn't help thinking, doing her best to keep her thoughts from registering on her face.

"Anyway," Gloria went on, "I could see that he was talking her up and she was laughing at everything he was saying. I noticed she was kind of walking funny, too."

"What do you mean, walking funny?" Luke asked before either Frankie or White Hawk had a chance to.

The blonde shrugged. "You know, like she'd had a few too many."

"Or like someone might have drugged her," Frankie suggested as the idea suddenly occurred to her. She looked at Gloria to see if the thought had jarred something for their witness.

"You think?" Gloria asked, her eyes growing wide. "Could it have been the guy she was with?"

"Good odds," Luke said.

Gloria appeared stunned. "He looked so clean-cut," she marveled.

"If we took you down to the station and put you together with our sketch artist, do you think you could describe him?" Luke asked, hoping that, just maybe, they had caught their first solid break.

The woman began to backtrack. "Maybe. It was kind of dark and Clancy was barking a lot so I wasn't paying *that* much attention, but yeah, sure. Why not?" She gazed up at Luke hopefully. "Can I get a ride with you?"

"Actually," Luke told her. "You'll be riding with all three of us. We only brought the one car."

"Oh, what a shame," Gloria replied with genuine feeling. She put her hand on his chest. "Let me just bring Clancy home and I'm all yours."

Frankie had absolutely no doubt that the woman meant that sincerely.

Chapter 12

"Does that happen often?" Frankie asked him as they stood outside of their witness's apartment, waiting for Gloria Hernandez to do whatever she had to do with her dog in order to accompany them to the precinct.

The question came out of the blue. Luke had no idea what she was talking about. "Does *what* happen often?" he asked.

"Women throwing themselves at you."

Luke looked at her as if she was crazy. And then he decided that this was some kind of a joke.

"Oh, yeah, sure," he told Frankie. "All the time. What's why I have to wear all this protective gear on me, to protect me from all the bodies hurling themselves at me."

"He doesn't let it interfere with the job," White

Hawk confided in a pseudo whisper, managing to suppress the wide grin that was attempting to surface.

"Well, that's heartening to know." Her response dripped with sarcasm.

Frankie would have gone on to say something more, but just then, their potential witness's apartment door opened and the woman they were waiting for stepped out.

"You changed your outfit," Luke noticed, surprised that the woman would take the time to do that.

Gloria Hernandez beamed at the observation. "Oh, you noticed," she purred. "A girl's gotta look her best when she steps out. These days you never know when someone might snap your picture," she told him, sidling up to Luke and wedging herself between the detective she'd set her cap for and White Hawk.

"You do realize that you're coming down to work with a sketch artist to recreate the man you saw last night, not to pose for a portrait," Frankie couldn't refrain from pointing out. She watched Gloria's face to see if her words had sunk in, even remotely.

"Of course I know," Gloria said, glancing at Frankie over her shoulder. "Just because I'm helping you find this man who did this terrible thing doesn't mean I have to look..." she paused as she gave the woman behind her the once-over before saying "...messy."

White Hawk leaned in toward Frankie and said in a low voice, "Welcome to the colorful world of Homicide."

Approaching the sedan, Gloria called out "Shotgun!" Then asked Luke, just to be sure, "You are the one driving, right?"

"He's the lead," Frankie told the other woman, assuming that answered the witness's question.

Luke glanced over his shoulder toward White Hawk. As if reading his partner's mind, he shook his head. "You have the car keys," he reminded Luke, wanting nothing to do with the overly amorous witness.

"This is so exciting," Gloria told Luke as she got into the car and almost snuggled into the passenger seat. "This is my very first murder. I mean, my first time being a witness in a *possible* murder." She flushed and laughed. "This isn't coming out right."

"As long as you can give the sketch artist something he can work with," Luke told her. "That's all that matters."

"No problem," Gloria promised, giving him a thousand-watt smile.

"There's a problem," White Hawk said more than an hour later, returning to the squad room. Luke had had his partner remain with Gloria while she worked with the sketch artist.

That left him, as well as Frankie, to compare the various victims' tox screens, looking for telltale similarities.

Luke stopped going through the file he had opened on his desk and looked up.

"What kind of a problem?" he asked, just a little leery. He expected White Hawk to tell him that their so-called eyewitness had started hitting on the sketch artist, but it turned out to be even worse than that.

"Unless Jimmy Stewart has come back from the dead to conduct a killing spree in Aurora," White Hawk complained, "it looks like we're back to square one."

"Jimmy Stewart?" Luke questioned his partner, totally confused.

"Look for yourselves," White Hawk told him, holding up the sketch that the department's artist had compiled from Gloria's description.

Luke frowned. "That certainly looks like Jimmy Stewart, all right," Luke agreed, none-too-happily. He looked at White Hawk for an explanation.

"Seems that Ms. Hernandez and her faithful dog, Clancy, had been watching a Jimmy Stewart marathon on the classic movie channel last night when Clancy felt the call of nature," White Hawk told him. "I should add that it turns out our so-called eyewitness saw the killer from a rather long distance."

Luke shook his head. So much for reliability, he thought. "Where's Ms. Hernandez now?"

"I thanked her for her service and sent her home with one of our police officers," White Hawk told him. And then he smiled broadly. "She didn't want to go without first seeing you, but I convinced her that you were otherwise occupied and couldn't be disturbed."

In Frankie's opinion, Luke seemed sincerely grateful. "I owe you one," Luke told his partner.

White Hawk's grin only grew wider as he said, "Yeah, I know."

Hearing every word, Frankie frowned. "So we're no closer to identifying Vanessa Jackson's killer than we were this morning."

"Well, thanks to you," Luke reminded her, "we know she used The Perfect Date website to wind up getting in touch with her killer. We can find out who she exchanged messages with, get a court order and have The Perfect Date people open up their files so that we can at least get the information they have on Vanessa's date."

Frankie looked at him doubtfully. "You think you can find a judge to give you that court order without hard-and-fast proof?"

Luke smiled. This was where being a Cavanaugh came in very handy.

"We have a couple of judges in our family tree," he said out loud.

"Wouldn't that be considered a conflict of interest for the judge?" she asked in all innocence.

Luke stared at her, stunned. "Seriously? *You're* asking *me* that?"

She realized that he was alluding to the fact that he was allowing her to stay on despite her own conflict of interest. She'd gotten so caught up in the case, she'd temporarily forgotten that.

"Sorry, lost my head," she murmured.

Luke was already letting her remark pass and was back to thinking about the court order.

"It might take us a couple of days to get one," he guessed. "In the meantime, we still have all these tox screens to go through and compare." And then he thought of something else. "Or we could follow up on that idea you had," he suggested.

"What idea?" Frankie asked. Things had been moving so fast, she'd actually lost track of things she'd said.

"Those yellow orchids," he reminded her.

"Oh, right." She flushed. How could she have forgotten about that?

"We could run a background check on the florist who delivered those vases," Luke said, thinking out loud. "Check out the people he has working for him. Might be a dead end," he allowed philosophically, "but we won't know that until we look into it. How about it, DeMarco?" he asked, looking at her. "You game?"

"Absolutely," she answered, already on her feet. She was anxious to get moving, to be out in the field. Sitting behind a desk, inertly turning pages and getting cross-eyed, had never been for her.

"White Hawk," Luke called out, turning toward his partner.

"Yeah, yeah," White Hawk replied with a sigh. "I know. Hold down the fort."

Luke clamped a hand on the man's muscular shoulder. "You're a good man, White Hawk."

"I just need a change of scenery obviously less than you two do," White Hawk responded agreeably.

The florist who had delivered all three vases turned out to be located all the way over on the other side of Aurora.

When Frankie went to open the door to the small, thriving shop, Luke had to pull her out of the way quickly. Otherwise she would have been directly on a collision course with a fast-moving messenger. His vision was obstructed by the rather large plant he was carrying out.

Frankie felt like the air had been all but knocked

out of her. Luke might have yanked her out of the way of the deliveryman, but he had wound up pulling her back right up against him.

Contact was immediate and hard, leaving imprints on both of them.

"You okay?" Luke asked her, releasing Frankie after a beat.

She drew in a long, shaky breath before answering. "I'm not sure," Frankie confessed.

Her body was throbbing. She could still feel the impact of his body against hers even after he had stepped back.

She supposed that was preferable to being knocked flat to the ground, but in all honestly, she wasn't altogether sure.

The next moment, Frankie managed to say, "I'm fine. It's okay."

"Hey, I'm—I'm really sorry," the deliveryman stammered. "I didn't see you standing there."

"That's because you're carrying a giant tree in front of you," Frankie commented, looking at what looked like a miniature palm tree in a decorative pot.

The commotion from the near collision brought out the manager of the flower shop. The man instantly began to apologize for his deliveryman.

"I'm so very sorry." He spared the deliveryman a dismissive glance. "He's new and still has some bugs to work out. I'm sorry if Roy alarmed you. Please, pick out an arrangement as a token of my apology. It'll be on the house."

"We're not really here to buy any flowers," Luke began to tell the shop manager.

Not to be put off, the shop manager guessed, "A

plant, perhaps?" He looked from Luke to the woman with him. "Or an arrangement of balloons to celebrate a happy occasion?" he asked hopefully.

Luke took out his badge and ID and held them out. He had a feeling that the man would just go on guessing what had brought them to the shop if he wasn't stopped.

"Detectives O'Bannon and DeMarco—she's the one your deliveryman almost mowed down," he added as Frankie belatedly fished out her own credentials. "We would like to ask you about some deliveries that were made from your shop."

The manager's bright smile faded by several watts. "I'm sorry. Our clients' privacy is very important to us. I'm afraid I can't really release any information without a court order. You understand," he added, looking from Luke to Frankie.

"I'm afraid I don't," Luke answered flatly. "The women those orchids were delivered to were the victims of a serial killer."

"Wait, what?" the manager cried, obviously shocked and dismayed by what he had just heard.

"Victims of a serial killer," Luke repeated deliberately. "So far we've connected three victims to your flower shop. There's a possibility that we might find more if we keep digging," he warned.

The manager, a man in his forties, looked as if he was about to have an anxiety attack right in front of them.

He grabbed hold of Luke's arm. "Wait, you can't mean that you think one of my delivery people actually—" Unable to bring himself to finish his sentence, he cried, "It's not possible. I've had each and every one of my people vetted. None of them have so much as a parking ticket between them—"

"We're not saying it's one of your delivery people," Frankie told him, cutting in. "What we think is that the killer might have sent the flowers from your shop. Yellow orchids." Frankie held up a picture she had taken in the last victim's home.

The florist examined the image on her smartphone, then shrugged, attempting to put distance between himself and the crime. "They might have come from here," he said vaguely.

"The tag that was attached to the arrangement said that they *did* come from your shop," she told him in no uncertain terms.

The man's shoulders sagged considerably when confronted with the information.

"All right, then, they did come from here." He bit his lower lip, debating what he was about to ask because it just connected him to this even more. "Do you have the address where they were delivered?"

"You don't quite have the hang of how a murder investigation works, do you?" Luke asked him. "We get a call and come to where the body is and everything goes from there. In this investigation, the victims were all found in their homes, so yes, we have addresses to give to you."

"Sorry," the florist said. He flushed as he collapsed into a chair behind the counter. "This just has me rattled so that I can't seem to think straight. Everything feels all jumbled in my head," he confessed. His eyes darted from one detective to the other.

Was it just nerves, or was there something more going on, Frankie wondered.

"I think we kind of got that," Luke told him. "Now, Detective DeMarco and I are going to give you the names and addresses of the last three murder victims. All three of the women had orchids delivered from your shop. I want you to check the addresses against your files and tell me the name of the person who paid to have the flowers delivered."

Luke enunciated every word to the man, as if he was talking to someone who had difficulty processing any sort of information—because it appeared that, at least for now, the man apparently did.

His hands shaking, the shop owner typed in each of the addresses where the orchids and vases had been delivered. Pulling up what he was looking for, he said, "The orders were all placed over the phone," he told the detectives in his shop.

"Naturally," Luke murmured. "How did they pay?" he asked out loud.

"By credit card, of course." The manager checked the screen to verify that. "The names on the credit cards were all different."

"And the cards all checked out?" Luke asked.

"Yes. The flowers don't go out until I run a check on the credit card," the manager explained, his voice sounding slightly miffed. It was obvious that he seemed to be coming around.

Luke processed this new piece of information. "Okay, so our guy is either a hacker, as well, or he just steals credit cards outright." He sighed. "Give me the names on the credit cards," he ordered.

"Okay. It'll take me a minute to print them out," the manager told him. "You're sure I won't get into any trouble for this?" he asked nervously.

"Not unless you were the one who killed those women," Luke answered, only to have the florist turn pale.

"No! No, of course not," the manager cried. He quickly printed out the transactions and handed the page to Luke. "Anything else you want me to do?"

"Not at the moment," Luke told him, folding the paper and putting it into his jacket pocket. "But we might be back if it turns out that the killer had orchids sent to his other victims."

"Oh, dear Lord, I hope not. Not that you won't be back, but that the killer sent more orchids from my shop." The very idea of being involved in any form with the heinous crime seemed to make the man shiver. "It's awful enough that he sent an arrangement of orchids to three of the women." The manager looked at Luke nervously. "You're sure that they all came from the same person?"

"The MO was the same and I don't believe in coincidences," Luke said, opening the front door. "Thanks for the list," he added as he followed Frankie out of the shop.

If the manager said anything in response, neither one of them heard it.

Chapter 13

The moment they were back in the squad room, Luke put in a call to Valri.

It took his cousin five rings to pick up.

"I almost hung up, Valri," he told her when he heard her voice.

"Little busy here, Luke," Valri answered, obviously preoccupied and in the middle of something as she answered her phone. "No time to talk."

"I won't keep you," Luke promised. "But—"

"Too late," she told him.

He talked faster. Though he was confident that she wouldn't hang up on him, he wanted to make good on his initial statement. "When you get a chance to go over those two laptops more thoroughly, see if you can find anything having to do with a site called The Perfect Date in either victim's search history."

He heard Valri laugh. "Have you finally gone through all the available women in the area to ask out?"

"You know, this job has turned you into a completely different person," he commented. "You really used to be so sweet."

Valri chuckled softly. "What you mean is that I used to be such a pushover."

"*I* never saw you in that light," Luke protested with just the right amount of sincerity.

"Uh-huh." After a moment, she asked, "What was the name of that site again?"

He repeated it for her slowly. "And I'd really appreciate it if you'd put that search on the top of your list."

"Of course you would." He heard his cousin sigh deeply before she told him, "All right, Luke, I'll see what I can do."

"That's all I ask, Valri."

"No, it's not," was his cousin's weary response, just before she terminated the call.

Frankie couldn't help but hear the exchange. "Problem?" she asked.

He replaced the receiver and looked across his desk at Frankie. "Valri's feeling overworked."

"There's a good reason for that," Frankie told him knowingly.

Luke decided that it was prudent not to respond.

Valri got back to him just as he and Frankie were about to leave the squad room. They were on their way to interview the friends and families of some of the other victims. Their main question entailed finding out if any of the victims had made use of that dating site, too.

Busier than ever, Valri didn't bother with any unnecessary preliminary conversation. Instead, she told her cousin, "Looks like you were right. According to search engines on the laptops, both victims accessed that dating site recently."

Luke could feel his adrenaline rising. "Did you get any profile names, or whatever it is they call people on this virtual mating game?" he asked.

Valri laughed. "Cousin, you are woefully undereducated when it comes to all things cyber."

"Sue me," he quipped. "I believe that meeting people should be done the old-fashioned, traditional way—like bumping into them at a club."

"Right." She didn't bother to point out that most of the family had met their significant other because of the job. But she knew that not everyone was fortunate that way. "To answer what I took to be your question, no, I couldn't find any male profiles that either one of the victims had saved. To be honest, something tells me that the victims weren't the ones to erase them," she added.

Luke could see where his cousin was going with this. "You think the serial killer erased himself?" he asked Valri.

"Not in the way you mean," she answered. "I think the killer hacked into their accounts from the comfort of his own home and erased the evidence."

Frankie noticed Luke frowning as he spoke to his cousin. "He could do that?"

Valri's laugh was audible enough for Frankie to hear where she was sitting.

"Oh, someday, when we both have a little time, I do need to take you under my wing and really educate you, cousin."

"Until then, Valri, I have you," Luke responded pointedly.

Valri sighed. "Yes, I know. Okay, if I've answered your questions for now, I've got to get back to the backlog of work I have waiting for me, thanks to you."

"I really appreciate this, Val."

He expected her to mumble something in response like "Yeah, yeah," and hang up. Instead, he was surprised to hear her say, "You can show it by making a donation to the baby fund."

"What baby fund?" he asked.

After a pause, Luke heard his cousin answer, "*My* baby fund."

"Wait, back up," he ordered, trying to assimilate the information that had just been thrown to him. He lowered his voice. "You're having a baby?"

Valri laughed. "Nothing gets by you, does it, cousin?"

The family was really growing by leaps and bounds, Luke thought. "Does Uncle Andrew know?"

Again she laughed. "Alex and I tried to keep it a secret," she confessed. "You know how well-kept secrets are within the Cavanaugh family. I think he's planning something next weekend."

"Uncle Andrew is always planning some kind of family gathering," Luke reminded her.

"But this time I'm sure he'll be putting the word out that there's a baby theme for the celebration next weekend," Valri told him.

"Next weekend?" Luke repeated. This really was the first he'd heard of it and he'd just been in contact with his mother this week. She was usually the first one to know these kinds of things and she hadn't said a word to him about it.

"Count on it," Valri assured him.

"So, what do you want, girl or boy?" Luke couldn't help asking as he lowered his voice again. Even so, he saw that Frankie's curiosity was really piqued.

"Yes," Valri answered ambiguously. "Gotta go," she told him just before hanging up.

"Girl or boy?" Frankie repeated, looking at the man across from her quizzically. "Okay, I was listening in," she admitted, although she'd only caught the latter part of Luke's end of the conversation. "Are we back to thinking our suspect might be a female?"

"What?" For a split second, the woman's question confused him—and then belatedly he realized what she was asking. "Oh, well, we're still ruling that out," he lied, then told Frankie, "Valri was just telling me that there's probably going to be another one of Andrew's bashes this weekend." For the moment, he didn't specify anything about his cousin's pending motherhood. Instead, he suddenly thought of extending the invitation to Frankie. "Hey, you want to come?"

Frankie felt she was being backed into a corner. "You don't even know that there's going to be a gathering," she pointed out. "You used the word *probably*."

"Oh, there'll be one," he assured her. "Uncle Andrew hasn't thrown a large party in a few weeks and he never misses an opportunity. It's definitely time for one—and according to Valri, he now has an excuse. Not that he needs one," he added. "The man just loves having the entire family around, loves cooking for them."

Frankie nodded her head. This wasn't exactly news to her. "So I've heard."

"And yet," Luke observed, "I don't recall ever seeing you at one of them."

Frankie didn't think that he would drop this topic until it was resolved to his satisfaction.

"There's a reason for that," she told him evenly.

"Which is?" Luke prodded.

"I've never *been* to one of them," Frankie answered simply. Anyone else would have accepted that and just let the subject drop. But O'Bannon wasn't anyone else.

"Why not?" he asked.

"You said they were family parties, right? Well, I'm not family."

And now I'm not part of anyone's family, she added silently, thinking again of Kris.

"Uncle Andrew used to be the chief of police," he told her, in case Frankie was the one person on the force who was unaware of that fact, "and he considers anyone in the Aurora Police Department to be part of his family."

"That's all very nice," she said, dismissing the whole subject of parties and attending them. "But right now we have a serial killer to catch."

"There will *always* be killers to catch," Luke told her. "The two things aren't mutually exclusive." He'd made up his mind. He wasn't going to give up until he had convinced her to attend. "I guarantee that you'll have a great time at the party. So, how about it?"

She had no idea why this was suddenly so important to him. Maybe it was part of the bonding process with the team. Frankie pressed her lips together and sighed. "If I say I'll go, can we get back to work?"

"Absolutely," he told her, then added, "But I will hold you to that, DeMarco. I think it'll do you a world of good."

"Fine, yes," she told him in exasperation. "Now, about this dating site," she said again, determined to get back to the topic at hand.

"What about it?"

Frankie knew she was going to have to choose her words very carefully in order to get O'Bannon to sign on to this. But she thought it would be their best shot at finding their serial killer.

"Well," she began slowly, "we've established that the serial killer definitely has a type."

The women whose photos were tacked onto the bulletin board looked so much alike, they could have been sisters, or at the very least, cousins. Anyone could see that.

"Yes. So?" Luke asked, studying her carefully.

"So." Frankie spread her arms wide in an effort to get him to look at her more closely—and actually *see* her, not as a detective, but as a woman.

His eyes narrowed. "What are you saying?" Luke asked sharply, although he thought he had a pretty good idea what she was intimating.

"That maybe if I sign up and post my picture with a made-up profile—"

"No," Luke said flatly.

She wasn't used to being cut off like that and she didn't like it. "You don't even know what I'm going to say," she said angrily.

Did she think he was dumb? "Oh, yes, I do, and we're not about to use you as bait."

Undaunted, Frankie tried again. "But we could save a lot of time and effort that way," she stressed. "We can get him to come to us."

For the sake of getting along, Luke decided to try to reason with her. "That's a long shot—"

"So? I'll take it," Frankie insisted.

Luke had no intention of being reckless in order to close another case. There were consequences to consider. Grave consequences.

"Look, we haven't gotten down to the bottom of the barrel yet. We've got other options open to us, other avenues that we can explore—"

He was just stonewalling her, Frankie thought, frustrated. "And meanwhile, another woman might be getting murdered because you're dragging your feet."

It took him a moment to keep his temper from surging. "Let's see if we can try narrowing down the suspect pool by using good old-fashioned detective work first, how about that?"

"And if that doesn't work?" she pressed. Why was he being so stubborn? Why couldn't she get him to agree to her plan? Was it just because she was the one who had come up with it and not him?

"Then we'll revisit your harebrained idea," Luke conceded between clenched teeth. "But not until then," he underscored. And then he told both White Hawk and Frankie exactly what he wanted them to tackle first, even before finding out if the other victims had signed up for that dating site. "Let's question the families and find out just how many of those women had a substance abuse problem that they managed to kick."

Frankie regrouped. What Luke had just suggested went along with what they had talked about earlier.

"And if they were in rehab," Frankie added. "We need to know the names of those facilities and what support groups the victims had frequented. Maybe the serial killer is lurking there, trying to bring these former addicts to permanent salvation."

Luke rolled the latter part of her statement over in his mind. "That's one possible motive. Another one is that he's using all those women he killed as surrogates, making them pay for something someone close to him had once done."

"You mean, like a girlfriend who overdosed?" White Hawk asked.

Frankie took the idea further. "Or a mother or sister. By killing them, maybe in his mind he's hurting them for hurting him."

Luke nodded, considering both angles. "That's why all the victims are so similar in appearance. The killer is getting even with the same woman over and over again." He looked at Frankie. "Which is why you're not putting your face out there on that dating site—even though that just might be his hunting ground."

Frankie sighed. "Okay, we'll do it your way—first," she agreed grudgingly.

First. He was easygoing by nature, but DeMarco seemed to be able to press his buttons faster than anyone he'd ever dealt with. "Did you forget who's the lead detective on this case?"

She offered him a wide smile. "Just keeping you humble," Frankie replied.

"Thanks for that," he said with more than a touch of sarcasm.

For the remainder of the week, Luke, Frankie and White Hawk split up the various names on the list of the victims' friends and relatives, and gathered as much information about the dead women's lives as they could.

A couple of the victims had no families, but they all had coworkers and friends who were deeply affected by their deaths. There was no shortage of people to talk to about the various victims.

"I don't know about the information you collected, but after speaking to the people who knew Kelly McClusky, Jane Gorman and Penny James, in my opinion these women came off like saints," White Hawk commented when they got together again to compare notes on what they had found out. "It seemed like because they'd all gone through substance abuse problems, the women were determined to make the world a better place in order to atone for their own lapse and fall from grace, so to speak. How about you?" he asked Frankie.

"I had the same impression. I have to say that I would have been more than willing to call any of these women a friend. They worked hard at their paying jobs and they did volunteer work, as well. I've got one helping out at a soup kitchen three days a week, another working at an animal shelter in her off hours."

"One of mine tutored underprivileged kids," Luke said. "Another one volunteered at least four times a week at a hospital."

"I've got one—Debra Evans—who read to the elderly in retirement homes on weekends," Frankie added. She looked at the other two detectives. "You know what all the victims have in common?"

"Offhand, I'd say they should all be canonized," Luke quipped.

"Maybe," she willingly allowed. "But they were also all too busy to find someone to date," she concluded. "That's why they wound up going to an on-line dating site. Filling out a profile and putting down what qualities they were looking for in a date was more efficient and time-saving. Doing it that way cut down on a lot of trial and error on the dating scene. It gave them a jump start, something that they all seemed to feel that they badly needed in order to weed out the men they felt weren't their type." She looked at Luke. "We've got to get our hands on the names— and photos—of the men who interacted with our victims on that dating site."

"First—" Frankie backtracked, knowing she was getting ahead of herself "—we need to make sure that all our victims actually signed up for this site. Once we verify that, we can go from there. I guess this means we're going to have to hit up someone in your family for a court order to get The Perfect Date people to open up their database for us."

Luke nodded. She was right, he thought. "We can do that at the party this Saturday," he told her.

She had walked right into that one, hadn't she, Frankie thought.

"The chief throwing another one of his famous gatherings?" White Hawk asked him. He obviously appeared to be pleased to hear this. "Linda's still talking about the last one we went to."

"As a matter of fact," Luke told his partner, even though he was looking directly at Frankie, "he is. I'll give you both the particulars as soon as I get them."

"Can't wait," White Hawk told him.

Maybe White Hawk couldn't, Frankie thought, but she definitely could.

Chapter 14

"Are you familiar with the term *blackmail*?" Frankie asked pointedly later that day, just as Luke was shutting down his computer.

Luke raised his eyes to meet hers. "Well, I know I only get to work with crimes having to do with dead people and I don't deal with the breadth of crimes the way someone in Major Crimes does," he told her. "But yes, I do happen to be familiar with what the word *blackmail* refers to. Why?" he asked.

"Because you're obviously guilty of it," she informed him.

"Well, I wouldn't have to resort to blackmail if you weren't digging in your heels the way you are." He gave her a penetrating look. "Why are you so afraid of coming to one of my family's parties?"

"I'm not afraid," she retorted. "Who told you I was afraid?"

He didn't have to pause to think before answering. "You did."

Frankie was about to protest that she had done no such thing then realized what he was basing his accusation on. "Because I didn't want to come to a big gathering?" she challenged.

"No, because you looked like a deer caught in the headlights over the idea of being around a *family* gathering."

Her eyes blazed as she told him, "I know you're the lead detective on this case, but you're also imagining things."

She looked magnificent when she was angry, he thought, fascinated with the way her eyes flashed. But he still wasn't going to let her win this.

"Am I?" Luke asked.

She shut off her computer with a flourish as she shot back, "Yes, you are."

"Okay," he conceded. "Then prove me wrong. Come with me to the party," he told her. "I'll pick you up at eleven."

For a second, Frankie was completely speechless. And then she pulled herself together.

"Eleven?" she questioned. "Isn't that kind of early? Is it a kids' party?"

"It's an *everybody* party," he replied. "Some of the family members have kids, and Uncle Andrew insists that they bring them. Like I said, everybody's welcome."

"What time will it be over?" she asked Luke. Maybe, because there were children, it was one of those two-hour parties. She could put up with two hours if that meant she could finally get O'Bannon off her case.

"When the last person goes home," he answered. Luke saw the slightly puzzled look on her face and explained. "There is no time limit on these things. Uncle Andrew just wants everyone to enjoy themselves. They're free to stay as long as they want—or go home whenever they feel like it," he added for her benefit.

"Well," Frankie admitted, "I have to admit I do like the last part."

Luke laughed. "Yeah, I had a feeling you would. So it's settled. I'll pick you up at eleven," he told her just as he began to leave the squad room.

Frankie sighed, then raised her voice so it would carry. "There's no getting out of this, is there?"

"Nope. Besides," he said as he made it out the door, "you don't want to insult Valri."

Frankie had already shut down her computer. She hadn't planned on going out of the squad room and down to the first floor with O'Bannon, but he'd aroused her curiosity. She really liked his cousin Valri and was impressed with her computer prowess.

Grabbing her purse, Frankie hurried to catch up.

"What does Valri have to do with it?" she asked.

Luke pressed for the elevator. "The party is for her."

"Her birthday?" Frankie guessed, saying the first thing that occurred to her.

The elevator arrived and he walked into the near-empty car. "Her pregnancy."

Frankie put her hand out to stop the doors from closing so that she could get in. "Her what?"

"Her pregnancy," he repeated.

That didn't make any sense to her. "But I just saw Valri yesterday and she looked as slender as a reed. Slenderer—if there is such a word."

"Be sure to tell her so." When she eyed him questioningly, he explained. "It'll make her feel good. According to her sister, Kelly, Valri already thinks she's getting fat."

"Then Valri really *is* pregnant?" Frankie asked. She thought of the Cavanaughs as workaholics as a whole. That didn't seem to leave much time for things like creating babies.

Just because you're married to your job doesn't mean that everyone else is.

"Well, she tells me that her doctor seems to think so. And so does her husband," Luke told her. And then he thought of something that might be keeping Frankie from coming with him to the gathering. "This doesn't mean you have to buy her a baby gift, so you can't use that as an excuse for not coming."

Frankie shot him a look. "I'm reserved, O'Bannon, not cheap."

"And why is that?" Luke asked her. "You being reserved, not cheap," he clarified.

"You might not have noticed this, but not everyone is outgoing," she told him, getting off the elevator and striding toward the back entrance.

"I know that," he agreed, walking right beside Frankie despite her attempts to get ahead of him.

"But the ones who aren't are really missing out on things."

"That's your opinion," she informed him coolly.

"Yes, it is," he readily admitted. "But it's based on a lifetime of observation. No man is an island," he told her. "And no woman is, either."

"So now you're paraphrasing John Donne? Very profound," Frankie commented dryly. Pushing the door open, she hurried down the steps.

"Also very true," he countered.

Lengthening his stride, Luke caught up to her in a couple of seconds. He had a feeling that the more Frankie resisted attending, the more she really needed to interact with his family on a social basis. He wasn't exactly sure why she was the way she was, if it only involved losing her cousin or if there was more to it than that, but he was certain that mingling with his family would help bring her out of her shell. He'd seen it happen before, when determined members of the family had brought other people into the fold. They came resisting, and they left happy that they had come.

"Look, I'm not asking you to sell your soul to the devil," he told her patiently. "I'm just asking you to come have a little fun. You need to learn to loosen up a little. Trust me, DeMarco, there's more to life than just work. And that's the part that makes the work worthwhile," he emphasized.

Feeling beleaguered, Frankie turned to face him. "I thought what made the work worthwhile was catching the bad guys."

Luke sighed. "Of course there's that, too. Look,

Frankie, I don't want to have an argument with you about this."

"You really could have fooled me." Exasperation echoed in her voice.

"I'll be there to pick you up at eleven," he said again, walking away.

"And if I'm not there?" she challenged.

"Then it'll be your loss," he answered.

Rather than continuing to try to convince her to attend, Luke fell silent and just kept on walking to where his vehicle was parked.

"You're under no obligation to go, you know that," Frankie told the woman who was looking back at her in her bedroom mirror. "You see these people enough as it is. You don't have to break bread with them or sit around and listen to them tell stories and look like a modern version of some Norman Rockwell painting come to life. You've got more important things to do.

"Oh, don't give me that sad face. It doesn't matter what *Detective* Lukkas O'Bannon said. You don't need to *socialize*, you need to solve this damn crime and get that evil SOB who killed Kris and all those other women," she told her reflection fiercely.

Still, Frankie reasoned as she blew out a long breath, if she didn't go to this party, O'Bannon would definitely give her a lot of grief about it on Monday morning. And this celebration, or whatever O'Bannon chose to call it, was for Valri, someone she did like.

Frankie looked up at the ceiling, as if that would

somehow help her make up her mind about this, one way or the other.

But just then the doorbell rang and suddenly the time for waffling and debating was over. Unless she intended to climb out the back window to make her escape, she was trapped.

Checking her overall appearance in the mirror, Frankie decided it was too late for any last-minute changes, anyway.

Resigned, she went to the front door.

Leaving the chain in place, she opened the door just a crack.

And there he was. O'Bannon. Standing on her doorstep, looking big as life.

Frankie made no effort to let him in. "We don't want any," she said.

"That's good, because I'm not selling any," Luke responded.

She continued to leave the chain in place. "Yes, you are. You're selling family and happiness and all that fairy-tale stuff."

Not to mention that, dressed in gray chinos and a light blue sweater, the man looked *really* good. She didn't want that fact to muddle her thinking.

"No, I'm not. I'm not selling it at all," Luke corrected. "I'm offering it to you for free."

There was a glint in his eye as he looked her over slowly.

Frankie felt herself growing warm. She wished he wouldn't look at her that way. It wreaked havoc with her concentration. "Nothing is free in life," she told him. "Everything comes with a price tag."

"In this case," he told her, "the price tag is that you just enjoy yourself."

There was a bigger price tag than that involved, she thought, and it was about causing her to lose her focus. "A lot you know," Frankie murmured under her breath.

The next moment, she pushed the door closed only long enough to take the chain off. Telling herself she was going to regret this, she opened the door.

"Okay, I'm ready," she said, much the way a condemned prisoner announced they were ready to meet the firing squad.

"You look great," Luke told her. "There's only one thing missing."

Here it comes, she thought, bracing herself for a lecture that would quickly devolve to a fight. "What?"

"Do you think you could maybe try to smile just a little and not look like you're being taken to your own execution?" he suggested.

She supposed that she *was* being a little petulant. "Sorry," Frankie muttered. Taking her shoulder bag, she locked up her apartment.

He went to take her arm, then stopped himself. For all he knew, that might make her bolt or be the ultimate deal breaker. He kept his hands at his sides.

"Don't be sorry, just smile." He led the way to his car. "Never mind," Luke told her the next moment, negating his previous request. "Just come. The smile will turn up of its own accord eventually." He opened the passenger door for her.

"Look," she said as she slid into the front passenger seat, "it's not that I don't like your family, it's just that…"

Luke buckled up on his side. Glancing at her, he hazarded a guess about her less-than-enthusiastic reaction. "It's not yours?"

About to protest, Frankie decided that there was no point in denying it. O'Bannon was clever enough to see through any lie she might come up with. If she conceded this, maybe he'd stop guessing.

"Something like that," she said with a shrug.

"Feel free to borrow anyone from my family anytime you feel the need," he told her loftily. "They're even a lot better outside of work than on the job."

"That's okay. You can keep your family intact. I tend to be a private person," she told him, trying to make Luke understand her reticence once and for all.

"Don't worry. Nobody is going to ask you to spill your guts," Luke promised. "You might not even have to talk at all if you don't want to. Hell," he laughed, thinking of several of the last parties, "Sometimes it's hard to get a word in edgewise once this group really gets going."

Luke was quiet for a moment as he drove to his uncle's house. He had an idea that he knew what might make her feel better about attending the gathering. "And we can leave anytime you want—your call," he told her. "Right after Uncle Andrew makes the toast."

"The toast?" she asked. Why would there be a toast, she wondered. Was this some kind of a tradition?

"Well, yes," he said, as if she should have figured

this out on her own. "To Valri and Alex—and their yet unnamed, barely formed baby." He spared her a glance. "So, does that make you feel any better?"

"I'm getting there," she allowed, even as she told herself that she was probably coming off as someone who needed to be handled with kid gloves. That was *not* the way she saw herself and yet here she was, behaving just like that.

"White Hawk will be there," he told her. He knew she got along well with his partner. Maybe this was the bargaining chip he needed to get her to relax.

"Then he really is coming?" she asked. She'd heard White Hawk mention attending with his wife, but at the time she'd thought he might have just said it to help convince her to come.

"He comes to a lot of these gatherings. As does Linda, his wife," Luke added in case she'd forgotten who Linda was. "I told you, to Uncle Andrew, *family* doesn't mean DNA, it means a feeling of kinship."

"Speaking of kinship, I might need a little moral support," he told her out of the blue. "Feel up to supplying it?"

"Why? What do you need moral support for?" she asked suspiciously. She had a feeling this was just his way of trying to distract her once they got there.

He debated just how much to tell her. "My mom's going to be there."

"You don't get along with your mother?" she asked. He hadn't said anything about that before.

"Oh, I get along with my mother just fine," Luke assured her. There was no misunderstanding the fondness in his voice, she thought. "She's my rock.

The only problem is, the rock is going to be there with another rock."

Completely lost now, Frankie stared at him. "Would you like to try to put that in English this time?"

He wasn't aware that he was frowning—but she was. "She's bringing a date."

Obviously a sore point, Frankie thought. "Is that unusual?"

"Just a little less usual than seeing Halley's Comet streak across the sky," he told her, then cutting through his own sarcasm, he said, "My mother doesn't date. She hasn't gone out with anyone since my father died and that was a long, long time ago."

"Then you don't like this guy?" Frankie guessed, trying to get a handle on the situation.

Luke felt that he had to give the man his due. "No, he's likeable enough. I've met him a few times."

In that case, Frankie didn't understand why he felt he needed any moral support. "Okay, then what's the problem?"

"She's my mother," Luke emphasized, as if that explained everything.

"Well, unless your name happens to be Oedipus, there shouldn't be a problem. You should be happy for her," she told him. And then Frankie suddenly stopped talking. She realized what Luke was up to. "I know what you're doing, you know."

He slanted a glance in her direction. "I'm driving to the party and confiding in you about my mother. Not exactly a big mystery," he pointed out.

"That's not what I meant and you know it," Frankie told him. "You're trying to distract me by talking about your supposed difficulty in coming to terms with your mother going out with someone. This way, you figure I'll get all caught up in your supposed situation and forget all about resisting going to this gathering."

"Distract you?" he repeated innocently. "I have no idea what you're talking about. That hadn't even occurred to me."

She laughed dryly. "Give it up, O'Bannon. Nobody is ever going to give you an award for an outstanding performance. They might, however, be tempted to throw rotten tomatoes."

"For your information, I already got my award," he informed her.

The man was fast on his feet. This was going to be good, Frankie thought.

"Oh?"

"Yeah," he replied, then told her what his award was. "You smiled."

Frankie instantly put on a serious face—although it wasn't as easy as she'd thought.

"No, I didn't."

"Yes, you did," he contradicted. "Just for a minute there, I saw the corners of your mouth curve ever so slightly. That's a smile in my book."

She sighed. "Okay, I asked you this before, but you really didn't answer me. Why does my smiling, my coming to this party, why does it matter so much to you?"

To Luke, it all made sense. "Because we work together, because you're part of the team and because I don't like seeing you unhappy."

Frankie shook her head, although she was aware

that he couldn't see her since Luke was looking straight ahead at the road.

"That still doesn't really answer my question."

"Well, that'll have to do," Luke told her. "At least, for now. Because we're here," he announced, waving a hand toward the house beside the driveway he had just entered.

Chapter 15

"Are you sure it's okay for you to park in the driveway like this?" Frankie asked a little uncertainly.

Granted, this was his uncle's house, and O'Bannon should be aware whether or not it was okay to park in the man's driveway, but it just didn't seem right, in light of what she was looking at. There were cars and vans parked all up and down both sides of the block as far as the eye could see.

"Just how did you happen to score this plum spot?" she asked. "And aren't you blocking whoever's car is in the garage?"

Luke grinned. At least she didn't have a sense of entitlement. "I mentioned to Uncle Andrew about, let's call it your *reluctance* to mingle, so he told me to park my car in the driveway. That way you'll have less distance to walk to the house and think about your getaway."

Frankie stared at him as she got out of the vehicle. "You *told* your uncle that I didn't want to come?"

He knew how to stay on her right side—by having her believe that she hadn't been presented in a bad light. "What I told him was that you wanted to work on the case today. He was the chief of police for a number of years, and he found that to be an admirable mind-set. He also agreed with me that it's important for you to unwind once in a while," Luke added. "That's when he told me to park my car in his driveway."

She supposed she should be flattered that her presence mattered to her host—if Luke wasn't making all this up. In any event, she felt guilty about the machinations that were involved. "This space should be for Valri. She's the one who's pregnant."

Had Valri had a vote in this, he knew his cousin would have sided with his uncle. "She sits at her computer all day. I'm sure she appreciates the chance to stretch her legs a little. And don't worry, that's her husband's car right over there," he told her, pointing out the car parked just past the mailbox. "She didn't have very far to walk."

"And the rest of all those cars?" Frankie had to ask, indicating the vehicles that were parked in every available space.

Luke confirmed what she was already thinking. "Yes, they also belong to other members of the family."

Frankie let out a long, low whistle. "Boy, the neighbors must love it when your uncle throws a party," she commented as she followed Luke up the winding path to the front door of the house.

"He does have his neighbors over on other days to appease them, so I'd say that they don't have much to complain about," Luke told her.

"The man thinks of everything," Frankie said with admiration.

"Pretty much," he agreed. Luke knocked on the door before turning the knob and opening it.

"Shouldn't we wait for someone to actually let us in?" Frankie asked. Invitation or not, she wasn't comfortable about just waltzing in like this.

"Someone just did," Luke told her with a grin. "Me."

Before she could say anything about that not being what she meant, a tall, robust-looking man who appeared far too young and vital to be sporting silver-gray hair the way he was, came over to them wearing a warm, welcoming smile.

"So," he said, addressing his words to Frankie, "you decided to come after all." There was pleasure in his voice.

Frankie glanced toward the man who had brought her before saying, "It was decided for me."

Andrew Cavanaugh nodded his head as he turned to Luke. "Honesty. I like that."

"For some of us, it's an acquired taste," Luke told his uncle. He became a little more formal as he made the official introduction. "Francesca DeMarco, this is my uncle, Chief Andrew Cavanaugh."

Andrew took her hand, enveloping it in both of his. "Do your friends call you Frankie?" he guessed intuitively.

She thought of Kristin, who had been her best friend. Kris had *always* called her Frankie.

"Yes," she replied.

"Then welcome to my home, Frankie," Andrew said to her warmly. "Make yourself at home. Luke can show you where everything is."

Ordinarily, Frankie would have been tempted to say that she already knew where the door was, but remarkably, she found that her ever-present need to flee was dissipating.

She smiled up at the towering patriarch and said, "Thank you." About to slip into the next room, Frankie suddenly stopped. She asked the host, "What is that wonderful smell?"

"Dinner," Andrew replied with a mysterious twinkle in his eye. "If you need something to tide you over until it's served, there are appetizers on several of the tables located just beyond the patio. Again, Luke can show you where they are." A timer went off, commanding his attention, and Andrew looked toward the kitchen. "If you'll excuse me, I have something to baste."

With that, he left them.

"He really does cook for all these people," she marveled. Being part of the police department, she'd heard about the former chief's cooking efforts, but she had more or less discounted the stories until now.

"What did you think, that it was just some urban legend?" Luke asked.

Putting a hand to the small of her back, he directed her through the house and the sprawling family room to the large sliding doors that led onto the patio.

"I thought it was just you Cavanaughs exaggerating," Frankie confessed honestly.

"Cavanaughs never exaggerate," he told her with a hint of a smile playing on his lips. And then he winked as he amended, "Well, maybe just a little—sometimes."

Having guided her to the patio, Luke gestured toward the teak bar standing over to one side of the yard.

"Want something to drink? You can have a soft drink, beer or something with a little more muscle," he told her, indicating a shelf that held several different alcohol bottles. "I know for a fact that that if you prefer flavored sparkling water, he's also got bottles of that. The appetizers are right over there," he concluded, pointing the tables out to her.

She was nothing if not overwhelmed. "Wow, your uncle certainly knows how to put out a spread."

Luke laughed. It was obvious that her comment pleased him. Like the rest of his generation, he had a great deal of affection for the former chief of police. "That he certainly does."

She turned toward Luke, still somewhat incredulous. "And you said he does this a lot?"

"Whenever he can get two or more family members together," Luke told her. "The man really thrives on this."

"But how can he afford to do all this?" she asked. In her estimation, all this food had to set the man back by a great deal.

"Oh, we all chip in," Luke said as if it was the most natural thing. When he saw her opening her purse and begin digging for her wallet, Luke put his

hand on hers to stop her. "By *all* I didn't mean you," he told her.

She couldn't resist looking at him in shock.

"I thought you said that I was family."

"Yes, but not paying family," he informed her. "Don't make me crazy, DeMarco. Just eat, drink and be merry." He fixed her with a look. "That's an order."

The last part made her balk. She raised her chin like someone braced for a fight. "You're not the boss of me," Frankie informed him.

Luke fixed her with a look. "I'm the lead, remember?"

"On the case," Frankie emphasized. "But we're not on the case now, are we? We're off duty. Isn't that the whole point of this? To be off duty and unwind?"

He gave her a penetrating look that went right down to the bone. "You were on the debating team in college, weren't you?"

Her response was to simply smile up at him.

"Hey, you got her to come. And she's smiling. You're more persuasive than I gave you credit for, O'Bannon."

The comment came from White Hawk who came up from behind to join them. He was holding a tall glass of beer in one hand and the hand of a very pretty dark-haired woman in the other.

"DeMarco," White Hawk said, turning to face Frankie. "This is my wife, Linda. Linda, this is De-Marco. She's been working with us on that serial killer case we caught."

The dark-eyed woman smiled at her. "Rick forgets that people have first names. Most of the time he just calls me Wife."

Frankie looked at the tall man. "Rick?"

"That's his first name," Linda told her. "I gather he didn't tell you himself."

"He did. I'm just used to thinking of him as 'White Hawk,'" Frankie confessed. Belatedly, she realized that she still hadn't told the woman her own first name. "I'm Frankie—Francesca," she amended.

Linda nodded "I like Frankie." White Hawk's wife put her hand out toward her. "It's nice to meet you, Frankie."

"Likewise," Frankie told her. Out of the corner of her eye, she saw Luke watching her with a self-satisfied look on his face that all but shouted *Knew you'd like coming here.*

White Hawk and his wife exchanged a few more words with them, then White Hawk saw someone he wanted to introduce to Linda and they excused themselves.

Frankie turned back to the buffet tables. She still hadn't sampled anything from the various dishes spread out across three tables and she could feel her stomach tightening in anticipation.

"What looks good to you?" she asked Luke.

The word *you* shot through his mind with the speed of a bullet. That took him completely by surprise because it had surfaced so readily, like a first response to a word in a word-association game.

"O'Bannon?" She turned to look at him when he didn't answer her question.

"Those are light," Luke told her, pointing out the small stuffed mushrooms covered with melted cheddar cheese that were arranged in rows. "You don't want to eat too much because you'll want to leave room for the main course. That is *always* worth waiting for," Luke assured her.

There were more and more people arriving now. Some, Frankie noted, stayed in the house, others came out into the yard, either for the appetizers, the beverages or the conversation.

In many cases, all three.

Before she knew it, the air became filled with fragments of different conversations and she found herself joining in.

It was hard not to.

The conversations were just that, conversations, not heated debates, not diehard opinions pitted against one another. Just people, talking, in a genial, welcoming atmosphere.

This was Malone's on a large scale, Frankie realized. And she was part of this, part of the family of cops who were all sworn to uphold the law while protecting the lives of the citizens within their city.

She had to admit she felt a sense of pride.

Listening, participating, and getting caught up in the vast camaraderie that abounded in and out of the former chief of police's house, Frankie felt good for the first time since she had stood over her cousin's body.

Really good.

And happy.

When the realization struck her, riding on a lightning bolt, she slanted a glance at the man beside her. Luke. The man who had coaxed, cajoled and all but hog-tied her to get her here.

The moment their eyes met, she could swear that she almost heard what he was thinking: *I told you so*.

But to his credit, he didn't say it out loud.

For that, she was grateful.

Halfway through the evening, she made her way to the woman who was the reason Aurora's former police chief was throwing *this* particular party.

Despite the fact that everyone here knew that Valri was pregnant, as she approached Luke's cousin, Frankie could only marvel at how really thin she looked.

"Congratulations," she said the moment that Valri looked in her direction. "Are you excited about the baby?"

Valri nodded, her eyes sparkling. Frankie could swear that the other woman was actually glowing.

"Excited, terrified, thrilled, the whole gamut of emotions—mostly all at the same time," Valri admitted.

Frankie dug into her oversize shoulder bag and finally found what she was fishing for.

"Here, I thought you might find this useful," she said, handing Valri what was obviously a gift-wrapped paperback book.

"Oh, you didn't have to get me anything, Frankie. Just having you here is more than gift enough," she said. "I know how hard it was to get you to come," Valri added, lowering her voice.

People always said things like that, that their presence was enough of a gift, but Frankie thought that the other woman actually sounded as if she meant it. She was touched.

As Valri tore off the wrapping paper, exposing a book that covered everything that a new mother could expect to experience during the baby's first twelve months, Frankie quickly explained, "I know there are lots of young parents in your family to turn to for advice, but sometimes it's just good to see it in writing." Then, in case she had overstepped her place, she added, "There's a gift receipt inside the book in case you want to exchange it for something else."

Frankie didn't get a chance to finish because Valri had thrown her arms around her and was now hugging her—hard.

"Why would I want to exchange it? It's a very thoughtful, not to mention very useful gift. I love it," Valri declared. Finally releasing her, Valri said, "Thank you!"

"Don't mention it," Frankie replied, color entering her cheeks. "Really, don't mention it." Displays of gratitude embarrassed her. She never knew what to say in response.

Valri stepped back. Their eyes met and Valri mouthed, "Thank you," again before turning away because she seemed to sense that Frankie actually preferred it that way.

"That was nice of you," Luke said, coming up behind her.

Frankie's heart slammed right against her chest and she whirled around. She'd thought that Luke was over by one of the buffet tables.

"Were you there the whole time?" It was almost an accusation. She hadn't wanted him to witness her giving Valri her present.

"The whole time," he confirmed.

"I didn't see you or hear you come up behind me." Why didn't the man make some kind of noise? Other men made noise.

Luke merely smiled. He was getting a lot more of a kick out of her reaction than he thought he would.

"That's what makes me such a good detective," he told her, tongue-in-cheek. "I blend in."

Frankie watched him dully. Blend in? Maybe here, she allowed, because there were so many good-looking men in the Cavanaugh family, but in general, in her opinion, there was absolutely nothing about Detective Luke Cavanaugh O'Bannon that allowed him to "blend in" with the average crowd.

The man was just too damn good-looking not to be noticed—so how had she missed him, she couldn't help wondering.

"C'mere," he said, surprising her by taking hold of her arm. "Dinner's about to be served and you definitely don't want to miss dinner."

Dinner. That meant it was already later than she'd realized.

Frankie suppressed a sigh. She had forgotten all about leaving early. That was because she'd been enjoying herself.

Just the way that Luke had predicted she would.

Damn the man, anyway. He was probably going to gloat about this.

But she made no attempt to separate herself and leave.

She didn't want to.

Chapter 16

"That was really your mother?"

Frankie shifted in the passenger seat to look at him as Luke drove her back to her apartment. It was way past midnight, a great deal later than she had initially thought she would be coming home.

But she couldn't complain. She had had a genuinely good time. Looking back, she had probably spent more time talking to people in this one evening than she had in the last year—probably even longer than that.

There were hardly any vehicles out on the road and he spared her a quick glance. "Yes, that was my mother. Why do you sound so surprised?"

"Well, from the few things you'd said about your mother, I expected to see this old, worn-out, tired-looking woman."

And Maeve O'Bannon was anything but old or worn out. If anything, the woman operated like a live wire.

"I never described my mother that way," Luke protested, switching lanes to make a right turn at the end of the block.

"No, you didn't describe her at all," Frankie agreed. "But you did say that she was a widow, that she'd raised five kids on her own and that she had driven an ambulance for years in order to make ends meet before she finally saved up enough to buy the company."

"So far, you've got it right," Luke agreed. "But why would—"

"Because that kind of life can wear a person out after a few years. But the woman I saw at your uncle's party was young," she told him. His mother had been dressed in a flattering silver-and-blue dress. "A lot younger than I thought she'd be." Frankie smiled, remembering. "And she certainly displayed a lot of energy on the dance floor with her boyfriend."

Luke flinched a little at the label she'd just given to his mother's escort. "Um, I think it's a bit early in the game to be calling him her boyfriend."

In this instance, Frankie was more than willing to be corrected. "What would you call him?"

Luke stared straight ahead at the road before him. "Fire Chief Carlyle—her date for the evening."

"So that was the first time they went out?" she asked, trying to get her facts straight. She assumed that if Luke's mother had been dating the fire chief on a regular basis, Luke would have been more comfortable with the situation.

"The second time," Luke corrected. Then, after a pause, he reconsidered the count and said, "Maybe the third."

"Three dates *means* that she's dating him. Which means he's her boyfriend," she concluded. And then suddenly, she replayed the man's name in her mind. It rang a bell. "Wait, did you just say Carlyle?" she asked. "And he's the fire chief?"

"Yeah, Craig Carlyle," he told her.

"That's Sierra's father, isn't it?" she asked, referring to his brother Ronan's fiancée. She'd met both—fleetingly—before.

He still kept his eyes on the road, refusing to register any sort of a reaction. "Yes, Mom works out of the same firehouse that Carlyle does."

Frankie was doing her best to read between the lines. There was something that the detective wasn't admitting, and she was doing her best to get a proper perspective on what it was.

"And this bothers you, your mother going out with someone?" she asked, trying to get to the bottom of all this.

"You know," Luke said honestly, "she even came to ask me if she should go out with the fire chief. I told her if she wanted to go out with him, then she should. It was her decision to make."

"But?" Frankie prodded. When he spared her a quick glance regarding the nature of her question, she elaborated. "It's really obvious that having your mother dating someone bothers you."

Luke shrugged. "It just seems strange, that's all. She's never dated before." Throughout his entire

childhood and adolescence, he couldn't remember her *ever* going out with anyone.

"Well, she must have dated at some point or you wouldn't be here," she told him.

"You know what I mean."

"Look at it from her point of view. Her kids are grown, her career is settled. I'd say that your mother has time for something new—and she's certainly earned the right to open a new chapter in her life," Frankie speculated as they drove into her apartment complex.

Luke pulled his car into the first parking space that was available in guest parking. Given that it was past midnight on a Saturday, there were only a few spaces left.

"You're probably right—and I'm glad for her. She did look happy," he acknowledged. Turning off the engine, Luke released his seatbelt and looked at her.

"So, what's your excuse?"

Frankie had no idea where that question had come from. "What?"

Getting out, Luke came around to the passenger side of his vehicle and opened the door for her. "You told me that you didn't go out on dates. I was just asking what your excuse was."

"I don't have the time." She slid out of her seat and deliberately avoided taking his hand. "My job keeps me busy." He, above all people, should know how demanding police work was.

"You don't work 24/7," he pointed out as he walked her to her door.

She stubbornly hung on to her excuse. "Currently, I'm working for this hard-ass who just doesn't let up

and keeps after me. Not to mention, I'm working a case that's really important."

Luke appeared unmoved. "*Every* case is important—and there'll always be another one." That was a simple fact of life that every detective learned early on. "I think you should take a page out of my mother's book and start enjoying life."

"I *am* enjoying life," Frankie insisted. "I enjoy putting bad guys away. Besides, didn't we have this argument before, centering around my coming with you to your uncle's party? I went, didn't I?" she reminded him.

"And you had a good time," Luke countered.

There was no way she could get away with denying that. "Yes," she agreed loftily. "I did."

"So, maybe you'll do it again." It wasn't a question but a statement of fact.

"If I'm invited," she allowed.

Luke decided to push things a little further. "How about if you're invited out on a date?"

"If that comes up, then I'll see," Frankie replied. Her mouth was beginning to feel like wet cotton, making it almost impossible for her to speak.

Luke was standing no closer to her than he had been a moment ago, yet it *felt* closer, somehow. It also felt as if there was less air around her than a moment ago. She could feel her body heating—or was that heat from his body that she felt?

She couldn't tell.

All she knew was that she felt hot, really hot.

Go inside before you do or say something you're going to feel stupid about.

Frankie fished around for her keys, coming up

empty several times before she finally found the right one and pulled it out, only to have it slip from her fingers and drop on the ground in front of her.

"Damn," she murmured under her breath.

Frankie stooped down to pick the key up at the exact moment that Luke did. The end result was that their heads bumped against each other.

The impact threw her off balance and Frankie would have fallen backward, bruising her dignity as well as possibly several other parts, if it hadn't been for Luke's quick reaction. He caught her by her arms, keeping her from sprawling on the ground right before her doorstep.

Regaining his own balance, Luke brought her up along with him.

It had been quiet in the development when they had first arrived. Now the area seemed to be as still as a tomb.

So still that she was sure Luke could hear the pounding of her heart. Any second, he was going to comment on it, joking about hearing the thunder of drums.

Except that he didn't make a joke. He didn't laugh or even say anything vaguely cryptic.

He didn't say anything at all because he couldn't. It was obvious that Luke had never learned the trick of talking and kissing at the same time, and he was far too busy doing the latter to attempt the former.

Frankie could feel her heart racing even while her knees took on the consistency of leftover whipped cream.

She had no idea how her arms came to be around his neck.

And when had his gone around her waist?

What was happening here? And why wasn't she pushing him away the way she should have been doing? she silently upbraided herself.

He shouldn't be doing this.

For some reason beyond his understanding, the woman he'd taken to his uncle's party was being exceedingly vulnerable. And he, he was breaking every rule he believed in by taking advantage of her.

That wasn't the way he operated.

And yet he couldn't quite make himself pull away. Couldn't make himself stop kissing Frankie. There was something very stimulating, very exciting about kissing this woman.

Damn it, get hold of yourself, O'Bannon. This isn't you!

Somehow, he managed to pull back, even though everything within him wanted him to continue what he was doing.

"What the hell was that?" Stunned, Frankie blinked, trying to clear her head and struggling or control. Struggling to steady her breathing and her racing heart.

"An aberration," he answered. He should have never given in to himself. "Sorry."

Her eyes met his. "Are you?" she asked, trying not to sound breathless. "Are you sorry you kissed me?"

"No," he admitted truthfully. "I'm not sorry. But I still shouldn't have done it," Luke added.

Key in hand, Frankie turned away from him and unlocked her door. Luke took that as a signal to leave. If he remained, he'd only complicate matters more by taking another inept stab at an apology and, most likely, he'd fail.

More than that, he'd be severely tempted to repeat his mistake.

It was better for both of them if he just made a quick getaway.

Luke had taken less than three steps toward where he had parked his car when he heard Frankie quietly ask him, "Would you like to come in for a nightcap?"

For a second, he thought he'd just imagined her voice. And then he turned back toward her, but he remained standing exactly where he had been.

"You don't drink." He hadn't seen her have anything but sparkling water all night—and only that one beer at Malone's, which she hadn't looked as if she'd enjoyed. "And I shouldn't, since I'm driving myself home."

"How about some coffee, then?" she suggested. "That shouldn't violate any laws."

"I don't think that's a good idea," he told her, referring to his coming in.

Frankie said nothing. She just remained standing in the doorway, looking at him.

He was going to regret this, a voice in his head told him. Regret crossing that threshold. But he knew that he would regret walking away even more.

"Oh, hell," he cried, crossing the threshold and following her into her apartment. "What kind of coffee do you have?"

She closed the door, then locked it before turning back around to face him. There was a look in his eyes that spoke to her. She saw what she needed to. "Does it matter?"

"Not a damn," he replied in all sincerity.

The next few moments were a blur.

Luke didn't quite remember how the distance between the two of them wound up disappearing, which of them crossed to the other or if they both just met somewhere in the middle.

What he did remember was thinking that she felt so good in his arms, as if she was meant to be there. As if she had *always* been meant to be there.

Unable to hold back, Luke kissed her over and over again. Kissed Frankie as if stopping meant he would have to stop breathing.

It was insane.

He was insane.

Where had this sudden, insatiable need for this woman come from? It wasn't as if he was some sex-starved prisoner who hadn't been with a woman in years. He'd always had a very ample love life and had had more than his share of women over the course of the last few years.

And yet, Luke was forced to admit, there had always been something missing, some ingredient without a name that hadn't been part of the mix, no matter how agile, how nimble, how beautiful the woman in his bed was.

There was always a challenge that wasn't being met.

Francesca DeMarco was a walking challenge, and he'd recognized that from the first moment that he'd laid eyes on her.

That was it, he thought with the sudden clarity of a sunrise. Her stubbornness, her feistiness, the challenge that she represented, *that* was what had been missing from his life.

Frankie made it up in spades.

But that still didn't give him the right to seduce her.

Cursing inwardly, Luke forced himself to stop and draw back from her a second time. He saw the confusion in Frankie's eyes as she stared up at him.

"What's wrong?" she asked hoarsely, immediately thinking that she had crossed some imaginary line, violated some rule and that was why he was pulling away from her.

"I am," he told her. "I shouldn't be doing this. I shouldn't be seducing you like this."

They had found their way to her sofa, leaving behind a few articles of clothing along the way. He began to get up now, but she caught his hand, holding it fast.

"I had the impression that we were seducing each other," she said.

"I—"

Still holding his hand, Frankie got up on her knees on the sofa cushion. Petite, delicate, she was still a force to be reckoned with.

"I want you to get something straight, O'Bannon," she told him, her eyes blazing. "If I didn't want this, it wouldn't be happening. You might be as good-looking as all hell, but I've got free will and that means I make my own choices, and heaven help me, I don't know why, but I choose you. Now stop treating me like I'm some sort of weak-wristed, addle-brained pushover who can be won by a set of dimples and a cleft chin. I am and have always been my own person.

"Now, are you going to finish what you started or

are you going to force me to tie you up so that I can have my way with you?"

Luke laughed, pulling her back into his arms. "You're crazy, you know that?"

"Well, there has been talk," Frankie allowed whimsically.

"I've had enough of talk," Luke told her. "How about you?"

"Finally, you've said something intelligent," Frankie told him. Looking up at Luke, her eyes spoke legions.

Chapter 17

She *knew* there were so many reasons for her not to be doing this. It was unprofessional. It might backfire on her and get her sent back to Major Crimes before her cousin's murder was solved.

Worse, it could get her called on the carpet and disciplined for unbecoming conduct. Her heretofore perfect record would be forfeit.

But the biggest reason she shouldn't be doing this was because she just didn't do this kind of thing. Ever. She didn't impetuously give in to the moment and make love with a man she hardly knew.

But somehow, none of those reasons mattered. Not in the face of this overwhelming, burning need that was only growing stronger. Nothing else mattered right now except following through on her desire to make love with Luke.

She couldn't think straight anymore.

She wanted to make love with him so badly that she could swear she was aching inside, and that was something that had *never* happened to her before. Having reached the ripe age of twenty-nine, Frankie had never felt that kind of overwhelming attraction that made her just blindly dive into the moment.

Relationships, if they happened in her life at all, were at best mild things that could easily be pushed to the back burner.

This, however, was something that was not about to be budged. And it was shaking up her world.

The moment Luke had kissed her, any resistance she might have had dissolved.

Warm shivers of anticipation rippled insistently through her body as she felt Luke's lips moving along her neck, her cheeks, her eyelids, before making their way back to her lips.

Frankie could feel her very soul fluttering.

For several moments, she was the wildly enthralled recipient, but then, suddenly she shifted her focus and became a participant in this exquisite dance of mounting desire, as well.

Her heart slammed against her chest as she kissed Luke over and over again, tugging at his shirt. She worked to remove it, even as her lips remained sealed to his.

The room began to spin. He caressed her, tugging away her dress and then other pieces of clothing that presented an annoying barrier, keeping him from touching her, from running his hands along her burning skin.

Frankie moaned as his lips touched her again,

skimmed her body, moving along to all parts of her, branding them and making them his own.

She could hardly breathe as another, stronger wave of anticipation washed over her. Frankie pressed her body against his, feeling its hot imprint along her flesh.

Luke didn't think it was possible for him to feel weak-kneed. That sort of reaction resided far back in his past. It had been a part of his early adolescence, when he was just coming into his own. When he had discovered that willing partners were all around him. All he had to do was look.

Even so, he'd never taken any of it for granted or as his due. Rather, he had always treated each and every one of the women he made love with as if they were special. And, in their own way, each one of them was.

But this one really *was* special.

A special kind of special.

Who would have guessed? he wondered. From the very first, the fiery detective with the smart mouth had aroused him and attracted him. Moreover, he saw her as a challenge. But the challenge had turned out to be so much more than he had anticipated.

Each passionate kiss just left him wanting the next one. And the next. His excitement grew to breath-stealing new heights.

He wanted her. Wanted her *now*. Wanted the mind-blowing, exhilarating feeling of final release that came when the very last of the mountain had been reached and conquered.

And yet, he wanted this dizzying, pulse-accelerating

feeling to continue, to grow as desire increased, doubling with every fraction of a moment, every intimate caress he both gave and received.

Luke struggled to pace himself, even as he felt himself rushing to the enticing climactic ending that beckoned to him like an irresistible siren's song.

With supreme effort, Luke began to steel himself. This wasn't just about him, it was about her. Her reaction. His first priority was her pleasure.

Just like his brothers, he had never been one of those men who wanted to "score," who only cared about his own gratification, his own pleasure, first and last. No, to him, making love had always been a mutual endeavor, something to be enjoyed together.

Ever mindful of her, he crafted Frankie's arousal as if he was fashioning a precious piece of fine jewelry, working at it patiently until he sensed that everything was just right.

And when it was, when he could see that she was unable to hold herself back a second longer, he drew his body up along hers. His eyes on hers, he parted her legs and began to enter.

The very next moment, he stopped. His eyes widened as he looked at Frankie.

Luke hadn't expected to discover any sort of an obstacle in his path.

But he had.

Stunned, he began to raise his head, a half-formed question on his lips.

Oh, no, she knew where this was going. He was going to retreat.

She couldn't let that happen. Couldn't let him just

stop, not when she was so very close to achieving that final exquisite leap to ecstasy. If he drew away now, it was all over.

Wrapping her legs around Luke's hard, muscular torso, she held him fast at the same time that she framed his face with her hands and pulled his mouth down to hers.

She kissed him. Kissed him over and over again until she burned away his question, his resistance and the doubts that had gotten in his way.

Her body moving against him urgently, she made him forsake his better judgment and thrust all the way into her.

The rest was inevitable.

The timeless dance to a rhythm only heard by the two people involved overtook them and surged forward until it was wrapped entirely around them.

Luke moved faster and faster. Working past the pain, Frankie emulated and echoed each one of his movements, determined to keep up.

Determined to reach journey's end at the exact moment he did.

With that very first thrust, there had been a flash of pain, but it faded quickly enough, replaced by surging passion and an overwhelming desire and need for the final burst of stardust that hovered just out of reach, waiting to bathe them both.

She sensed its closeness, could feel herself craving that final mind-numbing volley into ecstasy.

And then it happened. Fireworks both from within and without.

The shower of stars fell all around her. Her very skin felt as if it was on fire.

Frankie didn't want the moment to pass.

She clung to Luke, clung with every fiber of her being to the ensuing euphoria for as long as she could. Wishing it was longer.

But, eventually, her heart rate subsided. Her breathing returned to normal and the wave of almost unimaginable joy slipped into the background.

Luke's body relaxed against hers.

As she tried to tighten her arms around him, she could feel him separating himself from her. He rolled off to her side.

Frankie braced herself for what she knew would come.

Luke looked at her. Was that an accusation in his eyes? She felt disappointment taking hold of her.

"Why didn't you tell me?" he asked.

Willing herself not to break down, Frankie did her best to brazen it out. "Tell you what?"

Exasperation creased his brow. "Don't play dumb with me, Frankie. You're too smart for that." He raised himself up on his elbow, and still looking at her, he waited for an answer. But she remained silent. "Well?" he demanded.

"I'm sorry, what was the question?" she asked, clinging to ignorance for all she was worth.

She was going to make him spell it out, he thought, angrily. He was uncomfortable enough about this as it was.

"Damn it, Frankie, why didn't you tell me you were a virgin?"

She didn't know where to look and just wished she could disappear into thin air. This wasn't how the night was supposed to go. Why was he torturing her this way?

"You mean it wasn't in my file?" she asked sarcastically.

She eyed her scattered clothing, wondering if she could grab them and just hide in her bathroom. He'd have to take a hint and leave then, right?

Luke's expression darkened as he watched her. "I'm serious, Frankie."

"I realize that," she answered stiffly. "I also realize that you feel cheated and disappointed, so you can just take your clothes and leave. You're free to go. I'm not going to make you suffer a second longer in my company."

Luke made no move to do either. Instead, he stared at her, stunned almost speechless.

Almost.

"Cheated?" he echoed incredulously, then said, "Disappointed?" If possible, his stare only intensified. "Just what the hell are you talking about?"

Why was he drawing this out? Was that her punishment for not letting him know he was going to be making love to a woman who had absolutely no experience? "I'm talking about how you feel."

"How the hell would you know how I feel?" Luke demanded, then added, "Other than guilty."

"Guilty?" It was her turn to be confused. "Why would you feel guilty?"

"Because I took something from you. A woman's first time is supposed to be something special, something she could look back on with a fond memory."

And he had all but devoured her like a starving

man on a desert island, with no thought to creating a memorable experience for her.

"What makes you think this doesn't qualify?" she snapped, her voice echoing with the same intense anger as his.

"Because a hard-boiled egg takes longer to cook than what we just did."

That was so insane sounding, it caused a smile to surface and play on her lips. And then she gave in and laughed. "Maybe I should have hard-boiled eggs more often."

Lost, he blinked as if to clear his vision and stared at her. "What?"

"Look, you hardheaded idiot, in case you haven't noticed, I'm not complaining about what just happened. I don't know about you, but I had a really fantastic time." Frankie blew out a breath, desperately trying to find the right way to word this. "I realize you were expecting more, but—"

"More?" Luke repeated as if the word made no sense to him. How could she even *say* that? How could she even *think* that? "Any more and I would have probably exploded. I wouldn't have been able to handle *more*. You ever tell anyone this and I'll deny it," he warned, "but you're all the woman I can handle."

She stared at him "Then why are you yelling at me?"

"Because you should have *told* me that you were a virgin," he insisted.

"And just when was I supposed to do that?" she asked. "While you were kissing me so much that I was melting into a puddle, or while you were taking my clothes off and all I could think of was that I'd finally found someone I *wanted* to make love with and that I *really* hoped you wouldn't stop?"

His mouth all but dropped open. "Say again?"

"So I can feed that undernourished, starving ego of yours?" she asked, mocking him. She shook her head. "Oh, no, I don't think so."

But he wasn't about to let the subject go, not yet. "Are you telling me that you're a virgin because you've never met anyone in your life who you wanted to make love with?"

She closed her eyes for a moment, as if searching for inner strength. And then she opened them again. "If I say yes, are you going to run for the hills, or will you stay long enough to put your clothes on, then run?" she asked. "Because I really think you should get dressed first. There're cops out there who'll arrest you if you don't put your clothes on first."

Laughing, he caught her completely by surprise when he pulled her into his arms.

"I'm not running anywhere, naked or otherwise," he told her. Just to convince her, he brought his mouth down to hers.

After a very long moment, she wedged her hand between them, pushing him back just a fraction. "Then you're not leaving?"

He hovered over her, laughter in his eyes. "What do you think?"

"I think you need to show me."

"I can do that."

His smile melted away as he brought his mouth back to hers.

Frankie felt her blood heating almost instantly as

he began to do all the things that he had done before, except more slowly this time.

The slower he went, the more eager she became, desperate to scale another mountain and reach another climax.

When they finally achieved the mutual gratification he had fashioned for both of them for a second time, Frankie curled up against him, struggling to get her breathing normal again and under control.

Eventually she did. Which was when she sighed. "You are a revelation, Detective O'Bannon."

He laughed. "I could say the same thing about you, Detective DeMarco." He pulled her even closer to him, their bodies all but one, and then he pressed a kiss to her forehead. "But you really should have told me. How did you ever get to be twenty-nine without ever—ever—"

"Well," she said with a straight face. "First I turned one, and then two and so on. Before I knew it, I was twenty-nine and, well, you know the rest," she said, looking up at him.

"Not hardly, but you'll have to tell me sometime," he said.

"Nothing else to tell," she answered, a sigh escaping her lips.

Her warm breath drifted along his skin, reignited his fire.

To her surprise, he sat up. He was leaving, she thought with a sudden pang. She didn't want him to go. Still, she tried to tell herself that there was no reason to expect he would stay the night.

She had no idea what to expect, Frankie realized. For her, this was all brand-new, unexplored territory.

Because he had gotten up, she did, too. The next moment, she looked around for her clothes.

Luke watched her, puzzled, as she slid on her dress. "What are you doing?"

"Putting my clothes on. I thought that the neighbors might get upset if I was naked when I walked you to your car."

He still didn't understand. "Are you throwing me out?" he asked.

She blinked, the zipper on her dress only half up. Obviously their signals were crossed. "No, I thought you were leaving."

"No, I was going to go to your bedroom," he told her. "I thought, for a change, you might like to make love in your bed."

That would make three times tonight. "I thought you were tired."

He smiled at her, running his hand along her body. "Tired, maybe," he allowed. "But not dead." And then he thought that maybe this was her way of telling him she'd had enough for her first time. "Unless you'd rather go to sleep," he said.

Taking his hand, she began to head toward her bedroom in the rear of her apartment.

"Eventually," she told him.

"Sounds promising," he said. The next moment, he surprised her by sweeping her up into his arms.

Laughing, she laced her hands around his neck to anchor herself. "What are you doing?"

"Trying to help you conserve your energy," he

told her. "I don't want the walk to your bedroom to sap away your strength."

A wide smile played on her lips. "Very thoughtful."

"I told you, remember?" he reminded her whimsically. "I said that I'm a very thoughtful guy."

"I guess I forgot," she told him, pressing her lips against his neck.

Luke walked faster.

Chapter 18

The space beside her was empty.

Half asleep, Frankie had reached out to run her hand along Luke's arm. She had wanted to reassure herself that it all hadn't just been a dream, only to discover that she was alone in her queen-size bed.

Bolting upright, her eyes open now, Frankie sighed. She was usually a very light sleeper, but Luke had completely exhausted her last night. She supposed that was why she'd remained sound asleep when he had taken his leave.

Feeling let down, she kicked off the covers and got up.

Frankie was just taking out one of the oversize T-shirts she usually slept in from the drawer when she paused and took in a deep breath.

Coffee.

She smelled coffee.

But she hadn't put the timer on last night the way she usually did. She'd been far too busy. What was going on here?

Pulling on the T-shirt, Frankie took her service weapon with her as she hurried out to the kitchen to investigate.

It wasn't an intruder. It was Luke, standing at the stove with his back to her.

"What are you doing?" she asked.

"You're not supposed to be up yet," he told her, not bothering to turn around. "You're supposed to still be asleep so I can regale you with my culinary abilities when you do wake up."

She was still trying to process the fact that he hadn't left. "You cook?"

"That's what culinary abilities mean, Detective," he said, finally turning around. He saw the gun she was still holding. "Are you planning on shooting me if you don't like breakfast?"

Frankie set her gun aside on the counter. "I didn't know you cooked. You're a guy."

Luke laughed. "You figured that out, did you? What was your first clue?" He brought over two cups of coffee. "Oh, that's right, you saw me naked last night. I guess that gave it away." He placed one cup on the table in front of her, then set the other in front of his chair.

His eyes traveled along the length of her body, a sexy, appreciative smile curving his mouth. "I like your new look. You have underwear under that?"

Her eyes met his. There was a glint of mischief in hers. "No."

His grin was nothing short of wicked. "I like that even more."

She glanced past his shoulder toward the stove. There were eggs sizzling in the large frying pan. "You really are making breakfast," she marveled. She'd thought he'd just been putting her on.

"Growing up in my house, it was a requirement." Moving back to the stove, Luke turned off the burner beneath the frying pan, then divided the scrambled eggs into equal portions between two plates. There were two slices of buttered toast and three slices of bacon on each plate already.

Bringing the plates over to the table, he placed one before each of their chairs. "My mother insisted we all learn how to cook. We took turns making meals whenever Mom worked the night shift." He took a seat. "Sit. Eat. It's not poisoned," he assured her.

She sat down as gracefully as she could, given what she was wearing, then warily picked up her fork.

"This is good," Frankie marveled after taking her first bite. "I had no idea you had these hidden talents."

Grinning, Luke winked at her. "Stick around, kid. You ain't seen nothin' yet."

She knew it was just a playful line, thrown out with no real thought behind it, but she found herself hoping that there was more than a grain of truth to the words.

Careful, Frankie, you don't want to get carried away. One wrong move and he'll bolt out of your life like a racehorse on steroids in a fixed race.

"Look, I was thinking," Luke said, "after breakfast, why don't we—" The cell phone he'd left in his jacket, which was still lying on the floor, suddenly began to ring. Half a beat later, hers did, as well. "Answer the phone," Luke concluded with a sigh. Getting up, he asked, "What are the odds that those are two wrong numbers?"

"Not good," Frankie guessed. It took her a minute to locate her own cell phone.

Their voices almost blended as they each announced their names the moment they answered the calls.

Luke frowned as he listened intently to the person on the other end. He'd guessed correctly and he was far from happy about it—for a couple of reasons.

"Be there as soon as I can." Ending the call, he looked over toward Frankie. "Apparently, our serial killer decided not to take the weekend off. You get the same message?"

"No, actually I didn't," Frankie answered, putting her cell phone down on the coffee table for the time being. "That was Valri."

"Valri?" he repeated, puzzled. "My Valri? Why would she call you?"

"Well, apparently we bonded last night," Frankie told Luke. "Anyway, it seems that she knows some tech people who can access information..." She paused, looking for the right way to put this. "Let's say, off the record."

Frankie definitely had his attention. Rather than beat around the bush or resort to euphemisms, he said, "You're talking about hacking."

She got down to the heart of the matter—and the

reason Valri had called her the minute she'd gotten the information.

"What I'm talking about is that it turns out my cousin used the same online dating site as Ellen O'Keefe did and Valri's *associate* was able to get me—us," she corrected, knowing this had to be a joint undertaking, "the names of the men who responded to my cousin's dating profile."

Trying her best to rein in her excitement, she looked at Luke and said, "Kristin's killer's name is probably among those names."

He hated to rain on her parade, but he wanted Frankie to keep things in perspective. "If he didn't use an alias."

Frankie blew out a breath. He had a point, but she didn't want to think about that right now. "One step at a time," she told Luke, already hurrying back to her bedroom to get dressed.

"Our first step," Luke reminded her as he followed right behind Frankie, "is to get to the latest crime scene."

Standing in her closet, Frankie grabbed the first clothes she came across.

Damn it, she hated it when he was right. "I forgot about that," she said ruefully.

"I know," Luke responded sympathetically. "I wish I could, too." He thought for a second, trying not to react to the fact that she was quickly getting dressed in front of him. He forced himself to look away and concentrate on the case. Otherwise, it might be a while before they got to the scene of the crime. "Look, why don't you do what you have to do. I'll just say I couldn't get hold of you."

She pulled on a pair of jeans and a sweatshirt. "I'm not having you lie for me," she protested—although she loved him for suggesting that.

The thought startled her and she felt almost shaken. Focusing instead on what she had just found out, Frankie said, "Valri's forwarding the information to my smartphone. I can review it after we leave this new crime scene."

He appreciated her dedication. "Then let's get going."

With that, Luke crossed back to the living room to retrieve his jacket and his phone.

She was right behind him as they went out the door. "Aren't you afraid someone'll notice you're wearing the same clothes you had on last night?"

"Men don't notice that about each other," he told her.

He could see that Frankie was still concerned. Probably because she was worried that people would see them arriving at the crime scene together and put two and two together. He wanted to set her mind at ease.

"But if anyone does comment, I'll just say that I grabbed the first clothes I could get my hands on when the call came in. Not my fault they happened to be the same ones I wore yesterday."

He'd come up with that excuse so effortlessly, Frankie thought. "I take it you've done this before," she commented.

Luke chuckled. "Don't ask any questions you don't want the answers to," he said with a grin.

Of course he'd done this before, Frankie admonished herself. He had a reputation, she knew that. And now she was one of the many women he'd been with.

Let it go, Frankie. Let it go. You've got more important things to think about.

And she did. She owed it to Kris.

Even so, she couldn't stop herself from thinking about Luke and the night she'd just spent with him, as well.

This wasn't going to end happily for her in the long run. *It's not the final destination, it's the journey that counts*, she told herself and clung to that.

"He got another one," Sean Cavanaugh grimly told his nephew and Frankie when they walked into the seventh floor apartment where their latest victim had lived. "Sometimes I think this is the reason Andrew throws as many family gatherings as he does— to help us get the taste of death out of our mouths."

He looked over at what was clearly a covered body on the floor.

Moving toward the victim, Luke pulled up the sheet. The dead woman looked just like all the other women who had come before her. Dark haired and in her twenties. He carefully replaced the sheet and rose to look at his uncle. "Who found the body?" Luke asked.

"I did." A shaken, mousy-looking woman stepped forward. She seemed as if she was barely holding it together.

"That's Patricia Laihee," Sean told him. Both Luke and Frankie held up their credentials for the traumatized woman's benefit.

"Martha was supposed to meet me for breakfast

this morning," the woman continued. "When she didn't show up, I tried calling her a couple of times but it went straight to voice mail. Martha *never* shuts off her phone," Patricia insisted. "I had an uneasy feeling, so I came over to her apartment."

"How did you get in?" Luke asked, his voice low and almost soothing in an effort to keep the woman calm.

"I've got a key, but the door wasn't locked." The very memory was obviously agitating the woman. "When I came in, I found Martha on the floor. She was cold," Patricia cried. "And she wasn't breathing." Her eyes filled with tears as she regarded the strangers in her friend's apartment. "Why would she do this? Everything was finally going right for her. Why would she do this? Why would she kill herself?"

"You think she killed herself?" Frankie questioned, taking her cue from Luke. She had a feeling that one wrong word and the woman was going to break down right in front of them.

Patricia looked at her as if she didn't understand why that was even being asked. "There was a syringe on the floor next to her body. Martha must have overdosed."

"She took drugs?" Luke asked gently, prodding the woman along.

It took Patricia several attempts to pull herself together before she could finally answer the question.

"She used to," she replied, her voice strained. "But Martha was clean," she insisted. "I visited her every other day when she was in rehab, and she swore to me that she was never going to let drugs dictate her life again. That she was going to get clean and *make* something of herself." Tears were streaming down her face. "And I believed her. She was my best friend and I believed her," Patricia sobbed.

Luke looked in his uncle's direction.

Sean knew without asking what Luke needed from him. "I'll do a full tox screen," Sean promised. "Most likely, it'll be like all the others. No indication of any recent drug use, except for one large, fatal overdose administered in the last twelve hours," he said, his voice heavy.

"What does he mean, all the others?" Patricia asked. She directed her question to Luke, her eyes wide. "What others?"

Luke tried to be as tactful as he could. The woman before him was in a fragile state and he didn't want to add to her anguish, but he didn't want to just sweep her question under the rug, either.

"A number of former recovered drug addicts have been found dead due to a fatal overdose," Luke explained. "Except that someone else was responsible for killing them."

"I don't understand," Patricia said, bewildered. She looked around at the crime scene investigators. "Someone *did* this to Martha? Why? Why would someone kill Martha?" she cried.

"That's what we're trying to piece together," Luke told her.

Patricia ran her hands up and down her arms, as if trying to chase away a chill. "Do you think that he killed Martha here?"

"I'm afraid that it looks that way," Luke answered. He turned his attention to Frankie. "This is a very upscale building. Find out if the building manager can show you any surveillance videos from the last fifteen hours."

Patricia suddenly spoke up. "Martha has, like, a nanny cam set up in the living room. Does that help?" she asked.

"She has children?" Frankie asked. There was no sign of any children and she was immediately worried that something could have happened to them.

But Patricia shook her head. "No, she doesn't. Didn't," she corrected herself. "She was just worried that she might get robbed or that someone might break in when she wasn't home. The camera's in the spine of that book," she volunteered, pointing to a rather large anthology book on the top shelf of a bookcase against the opposite wall.

According to its title, the book supposedly dealt with nineteenth-century poetry.

Luke pulled on a pair of plastic gloves and removed the thick volume from the bookshelf. When he opened it, he found that the book had been hollowed out to accommodate a small, motion-activated camera.

Closing the book again, he handed it over to his uncle who slipped the entire anthology into a plastic evidence bag.

"Thank heaven for paranoia," Sean murmured in a low voice, taking care that the victim's friend didn't overhear.

"I'll have the lab get on this right away," he told his nephew and Frankie.

Luke called over the police officer who had been the first on the scene. "See that Ms. Laihee gets home," he told the officer.

Patricia suddenly spoke up. "When you catch this monster, I want to know."

"You will, I promise," Luke told her. Turning toward Frankie, he saw that she was staring into the next room. "You see something, DeMarco?"

"Orchids," she answered. If there was any doubt in either of their minds that this was the work of the same killer, the presence of orchids in a slender gray vase erased that. "Just like at the last few crime scenes." She thought of the florist they'd questioned. "As soon as you find anything on that nanny cam, I want a hard copy to show to the florist." She turned toward Luke. "I think maybe that bastard's luck is finally beginning to run out."

"You might be right," Destiny Richardson Cavanaugh said, coming in from the bedroom. "I just dusted the vase for prints. I found several."

"They probably belong to the deliveryman," Luke pointed out.

"Most likely," his cousin Logan's wife agreed. "But there's also a partial on it and that, hopefully, might just belong to someone else."

"How about the syringe?" Frankie asked suddenly.

"The killer probably held it with his handkerchief," Luke said.

"He probably held the cylinder that way," Frankie agreed. "But say she was struggling. He had his hands full with her and he was trying to push the plunger down. There might be a thumbprint there— or at least a partial of a thumbprint," she suggested.

Destiny dusted the small, round area as they spoke, then looked up with a smile. "Give the lady a cigar. We have a partial."

Almost afraid to hope, Frankie said, "Let's just see if it leads to something first, before anyone starts buying cigars."

Chapter 19

The second they were back in the car and she had buckled up, Frankie was on her smartphone.

Luke noticed that she had accessed something and was now scrolling intently from screen to screen. He recalled what Frankie had said earlier.

He began to drive back to the precinct. "Is that from Valri?" he asked.

Preoccupied, Frankie hardly heard his question. "Uh-huh."

"Find anything good?" Luke asked. Picking up speed, he drove his vehicle onto the freeway in order to get to the precinct faster.

Frankie didn't answer.

Switching his car into the extreme right lane, unofficially regarded as the slow lane, Luke spared her a quick look. Frankie was still scrolling.

"Detective DeMarco, I'm talking to you," he said, raising his voice.

"What?" Frankie looked up from her smartphone. "Oh, sorry, I was just reading the profiles of the men that were on my cousin's laptop. Valri's friend sent them to her and she forwarded them to me."

"And?" Luke pressed, still waiting for something they could work with.

"And," Frankie said, picking up on his lead-in, "it looks like there are definitely some candidates to consider here. We need to compare them to the ones who contacted Ellen O'Keefe, but I think we might finally be onto something."

Luke nodded, agreeing. "Okay. We'll put a list of these guys together so we can get them down to the precinct and start questioning them."

Now he had her full attention. "No!"

"What do you mean, no?" Luke asked, surprised at her reaction. Wasn't this why she had requested the list in the first place? "It's the fastest way to see if one of them is lying."

Frankie shook her head. "No," she said adamantly. "It's the fastest way to scare off the killer. He might even go into hiding, which could keep him from killing any other woman."

"That's not exactly a bad thing," Luke pointed out, picking up a little more speed.

Didn't he understand? she wondered. "No, but it also doesn't bring him to justice and it definitely doesn't keep him from killing women *in the future*."

The off-ramp was just ahead. For once, there was only a moderate amount of traffic. Even so, he spared just one quick glance in her direction.

"Your idea is to draw the killer out by posting a profile of a woman who matches his type." It wasn't a guess, it was the best way of going after their serial killer.

"Exactly," Frankie cried, relieved that he was coming around and seeing things her way.

"All right," Luke agreed. "I'll talk to the day sergeant and have him compile a list of policewomen who look like our killer's type, pick a volunteer and have Valri make up a backstory for her before posting her profile on the website."

She felt as if he had just pulled the rug out from under her. They'd already talked about this.

"Aren't you overlooking the obvious?" Frankie asked pointedly.

Exiting the freeway, he turned onto the through street that would eventually lead him to the precinct. Luke knew where she was going with this and he refused to go there.

"No," he told her firmly, "I'm not."

He was being deliberately stubborn, Frankie thought. But because he was the lead and because of the night they had spent together, rather than losing her temper, she laid out her argument.

"*I* look like his type," she stressed. "I have long, black hair, I'm in my twenties and, much as I hate the fact, I'm short. Just like all the victims," she concluded.

"But you're not a recovered drug addict," he said, reminding her of the most important thing all the victims had in common.

She didn't see that as a problem. "Valri can doctor

records, give me a history to match the other victims. She's good at that," Frankie stressed.

"You don't have to sell Valri's abilities to me," he told her, getting irritated. Why wasn't she being reasonable?

Luke pulled his car into his assigned parking space. Because it was Sunday, there were hardly any other cars in the lot. Vehicles belonging to patrolling police officers were out doing just that. Patrolling.

"I *know* the magic she's capable of doing with that computer of hers," he retorted, still referring to his cousin.

"Then what's the problem?" Frankie asked, getting out of the car. In her annoyance, she slammed the car door shut.

"The problem is that the guy we're trying to find is a serial killer," he answered, raising his voice again. "That means he *kills* people. Dark-haired women in this case," Luke shouted.

"I know. I pointed that out to you, remember?" she snapped.

No one could get to him the way she could, he thought, struggling to regain control over his temper. "Well, I don't want that dark-haired woman to be you, understand?"

Did he think that just because he could make her knees melt and that they had slept together, that gave him the right to order her around?

"You don't get to make that decision," Frankie snapped, glaring up at him.

"Neither do you!"

"Problem, children?" White Hawk asked, coming up behind them.

They had gotten so caught up in their heated argument, neither one of them had heard White Hawk's car pulling up in the row behind them.

Luke had completely forgotten that he'd put a call in to his partner to come into the squad room because the case had just grown by another victim.

Waving a hand at Frankie, Luke said angrily, "Super Detective here wants to go undercover so she can catch our perp."

Frankie turned toward White Hawk, trying to enlist his support on her side. "I look just like the killer's type," she insisted.

They both looked at White Hawk expectantly, each obviously waiting for the detective to take their side in this difference of opinion.

White Hawk paused for a moment before venturing to say anything. "She has a point," he began.

Her attention shifted to Luke. "See?" she asked triumphantly.

White Hawk wasn't finished yet. This time, he addressed Frankie. "As does he. O'Bannon doesn't want you risking your life or getting hurt."

Frankie threw up her hands. "It comes with the territory, we all know that. And you're both missing an important point. I *know* this case, this killer. I'm familiar with the way he operates. Any patrol officer you pick to go undercover to lure this guy out won't be nearly as prepared as I am."

White Hawk nodded. "She's—"

"You say she's got a point and I swear you'll be looking for a new partner," Luke warned the other detective, even as he knew that Frankie was ultimately right about this. She was far better equipped to take on this serial killer than someone new being read into the case.

White Hawk looked at his partner without saying a single word, but he didn't have to. His expression said everything for him.

Luke sighed, turning toward the building's entrance. "Okay, we'll review the profiles of the men who got in contact with our victims and then see where we go from there," he said cautiously, walking into the building.

With her biggest obstacle removed, eager and hopeful, Frankie's mood became buoyant. "I'll start working up a profile I can use."

No matter how he sliced it, he just didn't like her putting herself out there like this. "One step at a time," Luke reminded her.

"I'm just getting ready for the next step," Frankie told him cheerfully, heading through the double doors first.

"Thanks a lot for backing me up," Luke murmured to his partner as they both followed Frankie into the building.

"You know she's right," White Hawk told him.

Luke frowned. "Doesn't make it any easier to go along with," he grumbled through gritted teeth.

Frankie spent the next couple of hours sifting through the various profiles she pulled up from The Perfect Date's website. The profiles represented all the men who contacted either one or both of the two victims whose laptops were confiscated. To cover all their bases, she also went through all the men that the two women had gotten in contact with themselves—just in case.

"Why the latter group?" Luke asked, curious about her reasoning. "We're looking for the guy who singled his victims out."

She was doing her best to spread the net, the better to entangle the killer.

"Maybe he singled them out *after* they singled him out. Maybe when they got in contact with him, it wound up triggering something for him. We don't really know anything about this guy except that he has a vendetta against petite, twentysomething, dark-haired women who happened to be former drug addicts. We don't even know why."

She frowned as she looked at the list. There were a daunting number of names on it.

"He could have fallen for someone who matched the description and she turned him down or dumped him for someone else," Luke theorized.

"Or maybe he worked with her. He got her clean—like a rehab counselor—and she dumped him once she went back to her old life and felt she didn't need him," White Hawk volunteered, adding his voice to the discussion.

One theory was as good as the other, but it got them no closer to the actual killer.

"We can sit here and toss around theories until the cows come home. Meanwhile, the serial killer could be out there, looking for his next victim," Frankie reminded the other two detectives.

Luke knew she was eager to get her cousin's killer, but he wasn't about to condone her rushing in to tackle this.

"Being reckless isn't going to help you get this SOB," he reminded Frankie. "Getting yourself killed isn't going to help us get this guy, either. Now, we're going to do it my way or we don't do it," Luke told her, pinning her with a look. "Agreed?"

She pressed her lips together and sighed. "Do I have a choice?"

He was not about to dance around the answer. "No."

"Then agreed," Frankie replied grudgingly.

Luke's cell phone buzzed and he immediately swiped it open. Looking at the caller ID he saw that the call was coming from Sean.

"O'Bannon," Luke said, following protocol. "Do you have anything for us?"

"I've had a chance to review the video on the victim's nanny cam. You might want to come down and have a look."

"Be right there," Luke responded. Ending the call, he put away his phone.

Frankie's attention had instantly been piqued the moment she heard Luke's phone ring. "Be right where?" she asked.

"Sean has something he wants to show us that he found on the victim's nanny cam. Interested?" he asked, keeping a straight face.

He knew damn well that she was all but jumping out of her skin in her eagerness to go along with him to the lab.

"Interested?" Frankie echoed incredulously. "Just try and keep me away."

Luke laughed dryly. "Don't tempt me."

He was only half kidding.

The further they got into the case, the more Luke found himself wanting to keep her clear of it. Logically, he knew that he couldn't. He was more than aware of the fact that Frankie was a police detective and that all this was part of her job. But the night they had spent together had changed everything for him, even though he knew it shouldn't, knew it wasn't supposed to.

But it did.

In all honesty, he wanted to keep all his people safe, the ones who worked with him as well as his family. The latter group were all intricately woven into the tapestry of the police department. The sad, frustrating truth of it was that he could only be there for his people, lend them his support—and have their backs.

And pray that that was somehow enough.

All of this was why, when they got into the elevator and headed for the basement, he turned to Frankie and told her, "You're going to be wearing a wire."

Staring at him, she said, "Excuse me?"

"When you go out to meet these characters that you're finding on the website, you're going to be wearing a wire. Not only that, but I intend to be close by."

"You could stick yourself to my side and we can tell whatever guy we're setting up that we're twins who were never separated at birth."

He scowled at her. "This isn't funny, Frankie," he told her curtly.

"No, it's not." She sighed. Maybe she should be looking at the bright side of this. "I guess I should be touched."

"You *are* touched," he retorted angrily, hating that she had gotten to him like this. "Touched if you think you're going to do this without a wire."

Reluctantly, Frankie nodded. "All right, I'll wear a wire," she told him. "But nowhere obvious."

"All right," he agreed. "Nowhere obvious." A ghost of a smile touched his lips. "But I get to be the one who puts it on your body."

She gave him a wicked smile in response. "Deal. Now can we get on with this?"

Even as she asked the question, the elevator came to a stop in the basement and the doors opened.

"Absolutely," Luke responded. One hand on the door to keep it from closing, he let her get off the elevator car first.

Walking into the CSI lab, they found it almost eerily unoccupied. Sean and Destiny appeared to be the only two occupants, each working at their stations, examining the evidence that they had collected at the latest crime scene.

Sean was working in the video bay. Seeing them enter, he gestured for his nephew and the young woman to come over.

"Did you get a shot of the serial killer?" Frankie asked him eagerly.

"Yes—and no," Sean replied.

That did not sound as good as he had hoped. "Elaborate on yes," Luke requested.

"Lucky for us, we got the guy on video administering the fatal overdose to our victim," Sean said grimly. "We got the whole thing."

It was clear from Sean's expression that viewing

what was on the nanny cam, despite all his years in the crime lab, had affected him.

"Then we've got him," Frankie cried, unable to believe their good luck.

"Well," Sean told them, "that's where the *no* part comes in. Apparently this piece of filth has a keenly developed sense of self-preservation. He kept his back to the nanny cam the entire time."

Luke scowled. "Could he have somehow known about it and averted his face on purpose?"

"I really can't say—maybe it was just a sixth sense," Sean suggested.

"So, what do we know about him?" Luke questioned. "Anything?"

"Well," Sean replied, "we know approximately how tall he is and his hair color—neither of which is remarkable." To prove his point, he played the video for them. "He never shows his face to the camera."

So near and yet so far, Frankie thought, doing her best to suppress the huge wave of disappointment and frustration she felt.

Chapter 20

"Did we get any hits?"

Luke's question was directed at Valri as he walked into the computer lab.

First thing Monday morning, Valri, with input from Frankie, had fashioned a profile for Frankie that was similar enough to the profiles of the last *three* victims to, they hoped, attract their elusive serial killer.

Initially, they'd believed that only two of the victims had turned toward the dating service, but it turned out that Martha, the very last victim, had also posted her profile on The Perfect Date website. Presumably, it had been answered by the man whose back had been captured on the nanny cam.

Frankie's profile had been up for less than twenty-four hours and he wasn't expecting too much activity on it yet, but just to play it safe, he thought he'd check with his cousin.

"Apparently Frankie is a very popular lady." Valri turned her monitor in his direction so he could see the number of hits Frankie had gotten for himself. "She got more than a dozen—and counting." Turning her monitor back around to face her, she noted the expression on Luke's face. "What's wrong? You don't look very happy about this."

"No," Luke denied firmly. "This is what we want."

And, as a police detective, he was delighted with the way this was going. But as someone who had found himself extremely attracted to Frankie, he was less than thrilled about this development.

Valri frowned. "Luke, you may not be my brother, but I can still spot a Cavanaugh lying a mile away." She gave him a penetrating look. "Level with me, Luke. Is something going on between you and Frankie?"

"I think your nesting instincts are making you imagine things," he told her dismissively. "Review all the profile photos attached to those hits and rule out anyone with blond or red hair," he told her, thinking of the nanny cam video. "Make a list of the ones who are left and send that list to me."

"How about to Frankie?" Valri asked. "After all, this is her profile," she pointed out.

"And I'm lead on this case," he reminded her. In his opinion, that trumped Valri's point. "Send the list to me," he instructed firmly.

Valri inclined her head obediently. "As you wish, Detective O'Bannon," she said, deliberately sounding subservient. "It'll be on your computer as soon as I look over the profile photos."

"Then I'd better be getting back to my desk," Luke said, adding, "Thanks, Val," as he exited the computer lab.

The first thing he saw when he walked into his squad room was Frankie. She was standing over his desk, looking at his computer monitor. Lengthening his stride, he quickly crossed over to his desk.

"What are you doing?" he asked, even though it was more than obvious that she was looking at the email Valri had just sent.

She appeared to be somewhat overwhelmed. "Wow, I got this many hits?" Frankie glanced at him over her shoulder, sharing her surprise with Luke. "Are there that many men out there looking to connect?" she marveled.

"I wouldn't know," Luke answered with a dismissive shrug. "I never needed a computer to be my wingman."

Frankie's eyes were still glued to the computer monitor as she continued scrolling through the names. She blew out a low whistle. "It sure looks like I've got my work cut out for me."

"We," Luke corrected tersely. "*We've* got our work cut out for us." And he didn't want her to forget that. "I'm coming along on those dates, remember?"

"In spirit," she reminded him. "You're coming along in spirit, not in body."

He was not about to have an argument over this, especially not in the middle of the squad room.

"Okay, this is how it's going to work," he told her,

sounding far more like the team's leader than the man she had slept with. "We're going to run a background check on these characters so we know what we're up against. Once that's done, you're going to get in contact with these jokers and arrange to meet them in a coffee shop. White Hawk and I will be nearby at a table—"

"Separate tables?" she questioned with a smile. "Not like you two were out on a date?"

"Yeah, separate tables," he snapped. She was just trying to sidetrack him, and he intended to be there with her every step of the way. He didn't want to chance anything happening to her.

"What if my 'date' doesn't like coffee and wants to meet somewhere else, like for an intimate dinner in his apartment?" she asked, giving him an alternate scenario.

"No intimate dinner, no apartment," he said, shooting down her suggestions. "Your game, your rules. Tell him you feel better meeting him in a public place. Considering the times we're living in, that's not an unreasonable request."

Frankie sighed. "Okay, so he agrees to meet me in a coffee shop," she conceded. "Then what?"

"Then you use your spidey senses to tell you whether or not this guy's a few cards short of a full deck."

She tried again. As far as she was concerned, she was going with real-life scenarios. "What if the guy comes across like a perfect gentleman and after having coffee with me wants to go out on a 'real' date?"

"You order more coffee and keep him talking," Luke told her decisively.

She knew he was trying to protect her, and part of her was grateful for that. But she was also a police detective and she couldn't do her job if she was being protected. She needed to make him understand that.

"I think if we're going to catch this guy, I'm going to need to be a little more...accommodating first," she finally said, "in order to draw him out."

"Let's just get through this part first, okay?" Luke answered. He looked over toward White Hawk, who seemed obviously amused as he was taking all this in. He pulled him into the discussion. "I'm sending you and our bait here," he nodded at Frankie, "a copy of the list of potential dates that Valri put together. She narrowed it down to a dozen names. We each take four," he told them. "I'll take the top four. You take the next four and Frankie gets the last four."

"And what is it you want us to look for?" White Hawk asked.

"The usual," Luke told them. "Any prior arrests, any restraining orders, any complaints about stalking. In short, anything that indicates the guy doesn't play well with others," Luke specified. And then he thought of one additional thing. "Oh, and any indication that he might have tortured animals."

Frankie raised her hand as if this was a classroom setting. Now what, he wondered, trying not to lose his temper.

"What?"

"Seems to me that those are the kind of traits we'd put at the top of our list. At bottom, our serial killer is not a well-adjusted guy and the only way we're going to get him to come out of his so-called shell is to present him with another victim. The guy's not about to kill me in a crowded coffee shop," she pointed out.

"No," Luke agreed, "but he might just let something slip and give himself away if you keep him talking long enough."

"And if *that* doesn't pan out?" Frankie asked, playing devil's advocate.

"Then we'll strip you naked and dangle you in front of him like a piece of meat," Luke snapped in exasperation. "Satisfied?"

Frankie knew when to back away. Feigning contrition, she inclined her head and told him, "We'll shoot for a happy medium."

"The key word here being *shoot*," he murmured under his breath. Best-case scenario was to arrest the killer. Second-best case was to take him down before he could harm Frankie or anyone else. "Okay, start investigating," he ordered.

The next four hours were spent investigating the men on the list that Valri had compiled, going as far back in each man's life as possible.

In a couple of cases, that led to an uncomfortable dead end.

"This guy's name has got to be an alias," White Hawk said, calling Luke over to look at the photograph of a Patrick Jamison he'd pulled up on the monitor.

"He has no history beyond ten years ago. No school records, no work records. No driver's license. Nothing," he marveled. "That means that the guy's either an alien—like the ones from outer space—"

"Or he was put into witness protection as a kid,"

Frankie guessed, joining in. "Either way, he should go on the top of my dating list," she said euphemistically. "To either be cleared or arrested," she concluded, looking pointedly at Luke.

"I've got one like that myself," Luke said. "Bill Williams has no tax forms that go beyond eight years."

"Maybe he didn't have a job before then, so there was no need to file a tax form," Frankie suggested. "Does he have any school records prior to then?"

"Not that I can see. There's an out-of-state address dating back eleven years ago," he commented. "This is a lot harder than I thought it would be. I think I owe Valri a dinner out."

"You probably owe her a month's worth of eating out," White Hawk corrected.

Luke wasn't about to dispute that. He'd come to rely heavily on his cousin's computer skills. "You're probably right," he told his partner.

Several minutes later, Frankie spoke up again. "I've got one here who's a saint." Looking at the screen, she enumerated the name's list of attributes. "According to his background, Steven Miller currently teaches eighteenth-century poetry at the University of Bedford. He volunteers at a soup kitchen, and on Sundays he sings in the choir at his church."

"Do clocks stop when he walks by?" White Hawk asked.

"No, the guy's good-looking," Frankie answered, pulling up the man's photograph. "If you like pretty boys."

"Not my thing," White Hawk said dryly.

"He sounds almost too clean," Luke commented.

He didn't bother getting up and taking a look at the profile on Frankie's monitor. Instead, he said, "Okay, put him on the list, too."

Frankie smiled at him. "He's already on it."

In the end, they kept all twelve names, arranging the candidates in the order they believed was the degree of possibility that the man was the serial killer they were after, with the top name being the most likely.

Luke stared at the list once it had taken final shape. His gut was telling him that this wasn't the way to go, but then his gut wasn't exactly being impartial here, he thought.

He looked at Frankie.

"You sure you want to go through with this?" he asked her.

"Do I want to catch him?" she asked incredulously. "Absolutely. You bet." There was no hesitation on her part.

"No," he amended. "I mean do you want to go through with this and be the bait?"

"It's a little late in the game to be pulling out." She watched him uncertainly.

"Not pulling out, exactly," Luke corrected. "Officer Moretti looks enough like you to step in and take your place." His voice was picking up speed, as if he talked quickly enough, he'd get her to agree. "When she shows up, she can tell the guy that it was an old photo of her on the website. What?" he asked, aware that Frankie was staring at him incredulously.

"You actually went looking through the ranks for someone who resembled me?" she asked in disbelief.

Her eyes were blazing but he wasn't about to back down.

"I thought, in case you changed your mind, we should be prepared."

"I'm not about to change my mind," she informed Luke. "So change your tune and let's get this show on the road. I'll email back to these men and suggest we meet at…"

Frankie looked from one detective to the other, waiting for one of them to suggest a coffee shop they could use.

Luke thought for a moment, then said, "There's a popular coffee shop right across from the shopping center right off Main and Surrey. It's called Fast & Hot."

Another detective, Jorge Martinez, laughed as he passed by on his way to the break room. "That sounds like the way you like your women," he commented.

White Hawk shot the older detective a disapproving look. "Don't pay any attention to Martinez," he told Frankie.

She shrugged. "Doesn't bother me," she answered, even though the comment actually did bother her. "Okay," she said, turning her attention to Luke. "How do you want to do this?"

"I don't," he told her flatly.

But he knew they had to get this serial killer before another victim was added to the mounting body count and if the killer was setting his sights on Frankie, that meant that he wouldn't be killing another woman. And he and White Hawk would be right there to catch the serial killer before anything got out of hand.

Frankie was looking at him expectantly, waiting for orders.

"Write to each of these guys and make arrangements to meet them at Fast & Hot. We'll space them apart and do three a day. Or, more accurately, three in the late afternoon. Presumably they all have jobs, so tell them you'll meet with them at, say, 5:30, 6:30 and 7:30."

She looked at him innocently. "What if the 5:30 guy doesn't want to leave by 6:30?"

"See that he does," Luke instructed. "Tell him you have a family emergency and you'll get back with him. This pre-date meeting is just to test the waters, understand? Any guy who stands out as a possible suspect, you'll call him back, apologize for having to leave so abruptly and say that you'd like another opportunity to get to know him better."

"Sounds like a plan," she told Luke.

"I know—but I wish there was someone else executing it," he told her honestly. "I know you'll be wearing a wire for this, but if at any time during this pre-date you feel spooked by the guy you're talking to, I want you to let us know and we'll pull you out of there fast."

"And just how do you propose I let you know that I feel spooked?"

"The usual way," Luke replied. "I'll give you a safe word. Just say it and White Hawk and I will be at your side before you know it."

"Like the cavalry," she commented. Something

she knew that her cousin certainly could have benefited from. "Okay, what's the safe word?"

"Cupcakes," Luke told her. "Just say *cupcakes* and you're out of there."

"Cupcakes?" she repeated as if he had just said a foreign word.

Luke nodded. "Uh-huh."

She surprised him by laughing. "Now you have me wanting one."

For the first time since this undercover operation had gotten started, Luke grinned. "We'll stop at a bakery on the way home and I'll get you a whole box of them," he promised.

"On the way home," she repeated. "Whose home?" she asked. "Mine? Yours?"

"Take your pick," Luke told her. "Unless you just want to go home with the cupcakes," he said, thinking that she might be feeling too much pressure if they got together again so soon.

"No, you'll make a nice side dish," she told him, doing her best to keep a straight face.

But even as she said it, she knew she was getting carried away.

As attracted as she felt to this man, Frankie understood that this was just temporary on his part. And although she intended to enjoy herself for as long as this lasted, she wasn't about to fool herself into thinking that there was anything permanent on the horizon. Not when it came to Luke. The reputation he had existed for a reason.

He was a player.

A charming player, but nonetheless a player. At

some point in the scenario, players picked up their marbles and went on to another game.

"Okay," she declared. "I'd better get busy and write back to my perfect dates before they all lose interest and decide that they want to go on to some-one else."

"They're not going to lose interest that fast," Luke told her.

How about you, Luke? she asked him silently. *How fast are you going to lose interest and seek out some greener grass?*

With effort, she pushed the thought out of her mind. She had work to do.

And a serial killer to catch.

Chapter 21

In the end, when the workday was over, Frankie wound up driving home alone.

Walking into her apartment, she tried not to think about it, but somehow, her apartment felt lonelier and emptier than it had before she had allowed Luke into her life.

"Certainly didn't take long, did it?" she murmured under her breath as she locked the door behind her and slipped the chain into its metal slot. "Wonder if this was some kind of record for him?"

The "him" was Luke.

After they left the squad room on Sunday, he had followed her to her apartment. His thinking at the time, he'd told her, was that after they'd had dinner he'd leave and drive home.

But dinner—which turned out to be Chinese

takeout—was followed by "dessert," a very long, sumptuous, steamy dessert. Ultimately, Luke didn't leave her apartment to go back to his place until it was well into the wee hours of the morning.

"Thought that was going to be an ongoing thing, didn't you?" Frankie mocked herself as she rummaged through her refrigerator.

Nothing looked good to her, so she took out the remainder of the loaf of bread that was there and put the last two slices into her toaster.

"Well, surprise. I guess you scared him away by sticking to your guns and insisting on doing what you're being paid to do—catching a killer."

She supposed that if she had backed down and gone along with his idea of using a police officer to go under cover, maybe Luke would be here tonight. But that would be selling out.

Worse, she'd be letting Kristin down. When she had walked into Kristin's apartment and found her lying on the floor, dead, she'd vowed that she would find the person who had killed her cousin, and no matter how long it took, she fully intended to do just that.

If that lost her O'Bannon, well, so be it.

Frankie fought to block out the deep, bitter pang she felt.

There were more important things than ripped arms, a hard, muscular chest and a killer smile—not to mention a man who made her want to make love until she couldn't breathe from exhaustion.

"C'mon, DeMarco, get a grip," she ordered. "You know that O'Bannon would have left sooner or later—

it just turned out to be sooner than later, that's all. Deal with it!"

Struggling not to cry, she buttered her toast, put it on a plate and took it to the living room. With a resigned sigh, she planted herself in front of her TV monitor and went channel surfing, searching for something that would sufficiently numb her mind as well as her aching heart.

Frankie spent the next half hour nibbling on toast she didn't taste and flipping from one program to another.

She couldn't find anything to watch, anything to even mildly distract her from her thoughts.

Pushing aside the plate of half-finished toast on the coffee table, she decided that she might as well just go to bed and begin the frustrating task of trying to fall asleep. No easy feat, considering that she felt wound up enough to snap right in half.

Frankie had just gotten up and shut off the TV when she heard the doorbell ring. Her first instinct was just to ignore it. She didn't feel like talking to anyone, and besides, it wasn't as if she had friends who were inclined to come over at the drop of a hat. Everyone she knew worked at the precinct, and none of them would have any reason to visit at this hour.

The person on the other side of the door was either selling something—solicitors seemed to be driven to come by at all hours—or someone who had mistaken her apartment for someone else's and ultimately needed to be steered in the right direction.

But whoever had rung her doorbell was obviously persistent because they rang it again.

And then again.

When she didn't answer the third ring, it was followed by a rather urgent knock on the door. The banging just darkened her mood.

Whoever it was was going to be sorry, Frankie silently promised as she paused to pick up her service revolver before heading for the door.

"Who is it?" she called out through the door even as she cocked her gun.

"The cupcake fairy."

She stared at the door in disbelief. "Luke?"

What was he doing here now? When they'd left the precinct, he'd told her that he had something to take care of just before he drove off in the opposite direction.

She heard him say, "Okay, you guessed my secret identity. Now c'mon, Frankie, open the door. They're getting cold."

He wasn't making any sense. It was an unusually warm evening, given the time of the year. "What's getting cold?" she asked as she removed the chain, unlocked the door and pulled it open.

She had her answer before Luke was able to say another word. Or rather, she smelled her answer.

And the aroma made her mouth water almost immediately.

Luke regarded her for a moment. Intentionally or not, she was blocking the doorway. "Can I come in?" he asked, taking nothing for granted.

Reacting immediately, Frankie quickly stepped to one side. "Oh, yes, sure," she said, letting him walk in. "Did you just pick those up from the bakery?" She nodded at the eight-by-ten covered pan he was holding in his hands. The lid was see-through and she could still see the dozen cupcakes in the pan even though they were giving off heat and fogging up the lid.

"No, I just pulled them out of my oven," he told her with a smile.

She looked at him quizzically. "You asked your mother to come over and make cupcakes?" As far as she could see, that seemed to be the only viable explanation since he was telling her that they weren't store-bought.

He shot down her theory. "This is the thing I had to do in my kitchen rather than driving straight to your place right after work."

She was still chewing on what he'd told her. "You baked those," she said in disbelief.

He nodded. "Yes."

"You actually bake?" she asked in awe.

She was still having trouble wrapping her mind around that. Luke came off like such a he-man type. A hunky-looking protector who could fight with one hand tied behind his back.

Hunky protectors didn't bake.

She had just gotten herself to come to terms with the fact that he could cook breakfast.

"Haven't figured out how to fakely bake anything, so, yes, I actually bake," he told her. He took the pan of cupcakes into her kitchen and removed the lid, placing it next to the pan. He tilted the pan slightly to allow her to look over its contents. "Care to try one?" he asked.

She regarded the cupcakes for a long moment. "It's not going to knock me out for a week is it? So you can get Moretti to step in," she explained when he looked at her, confused.

"No," Luke assured her, then looked at Frankie thoughtfully. "Although, now that you mention it, that doesn't sound like such a half-bad idea."

The aroma was really getting to her. She could almost feel her mouth watering.

Frankie gave up resisting.

"Why would you go to all this trouble?" she asked, taking a couple of plates out of the cupboard and then two forks from the utensil drawer directly below it.

Luke shrugged. "You told me that saying the safe word made you hungry for cupcakes, so I thought I'd make you some of my mom's special ones."

"Special?" she questioned. Just what did he mean by special?

A smile was playing on his lips.

"Taste them," he told her.

"And you're sure they won't put me to sleep?" she asked, hanging on to a shred of suspicion as she picked up one of the cupcakes and put it on her plate. She carefully proceeded to separate the cupcake from the paper that was wrapped around it.

"I'm counting on the fact that they won't," he answered, a wicked look in his eyes. "Here, I'll have one myself. Will that put your fears to rest?"

She didn't answer him. Having taken the wrapper off her cupcake, she was too busy savoring what she had just bitten into.

"What is that taste?" she asked. It all but made the inside of her mouth sing.

His grin spread. "Good, huh?"

"Good?" she echoed. That seemed like much too

weak a word to use to describe what was going on in her mouth. "It's *fantastic*. I don't think I ever tasted anything like it before. Certainly not in a cupcake." She took another bite. And then another before asking, "Is there some kind of a secret ingredient?"

He thought of the recipe that had been handed down to his mother, who had proceeded to put her own signature on it.

After debating for a moment, he answered her. "I guess you could call it that. There's half a cup of Amaretto and a quarter cup of rum in them."

"Ah, you're trying to get me drunk," she concluded, teasing him.

"Well, if you ate all twelve cupcakes at one sitting, maybe just a little," he allowed, lightly feathering his fingers through her hair. "But to be honest, I'd really rather have you wide awake and clearheaded."

"You mean, for tomorrow?" she asked.

Luke didn't want to think about tomorrow. Frankie would be meeting the first three men who had responded to her profile tomorrow. That meant possibly putting her life at risk. If he dwelled on that, tonight would be ruined. "No, I was thinking more like for tonight."

"Oh?" Rising, Frankie abandoned her chair and came around the table to his side. Lowering her voice by a couple of decibels, she asked, "What about tonight?"

The sound of her sexy voice turned him on even more—as if he needed that. Luke pulled her onto his lap. "What do you think?"

"Do I *have* to think?" Frankie asked, wrapping

her arms around his neck. "That sounds tiring and I want to save all my energy for something else."

He laughed softly just before he kissed her. "A woman after my own heart."

If you only knew, Luke O'Bannon, Frankie thought, just before getting lost in his kiss.

It was more than two hours later that he turned to her in her bed and said, "I should be getting up and going home."

She really loved the feel of his body against hers beneath the sheets. Taking a breath, she could feel herself getting aroused all over again.

"You should," she reluctantly agreed, turning into him just as she drew in another deep breath and stretched so her body all but imprinted itself on his.

He laughed softly. His body was reacting to the silent invitation hers was issuing.

"If that's the way you think you're going to persuade me to go, you realize that you're going to fail, don't you?"

Frankie pretended to sigh as she snapped her fingers. "Oh, darn." The next moment, with lightning speed, her mouth was pressed against his. The kiss lasted a good two minutes. "How's that? Ready to go now?"

"That all depends on what you mean by ready to go," he answered, pulling her into his arms again.

She was melting against him. "I mean anything you want me to mean."

Luke wished that she could be that cooperative in the squad room, but a man couldn't have everything, he thought philosophically, and right now, he had more than he'd ever dreamed he would.

He didn't leave until five the next morning.

Once in the squad room, he, White Hawk and Frankie spent the morning reviewing the case files again. Luke felt that it wouldn't hurt to be as familiar as they could be with the killer's mode of operating.

The afternoon was spent prepping Frankie.

The closer the time came for her first meeting at the coffee shop, the more uneasy Luke felt about the whole undertaking.

"It's going to be all right," Frankie assured him. She could feel the tension emanating from him as they got into the car to drive over to the Fast & Hot coffee shop. She held out her wrist for him to view. "Sean wired my bracelet. You and White Hawk will hear everything that's said in those earpieces he gave you."

He knew that. Knew all the details better than she did.

That still didn't help reassure him.

"Why are you so calm?" he asked her.

"Because I want to catch this SOB so bad I can taste it," she told him. "And this is the only way it's going to happen—with luck," she added, even as she made a show of crossing her fingers.

Crossing her fingers wasn't going to be nearly enough to keep her safe, Luke thought. Only keen vigilance would accomplish that.

Luke glanced at his watch. It was ten after five. Her first so-called meeting was at 5:30 p.m.

"Almost showtime," he told her. He parked their vehicle around the corner from the coffee shop. "I'll go in first. Then you follow. White Hawk will go in the shop last."

"I know," she told him with a patient smile. "You already said that. Twice."

"The landing on D-Day had less planning behind it," White Hawk commented from the backseat.

"D-Day wasn't my responsibility," Luke retorted. Then, forcing himself to calm down, he looked at Frankie. "This is." With that, he opened the car door but made no move to get out. It was almost as if when he did, he felt that he would lose some control over the situation. "Remember, give me a couple of minutes. Then you follow. White Hawk will be behind you."

"Breathe, O'Bannon," Frankie counseled, patting his cheek.

With a grunt, Luke got out of the car and started walking.

"Never saw him this nervous before," White Hawk commented as he watched his partner walk up the street and turn a corner. "Actually, I don't think I ever saw him nervous."

"Probably because he's working with me for the first time and he's not sure I can handle myself," she told the other detective.

"Yeah," White Hawk said, a touch of sarcasm in his voice. "That must be it." Just like his partner had a few moments ago, he looked down at his watch. "You'd better get out and be on your way. If you don't walk through those doors in the next three minutes—" he nodded in what was the general direction of the coffee shop "—O'Bannon's liable to go into cardiac arrest."

She really couldn't tell from White Hawk's deadpan voice if the detective was kidding—or not. Either way, Frankie got out of the vehicle and walked down the street before turning the corner, just as Luke had done before her.

She might appear calm, but every bone in her body felt like it was on high alert. Because each of the three men she was meeting at the coffee shop tonight just might be *the* one—and not in the romantic way that The Perfect Date website meant, she thought.

Almost before she knew it, she found herself approaching the coffee shop.

Taking a deep breath and widening her smile, Frankie pushed open the coffee shop door and walked in.

Ready or not, here I come, she thought, silently addressing the shop's occupants.

Chapter 22

Half an hour into her second coffee date, Frankie realized everything that she had been missing by avoiding the whole dating scene.

And she was sincerely glad that she had.

She was grateful, too, that despite avoiding all the awkward conversations and uncomfortable moments, she had still managed to connect with Luke. Connect with him in a good way.

For however long this personal relationship between them lasted, she felt that she had lucked out. Because, for the most part, this dating thing was really hard work.

Definitely harder than real work, she thought as she listened to Wade Bochner, the clean-shaven aerospace engineer, talk about how disappointed he had felt when his first marriage fell through.

She did her best to say some sympathetic things and look as if she cared about the nightmares he'd been having since his divorce.

On cue—and none too soon in her opinion—her cell phone rang. Frankie answered it on the third ring. "I'm sorry, I have to take this," she apologized to Wade.

As she pretended to listen to the person on the other end of the line, she was quick to express the proper amount of distress.

"Oh, Lord, is he all right? Oh, okay. Yes. Yes, of course, I'll be there as soon as I can." Ending the call, she put her phone away and looked properly apologetic.

"I'm sorry. That was my mother. My father was having chest pains and lucky for him, my mother bullied him into going to the ER. According to the emergency physician, she got him there just in time. The worst is over, but they're going to keep him there overnight for observation, just in case. I told her I'd meet them there."

"I heard," the engineer responded, appearing somewhat dejected. "Is there anything I can do?"

"If you're in the habit of praying, that would be appreciated," she told him.

"Then your father really did have chest pains?" he asked, surprised. "Because, well, I thought this was just an elaborate brush-off," Wade confessed. "You know, a girlfriend calling, giving you an excuse to beg off."

"I'm not that creative," Frankie told him. She glanced at her watch. "And now I've really got to go. My mother's going to pieces."

"Sure, sure, I understand. Email me when everything settles down. I'd like to do this again—not the part where your father has chest pains, but the rest of it," he told her, stumbling over his tongue.

"Of course. Yes, but I've really got to go," she told Wade. With that, she left the coffee shop quickly.

Frankie hurried down the street and got into her car, just in case Wade had left the coffee shop and was watching her. She slowly circled the entire block, waiting for Luke to call and give her the all-clear sign.

Twenty minutes later, she was back in business, listening to Roy Anderson, an accountant, tell her how he thought that trendy coffee shops like the one they were in charged too much for what they served. He felt the different kinds of coffees that Fast & Hot offered were pretentious.

And by the end of the day, while relieved that the three minidates were over, Frankie felt that none of the three men met the criteria of a serial killer.

It was the same the next day. And the next. By Friday, the end of the fourth day, she was convinced that maybe she, White Hawk and Luke were barking up the wrong tree altogether.

"Maybe we need to consider that the killer found his victims some other way than through a dating site," Luke suggested.

"I don't know," she said, not ready to give up just yet. "I think maybe we should widen the net, get in contact with some of the men on the list that we ruled out."

She could tell by Luke's expression that he didn't

agree, and she did her best to try to convince him that she was right.

They'd all driven to the coffee house separately this time. White Hawk had gone home for the evening and she was standing outside of the coffee shop, trying to make Luke see her point.

"It's too much of a coincidence that the last three victims were all on that dating website—and we don't believe in coincidences, right?" Frankie stressed.

"Right," he said, but with a certain lack of conviction. "I'd like to have another go at that florist before you start putting yourself out there again. Maybe he knows more than he told us—or maybe he's our serial killer."

She'd thought that initially, but on reflection, she felt that she'd been wrong to suspect the man. Still, she didn't want to just butt heads with Luke. "We can do both."

"Let's put a moratorium on the dating site thing until we rule the florist out once and for all," he told her. "I'll have White Hawk tail him for a few days to make sure he's really on the up-and-up. While White Hawk's doing that, I'll check out a couple of other things. When we rule all that out," Luke concluded, "*then* we can get back to your coffee dates."

Frankie knew what his objection was. He didn't want her meeting the men from the website without backup. "I don't have to stop ruling out guys from the dating website just because you and White Hawk aren't going to be hovering around me like undercover guardian angels. I can take care of myself, you know," she insisted.

For a moment, Luke's temper got the better of

him and he wound up shouting at her. "At this point, the guy's killed nine women," he stressed. "Maybe even more women that we haven't uncovered yet. I'm sure that at least some of those women thought they could take care of themselves, too. Get it through your head, DeMarco, you're not some super cop who can bend perps with her bare hands. You're five foot one, for heaven's sakes," he reminded her. "You barely cast a shadow."

Frankie narrowed her eyes until they were almost laser pinpoints. "I went through academy training, same as you!" Her point was that she knew how to protect herself.

He struggled not to shout at her again. "Look, we're not arguing about this—"

"You could have fooled me," she retorted. Turning her back on him, she marched over to where she'd last parked her vehicle.

Luke was right behind her. "We went through the twelve top candidates. Coffee shop dating is on hold until I say otherwise," he ordered.

"Yes, Your Highness," Frankie said in a singsong voice. Getting into her vehicle, she slammed the door shut.

She drove away from the coffee shop before Luke could say anything else to her.

Angry, he watched her go.

Damn, but she was the most infuriating woman he had ever had to deal with. This undercover gig to find a serial killer was putting a strain on both of them. He needed a cooling-off period, as did she. With the weekend here, they could use the two days apart to get back into gear—

If that was possible, he added to himself, fighting the urge to take off after her. He wanted to give her a piece of his mind since she seemed to be so free with hers.

Taking a deep breath, Luke got into his own vehicle and after a long moment, he turned it around and pointed it toward his home.

Trying to calm down, Frankie struggled not to let her temper get the better of her—especially since the angrier she became, the harder she pushed down on the gas pedal. She was doing sixty-five on a regular road before she realized it.

Coming to a stop at a red light, she took several deep breaths, then slowly let them out again. She was desperately trying to simmer down before she either hit something or got pulled over for speeding.

That would be just her luck. Because somehow or other, Luke would find out and then he'd really call her reckless—with reason. She'd never hear the end of it. If she got a speeding ticket, that would just give him something to prove his point. That she was impetuous, given to taking chances and not thinking of the consequences.

But she did think of the consequences. She just thought that, in this case, the possible consequences were worth it. Worth it if she could finally catch Kris's killer.

"Give it a rest, Frankie," she told herself out loud. "Monday morning he'll have calmed down and you'll get him to see things your way. The killer's *got* to be in those profiles. He just has to be."

After pulling into her parking space, she sat for a

moment, her eyes closed as she struggled to center herself. "A killer hiding behind a profile of respectability." She opened her eyes again, determined as she looked into the night. "And I'm going to find you," she promised.

Once out, Frankie pressed her key fob. Her car made the appropriate noise, telling her that it was locked. She proceeded up to her apartment.

She unlocked the door and went inside. She put her keys in her pocket as she paused to lock up again. Just because she was angry was no reason to get careless, she told herself.

O'Bannon made her angry. Added to that, she felt really drained.

She didn't know if it was from the tension she'd felt going through those so-called dates, or because of the argument she'd just had with Luke.

Maybe both, she thought, too tired to figure it out. Either way, she intended to finish off the leftover Chinese food in her refrigerator and then go to bed. She wanted to forget about Luke's Neanderthal attitude and the last four days of marathon dating.

She needed to recharge her batteries.

Kicking off her shoes, Frankie went to the kitchen and took out the two half-empty cartons of Chinese food. She was going to take them to the table, then decided that there was no point in getting any plates dirty. She could eat out of the carton while standing at the sink. Somehow, it seemed more efficient that way.

O'Bannon was getting to her, she thought in annoyance.

She'd hardly gotten started on the first carton when she heard her doorbell ring.

Luke!

He'd come to apologize, she thought, feeling her pulse accelerating a bit. Well, O'Bannon was going to have to suffer a little bit before she saw her way clear to forgiving him.

She didn't answer the door right away, and to her surprise, the doorbell didn't ring again. She stifled the impulse to open the door. If he wanted to play games, she'd wait him out.

Walking back into the living room, she swallowed the gasp that rose to her lips. She hadn't heard him come in. Somehow, the man standing in her living room had broken in despite the security locks she had on all her windows and doors.

It wasn't Luke.

It was the college professor, her second to the last "date" of this evening.

"Bill, what are you doing here?" she asked, startled to see him there. "How did you know where I lived?" She hadn't used her real name in the profile and she hadn't given any of the men she'd met her real address.

Her gut tightened.

The college professor held up a small black notebook. "You left this behind at the coffee shop when you hurried off to the hospital. I thought you might need it."

He was lying.

Frankie could feel herself growing more agitated. She'd left her weapon on the side table.

"That's not mine," she told the man calmly.

"It was under your chair," he said, holding the notebook out to her.

"Still not mine." Maybe it was an honest mistake on his part, but she wasn't about to be sidetracked. The man had broken in. "And you haven't answered my question. How did you know where I lived?"

"I guess I'm just a resourceful guy." The smile that she had thought of as shy and boyish when she was sitting across from the man at the coffee shop now made her uneasy as her blood ran cold. "And patient," he continued. "I watched you, you know. You didn't really rush off to the hospital. Instead, you doubled back and went to the coffee shop again. So I waited across the street until you left again— for real, this time."

His eyes narrowed as an expression of cold satisfaction crossed his face. "I guess that guy you picked up at the coffee shop didn't work out, did he? I saw the two of you arguing. You looked really mad. So I followed you home. I thought maybe you needed someone to comfort you. I'm good at that, you know, comforting women when they're all upset."

He was crowding her. Crowding her without taking a single step in her direction. This was his method of intimidation. He was out of luck, though. In her case, it just succeeded in making her angrier.

"No, I'm fine, thank you," she told him curtly, then said in a low, authoritative voice, "You need to leave, Professor Williams."

"No," he contradicted in a steely tone. "I think I need to stay. Besides, I brought something for you," he told her.

The man refused to give up. Frankie dug in herself, trying to keep him talking until she could get to her weapon. "I already told you that's not my notebook."

"No, I brought you something to make you feel happy," he said. "You know, just like in the old days."

He was crazy. She could see it now. There was a strange look in his eyes, as if he was seeing something that wasn't there.

"I don't know what you're talking about," she told him. She tried to keep him distracted as she slowly edged her way to where she had left her weapon.

"Sure you do," Williams insisted. "I read your profile. Very honest of you to admit you had a drug addiction once. But the trouble with addictions, you know, is that you're never really over them." He took out a small case from the pocket of his jacket. He flipped it open. There was a syringe inside the case. Williams held it up so that she could get a better look at it. "See? It's all ready for you. Don't you want some?" he asked in almost a seductive voice as he took a step closer to her.

Instead of moving toward her weapon, she was forced to take a step back.

"No, I don't!"

"Yes, you do," he coaxed. "You're a drug addict. All drug addicts crave that hit, that sweet rush as the drug goes into your vein, then seductively moves all through you. Lisa wanted it."

"Lisa? Who's Lisa?" she asked Williams, hoping she could distract him and get him to tell her about the woman. Was that another of his victims? Or was this Lisa the reason he had gone on this killing spree in the first place?

"Just another useless addict," he said in disgust. His eyes almost blazed as he said, "Like you!"

Williams lunged for her but Frankie managed to jump out of the way at the last moment. Still unable to get to her weapon, she pressed the panic button on the key fob in her pocket, hoping that someone would hear her car alarm and call the police.

Williams put two and two together when he heard the alarm go off. "That's pathetic," he jeered. And then he mocked her. "Nobody pays attention to car alarms. Don't you know that, Lisa?"

"I'm not Lisa!"

"Yes, you are. Yes, you are," Williams cried more insistently. "We were supposed to get married and then you went on that bender and you left me!" he shouted at her, his face contorting into a mask of dark anger. "Left me standing at the altar like some pathetic fool!"

The rest happened so fast that it became just one huge blur.

Her brain struggled to sort it all out after the fact.

She'd never had the opportunity to lock her front door after Williams had come in. It flew open now, and suddenly Luke was there, aiming his gun at the so-called mild-mannered college professor who was trying to plunge the syringe filled with some narcotic into her arm.

"Drop it!" Luke ordered. "Drop the syringe!"

Rather than do as he was told, Williams flew into a rage and tackled Luke as if they were on a football field. The syringe and gun went flying.

Since he obviously felt the gun gave him a better advantage, Williams made a dive for the weapon.

Grabbing the gun, he aimed it at the woman he thought had betrayed him.

He aimed the gun at Frankie.

At the last moment, Luke managed to keep the professor from killing the woman Williams thought in his delusion was his fiancée. Luke blocked the shot with his own body.

The bullet dug into his flesh. Blood started pouring everywhere.

Frankie had never screamed before in her life. Until this second, she'd thought she was unable to scream, that there was something that almost paralyzed her and kept the sound from coming out.

Terrified, she screamed now. "Luke!"

Ducking, Frankie was able to finally secure her own weapon. Holding it with both hands, from her position on the floor she fired at Williams, hitting him in the chest and the knee.

Chapter 23

Moving quickly, Frankie pulled Williams' arms behind his back and handcuffed him, looping the handcuffs around one of the sofa's legs. That way, she didn't have to worry about him fleeing.

Williams released a torrent of curses, calling her every vile name under the sun. He didn't matter. Nothing mattered except for Luke, who was lying on her floor, bleeding.

Bleeding and not moving.

Panic filled her as Frankie fumbled for her cell phone. Dialing 911, she held her phone against her ear with her shoulder as she desperately tried to rouse Luke.

The second she heard a voice on the other end, she started talking. "This is Detective DeMarco. I've got an officer down," she cried. "I need an ambulance."

She rattled off both her address and her badge number. "Hurry! Hurry!"

"Backup's already on the way," an incredibly calm dispatch officer on the other end told her.

The news caught Frankie off guard. "Who called it in?"

"Detective O'Bannon," the woman answered.

Frankie dropped her phone as she heard the sound of approaching sirens in the background. She clutched Luke's hand tighter. "Always one step ahead of me, aren't you?" Fear had her heart pounding and she could feel tears filling up her throat. "Open your eyes, O'Bannon. Damn it, open your eyes!" she pleaded.

But he didn't.

Luke continued to lie there, unresponsive and bleeding. Desperate, she tried to stop the bleeding with her hands. Blood seeped through her fingers.

"C'mon, damn you, wake up!" she ordered.

A cold chill swept over her. Luke wasn't responding. What if he didn't regain consciousness? What if he died on her?

Her breathing grew shallow and ragged. "Oh, no, you don't get to make me care about you and then just duck out on me like this. You come back, you hear me, O'Bannon? This isn't about you, it's about us. You *made* it about us, damn it! Now you come back and live up to your promises or I swear that wherever you are, I'll find you and make your life a living hell. You hear me, O'Bannon?"

She wanted to shake him, to wake him up, but she was afraid that any movement like that would be fatal.

There was a commotion behind her. From the sounds, she could tell that other officers and detectives had arrived, responding to Luke's call for backup.

Holding his hand, Frankie was afraid to look away. Afraid that if she took her eyes off Luke for even one second, he'd slip away from her and be gone.

"Listen to the sound of my voice, Luke. You stay with me, you hear me? Open your eyes and stay with me! Stay with me," she pleaded, her tears falling on his face.

And then, as the ambulance arrived, she thought she saw Luke's lips moving. Her heart slammed against her chest. He was alive! "Luke? I'm here, Luke, I'm right here. Talk to me!"

She lowered her ear right next to his lips so that she could make out what he was saying. The whisper was so soft, she could just barely make it out.

"If...I...stay...will you...stop...yelling...at me?"

He looked as if his chest hurt with each word he pushed out.

"Okay," Frankie sobbed, tears streaming down her cheeks. "I'll stop yelling. But you can't leave me, you hear?"

"Deal," he managed to get out before he lost consciousness again.

"We'll take it from here, detective," the ambulance attendant told her gently, trying to move Frankie out of the way as he and his partner lined up the gurney.

"You're not taking him anywhere without me," she said, her voice hoarse. "I'm going with him to the hospital. And to drag him back from the bowels of hell, if I have to."

"Hopefully, that won't be an issue," the other EMT said as he and the first attendant picked Luke up from the floor and placed him on the gurney.

"What about me? I need a doctor!" Williams screamed. "The bitch shot me!"

Frankie glared at the man as the newly arrived White Hawk put fresh cuffs on him after freeing him from the sofa.

"You're lucky I didn't disembowel you," she retorted. The paramedics began to move Luke's gurney. "We got our serial killer," she told White Hawk as she hurried alongside Luke's gurney. "The syringe he tried to use on me is over there." She nodded in its general direction.

After that, her entire attention was totally focused on Luke.

Except for that one brief instance when he'd whispered to her, Luke remained completely unresponsive as they rode to the hospital.

"But his heart's beating, right?" Frankie asked the attendant riding in the back with them. "It *is* beating." It was as if she said it with enough conviction it would be true.

The attendant smiled sympathetically at her. "Given the situation, I don't think it would dare not to."

She knew the paramedic was trying to be kind and lighten the moment, but she couldn't get herself to reply. Panic was tightening her air passage.

Sitting beside the gurney, she continued clutching Luke's hand. "Keep it beating, O'Bannon. You keep it beating, you hear me?" Lowering her voice, she whispered, "Please?"

* * *

A surgical team was waiting for them by the time the ambulance pulled up by the emergency room's doors. Doing her best not to break down, Frankie continued to hold Luke's hand as she hurried beside his gurney.

She accompanied him as far as they would let her. And then a towering woman—one of the emergency nurses on duty—materialized to block her way.

"I'm sorry," the austere-looking woman told her gruffly. "You have to stay out here. You can't come into the OR."

"I know that," Frankie practically snapped at the nurse, frustrated. This was her fault. *Her* fault. If Luke hadn't tried to shield her, he wouldn't have been shot. "But you fix him, you understand?" she ordered the nurse. "You bring him back to me breathing."

"The doctor'll do his best."

"No," Frankie informed her angrily. "Not his best. He'll do *it*. He'll save Detective O'Bannon. Or I'll come after both of you."

Looking a little nervous now despite the difference in their sizes, the ER nurse backed away and went through the OR's swinging doors.

Weak, drained, unable to stand, Frankie leaned against the wall and then slowly slid down until she was sitting on the floor. She leaned her head against her knees and dissolved into tears.

That was the way Brian Cavanaugh found her, less than half an hour later. Rather than raise her to her feet, the chief of detectives sank down on the floor beside her.

"He's going to be all right, you know," he told her

kindly, starting the conversation as if they'd been talking for hours. "We've got a contract with this hospital that forbids them from allowing any of our people to die, so they don't," he concluded, hoping the irrational statement would get a hint of a smile from her. Instead, he watched as tears slid down her cheeks.

Brian slipped his arm around Frankie's shoulders in a paternal act of comfort. "They'll fix that boy," he told her, "and he'll be good as new."

"How do you know that?" Frankie challenged, sick with worry. "How do you know that?"

"I just do," Brian answered quietly. "I just do."

In less than half an hour, while Luke was still in surgery, they started coming. The members of his family, by blood and by badge. Word had spread fast. The hallways began to fill up.

"Oh, dear Lord, they brought us another one," Constance Abernathy, the head nurse on the ground floor groaned as she looked around the area just outside the OR. Recognizing the chief of detectives, she approached Brian in hopes of securing an ally just this once. "Chief Cavanaugh, would it do any good if I asked your people to use the waiting rooms the way they're supposed to?" she asked.

"You could ask," Brian replied with an understanding smile. "But I really doubt that it'll do any good."

The nurse sighed, shaking her head. "That's what I thought. Well, at least try your best not to block the doors," she requested before she retreated.

By the time Luke's mother knew what had happened, Luke was out of surgery and being taken to the recovery room. She arrived at the hospital just as Luke's surgeon came out to report on his condition.

The entire area turned as one, their attention focused on the man in green scrubs.

"All I can say," Dr. Goldfarb said, addressing Brian and the ashen-faced women on either side of him, Maeve and Frankie, "is that he has the Cavanaugh luck. It was touch-and-go for a bit, but we got the bullet and we managed to stop the internal bleeding. He'll be fine. He just needs some rest."

Maeve threw her arms around the doctor's neck. "Thank you!" Then, releasing him from her grasp, she anxiously asked, "Can we see him?"

"He'll be unconscious for a while, even after he gets out of recovery." He looked around at the crowded area. "There's no point in all of you waiting around here through the night. Go home, people. I'll have his nurse give you a call, Chief," he said, addressing Brian, "once your boy's regained consciousness."

"If you don't mind, I'll stay," Frankie said to the doctor. Her tone told the surgeon that even if he did mind, it didn't matter. She was staying.

Dr. Goldfarb nodded, sensing that arguing would do no good. "I'll have someone give you his room number once he gets one."

"Dear, you look worn out," Maeve told her kindly when the surgeon had left. "Are you sure you want to stay here at the hospital?"

There was no question in Frankie's mind that she was staying. "I've got no place else to be."

Maeve sighed and nodded. Turning toward Brian,

she murmured, "Looks like my boy's got himself a stubborn one."

Brian chuckled softly. "I'd expect nothing less."

Frankie set up camp in Luke's room, prepared to wait as long as it took to see him open his eyes again.

In the midst of her vigil, White Hawk came to tell her that the man who had tried to kill her was being arrested and officially charged not just for her attempted murder, but with the murders of nine women.

"Just thought you'd want to know that it looks like the case is closed. Williams became unhinged with his lawyer sitting right there, screaming that it was all Lisa's fault."

She should be feeling better about this than she did, Frankie thought. She'd lived up to her promise to Kris. But all she could think about was being able to see Luke open his eyes. He still hadn't done that.

"Did you find out who Lisa really was?" she asked White Hawk, since he'd been nice enough to come and give her an update.

"Once we got a warrant to search his home," he answered. "Apparently, Lisa was his fiancée, just the way he said. She left him standing at the altar. When he went to confront her, he found her on the floor, a syringe in her arm. She'd died of a drug overdose after having been clean for over a year.

"Turns out this Lisa looked just like all the women he'd killed. My guess is that Williams searched out women who had kicked the habit. He tried to make them pay for what Lisa had done to him. Sick bastard," he commented, shaking his head.

The victory still felt hollow to her. But at least she could comfort herself knowing that Williams wouldn't be killing any other women. "I second that observation," she told White Hawk.

About to open the door and leave, White Hawk stopped for a moment and looked at her. "Why don't you go home, Frankie?" he suggested. "I'll take over watching him for a while and I'll call you the minute O'Bannon opens those piercing green eyes of his."

But she shook her head. "Not that I don't appreciate the offer, but that's all right. I wouldn't be able to sleep anyway. I'd rather be right here—so I can read him the riot act the minute he wakes up for jumping in front of that bullet the way that he did."

"Could be why he's still sleeping," White Hawk guessed, looking at his partner. He patted her shoulder. "Take it easy on yourself, Frankie," he told her just before he left the hospital room.

With a sigh, Frankie settled back in her chair, prepared to go on waiting indefinitely.

"Is he gone?"

Frankie swallowed a yelp as she bolted upright. For a second, she thought her mind was playing tricks on her. She'd been sitting here, keeping vigil for close to two days now. Other people had dropped in, bringing her food. Eventually, they left, but she had stubbornly refused to go. She'd wished Luke into consciousness so often that she was certain she'd imagined his voice just now.

And then his eyes opened.

She drew in her breath, willing herself to remain calm rather than hugging him as hard as she could. "You mean White Hawk?" she asked. "Yes, he's gone. You were awake?" She heard her voice go up, but she couldn't stop herself. "Why didn't you say something?"

Luke took a deep breath and found that that really hurt. He was going to have to be careful for a while and that didn't sit well with him. He was used to thinking of himself as invulnerable.

"Because I wanted to talk to you first," he told her. "Alone." He had her attention. Now he had to find the right way to say this. "Did you mean all that?"

She had no idea what he was referring to. She'd talked to him a lot in the last two days, hoping to wake him up. "All what?"

"What you were shouting at me just after I took that bullet for you." He didn't know if she understood, so he elaborated further. "That you cared about me."

"You heard that?" she asked him, stunned. At the time she'd been sure that he was at death's door, cracking it open.

"Yes. I heard you offer to go down into the bowels of hell to drag me back, too." He smiled and found that at least *that* didn't hurt. "Not the most romantic proclamation, but I've got to admit, it's original."

"If you heard all that, why didn't you say something?" she demanded. She'd been half out of her mind with worry.

"I wasn't exactly in any shape to carry on a conversation," he reminded her.

Her knees felt oddly weak. She had to grip the armrests in order to push herself up out of the chair. "Well, since you're conscious, I'd better let your family know." Turning, she began to head for the door.

"I love you."

That stopped her cold in her tracks. And then her heart accelerated. Frankie turned slowly around to look at him.

"That's the pain medicine talking," she told him warily.

"No," he corrected, "that's the man who came back from the dead talking. C'mere," he beckoned her over. She approached him as if she was crossing a layer of thin ice, thinking that, at any moment, she'd go plunging into the water. "I don't want to waste time anymore, Frankie," he told her. "I love you and I gather that since you've been sitting here for—how long?" he asked.

"Two days," she answered.

"For two days," he continued, "that you have feelings for me, too." He looked at her. "Do you?"

"You're a damn idiot, you know that?" she cried. Leaning over him, tears streaming down her face, she ordered, "Shut up and kiss me."

"Is that a yes?"

"Yes," she sobbed just before she sealed her mouth to his.

Epilogue

She decided to give Luke some space.

After everything he'd been through, Frankie felt that he needed to be left alone. So she stepped back and let his family—his mother and his siblings—take Luke home en masse. Though she ached to see him, she refrained, thinking it best if she held herself in check.

Instead, she filled up her time doing paperwork, both her own and Luke's. She deliberately did as thorough a job as she could writing up both reports. Together with the one that White Hawk wrote, she felt that a clear, concise picture of everything that went down was presented.

There was enough evidence, Sean told her after everything had been catalogued, to put Williams away for the rest of his life.

We got 'im, Kris, Frankie thought as she left the precinct after putting in an extra-long day. *We got the SOB who killed you.*

She let out a shaky breath. It wasn't going to bring her cousin back and revenge didn't taste nearly as sweet as she'd hoped it would, but at least she had the satisfaction of knowing that Williams would never cause another family grief, never rob another young woman of her future.

It was when she came to a stop at the second red light that Frankie realized she wasn't driving home. At least, not to *her* home. Lost in thought, she'd automatically wound up driving toward Luke's house.

At the next light, she seriously considered making a U-turn so she could head to her apartment complex.

You can't avoid him forever.

White Hawk had told her that Luke was making progress, getting better faster than the doctor had thought he would. "He's been asking after you," Luke's partner had told her tonight, just as he was leaving the squad room.

There was no judgment in his voice, no note of curiosity as to why she hadn't gone to see Luke when everyone else obviously had. White Hawk had only stated a fact and let her digest it, leaving her to make of it what she would.

Pressing her lips together, Frankie gave up the idea of retracing her steps and continued driving to Luke's house.

Luke's mother opened the door when she rang the bell. The woman's face instantly lit up.

"Frankie, come in!" Maeve invited warmly.

Feeling awkward, Frankie remained standing on the doorstep. Maybe this was a bad idea, after all.

"I don't want to intrude. I just wanted to find out how he was doing," she explained, paving the way for her retreat.

But Maeve grabbed her hand and tugged Frankie across the threshold.

"Come see for yourself, dear." She was leaving Frankie with no choice.

Her cold feet froze over and she shook her head. "No, really, I don't—"

"Oh, come on, dear," Maeve urged. "You can keep him company. I have to be going. I have a shift to cover," she explained. "And Luke's been asking for you," Maeve added, lowering her voice as if she was sharing a secret with a beloved friend.

Grabbing her purse, she switched positions with Frankie with the practiced ease of a professional magician.

"Go to him." It was almost an order. She uttered it in her wake.

And then the door closed. Maeve was gone, leaving her standing inside.

When had she gotten to be such a coward? Frankie silently demanded. Maybe when the stakes had gotten so high. The next moment, Frankie lost her one and only opportunity for retreat.

"Who was at the door, Mom?" Luke called out, slowly making his way into the room.

Frankie ran her tongue over her dry lips. Turning around to face him, she answered, "I was."

"I can see that," Luke said. With effort, he lowered himself down onto the sofa. "The prodigal detective returns," he quipped. His eyes swept over her, taking full measure. She looked even better than he remembered. "You know, everybody's come by to see how I was doing since I got home from the hospital. Except for the serial killer, of course. And you." His eyes held her prisoner. "Williams is in prison. What's your excuse?"

Frankie shrugged, dismissing the question. "I was filling out our reports. Yours and mine."

He'd been home almost five days. "How? Were you writing them longhand by using a pen in your teeth?"

She glanced away. "I was being thorough."

He knew better than that. "No, you were being a coward."

Her head jerked up. "What?" she demanded, her eyes suddenly blazing.

There was the woman he loved.

"You heard me. A coward," Luke repeated, then elaborated on his assessment. "You let down your guard and said some things, and now you're trying to run from the consequences."

She thought back to the ambulance ride, to how terrified she'd been that he was going to die. "Look, about that, we both said things in the heat of the moment and we need to clear the air. I want you to know that I'm not holding you to any of it."

Luke remained silent for so long, she thought he was letting her know that he wanted her to leave. Just as she began to rise, he said, "Maybe I want you to hold me to it."

Frankie didn't believe him. Didn't believe in

happily-ever-after when it came to her. "You don't know what you're saying."

Luke sighed. "How long are you going to keep doing this?"

"What do you mean? Doing what?"

"I mean, how long are you going to keep denying what's right in front of you? Frankie, I took a bullet for you. In some countries, we'd practically be engaged. What do I have to do to convince you that you mean the world to me? That nothing is more important to me than you are?"

She was afraid allow herself to believe that. Really afraid. "I—"

"Now, if you don't feel the same way that I do, all right, I can accept that," he told her. "But if you're just running scared, then no, I *can't* accept that. I love you, Frankie. And it's not the pain medication talking," he said, recalling what she'd told him the first time he'd said the words, "because I'm not on any pain medication. That's just me talking. So, what do you say?"

She was afraid of what would happen if she said yes, but more afraid of what would happen if she said no and turned away.

"Is it always going to be like this?" Frankie asked. "You drowning me in rhetoric?"

"No, not always," he answered, the corners of his mouth curving. "Sometimes I won't say a word."

"When?" she asked, sinking down next to him on the sofa. "When we're asleep?"

"No." He threaded his fingers through her hair, caressing her cheek. "When we're making love."

The warmth was starting. The warmth that even

now was flowing through her body. The warmth that only he was capable of creating within her. "I think I can live with that."

"Can you live with me?" he asked softly.

For a second, her heart stopped beating. It felt as if every fiber of her being was holding its breath. "You're asking me to live with you?"

He started to laugh, but it hurt too much so he stopped. "I'm asking you more than that, DeMarco. I'm asking you to marry me."

Her heart launched into triple time as she stared at Luke, not sure that she'd heard him correctly. "You're what?"

Luke took her hands into his. "I'd drop to one knee if I could, but if I did, you'd have to help me up again." Before she could say anything, Luke was asking her that all-important question he'd been rehearsing in his mind ever since he'd opened his eyes in the hospital and seen her sitting there. "Francesca DeMarco, will you marry me?"

Frankie's mouth dropped open. For a moment, it was too dry for her to say anything. And then she asked, "You're serious."

"Completely," he answered. "And I'll keep asking you until you say yes."

"I thought you said that you could accept my not feeling about you the way you felt about me," she reminded him. She wanted to be absolutely sure he wanted her before she accepted his proposal, that he wouldn't suddenly change his mind.

"I lied."

Frankie couldn't maintain any of her barriers any longer. "Then I guess I should say yes, shouldn't I?"

He grinned at her. "I like the sound of that. Know what else I like?" he asked.

"What?" she uttered breathlessly.

He didn't bother answering her.

He showed her instead.

Showed her for the rest of the evening. And then the following morning, as well.

* * * * *

Don't forget previous titles in the
CAVANAUGH JUSTICE *series:*

CAVANAUGH ON CALL
CAVANAUGH IN THE ROUGH
CAVANAUGH COLD CASE
CAVANAUGH OR DEATH
HOW TO SEDUCE A CAVANAUGH
CAVANAUGH FORTUNE
CAVANAUGH STRONG

Available now from Harlequin Romantic Suspense!

A JOGGER SPOTTED the body floating in the Anacostia River just south of the John Philip Sousa Bridge.

"I hate these kinds of calls," Lieutenant Sam Holland said to her partner, Detective Freddie Cruz, as she battled District traffic on their way to the city's southeastern quadrant. "No one knows if this is a homicide, but they call us in anyway. We get to stand around and sweat our balls off while the ME does her thing."

"I hesitate to point out, Lieutenant, that you don't actually *have* balls to sweat off."

"You know what I mean!"

"Yeah, I do," he said with a sigh. "It's going to be a long, hot, smelly Friday down at the river waiting to find out if we're needed."

"I gotta have a talk with Dispatch about when we're to be called and when we are *not* to be called."

"Let me know how that goes."

"To make this day even better, after work I have to go to a fitting for my freaking bridesmaid dress. I'm too damned old to be a damned bridesmaid."

His snort of laughter only served to further irritate her, which of course made him laugh harder.

"It's not funny!"

"Yeah, it really is." With dark brown hair, an always-tan complexion and the perfect amount of stubble on his jaw, he really was too cute for words, not that she'd *ever* tell him that. Everywhere they went together, women took notice of him. For all he cared. He was madly in love with Elin Svendsen and looking forward to their autumn wedding. Wiping laughter tears from his brown eyes, he said, "I won't make you wear a dress when you're my best-man woman."

"Thank God for that. I need to stop making friends. That was my first mistake."

"Poor Jeannie," he said of their colleague, Detective Jeannie McBride, who was getting married next weekend. "Does she have any idea that she has a hostile bridesmaid in her wedding party?"

"Of course she does. Her sisters left me completely out of the planning of the shower, no doubt at her request. I'll be forever grateful for that small favor." Sam shuddered recalling an afternoon of horrifyingly stupid "shower games," paper plates full of ribbons and bows, and dirty jokes about the wedding night for two people who'd been living together for more than a year. The whole thing had given her hives.

But Jeannie... She'd loved every second of it, and

seeing her face lit up with joy had gone a long way toward alleviating Sam's hives. After everything Jeannie had been through to get to her big day, no one was happier for her—or happier to stand up for her—than Sam. Not that she'd ever tell anyone that either. She had a reputation to maintain, after all.

She'd been in an unusually cranky mood since her husband, Nick, left for Iran two weeks ago for what should've been a five-day trip but had twice been extended. If he didn't get home soon, she wouldn't be responsible for her actions. In addition to worrying about his safety in a country known for being less than friendly toward Americans, she'd also discovered how entirely reliant upon him she'd become over the last year and a half. It was ridiculous, really. She was a strong, independent woman who'd taken care of herself for years before he'd come back into her life. So how had he turned her into a simpering, whimpering, cranky mess simply by leaving her for two damned weeks?

Naturally, the people around her had noticed that she was out of sorts. Their adopted thirteen-year-old son, Scotty, asked every morning before he left for baseball camp when Dad would be home, probably because he was tired of dealing with her by himself. Freddie and the others at work had been giving her a wide berth, and even the reporters who hounded her mercilessly had backed off after she'd bitten their heads off a few too many times.

During infrequent calls from Nick, he'd been rushed and annoyed and equally out of sorts, which didn't do much to help her bad mood. Two more days.

Two more long, boring, joyless days and then he'd be home and things could get back to normal.

What did it say about her that she was actually *glad* to have a floater to deal with to keep her brain occupied during the last two days of Nick's trip? *It means you have it bad for your husband, and you've become far too dependent on him if two weeks without him turns you into a cranky cow.* Sam despised her voice of reason almost as much as she despised Nick being so far away from her for so long.

Twenty minutes after receiving the call from Dispatch, Sam and Freddie made it to M Street Southeast, which was lined with emergency vehicles of all sorts—police, fire, EMS, medical examiner.

"Major overkill for a floater," Sam said as they got out of the car she'd parked illegally to join the party on the riverbank. "What the hell is EMS doing here?"

"Probably for the guy who found the body. Word is he was shook up."

Dense humidity hit her at the same time as the funk of the rank-smelling river. "God, it's hotter than the devil's dick today."

"Honestly, Sam. That's disgusting."

"Well, you gotta figure the devil's dick is pretty hot due to the neighborhood he hangs in, right?"

He rolled his eyes and held up the yellow crime-scene tape for her. Patrol had taped off the Anacostia Riverwalk Trail to keep the gawkers away.

The closer they got to the river's edge, the more Sam began to regret the open-toe sandals she'd worn in deference to the oppressive July heat. The squish of Anacostia River mud between her toes was almost as gross as the smell of the river itself. She had her shoulder-length hair up in a clip that left her neck exposed to the merciless sun.

Tactical Response teams had boats on the scene, and from her vantage point on the riverbank, Sam could see the red ponytail belonging to the Chief Medical Examiner, Dr. Lindsey McNamara. She was too far out for Sam to yell to her for an update.

"Let's talk to the guy who called it in," she said to Freddie.

They traipsed back the way they'd come, with Sam trying to ignore the disgusting mud between her toes. Officer Beckett worked the tapeline at the northern end of the area they'd cordoned off. He nodded at them. "Afternoon, Lieutenant. Lovely day to spend by the river."

"Indeed. I would've packed a picnic had I known we were coming. Where's the guy who called it in?"

"Over there with EMS." Beckett pointed to a cluster of people taking advantage of the shade under a huge oak tree. "He was hysterical when he realized the blob was a body."

"Did you get a name?"

Beckett consulted his notebook. "Mike Lonergan. He works at the Navy Yard and runs out here every day at noon." He tore out the page that had Lonergan's full name, address and cell phone number written on it and gave it to Sam.

"Good work, Beckett. Thanks. Keep everyone out of here until we know whether or not this is a crime scene."

"Yes, ma'am. Will do."

"Why would anyone run out here during the hottest part of the day?" Sam asked Freddie as they made their way to where Lonergan was being seen to by the paramedics.

"For something called exercise, I'd imagine."

"When did you become such a smart-ass? You used to be such a nice Christian boy."

"Things began to go south for me when I got assigned to a smart-ass lieutenant who's been a terrible influence on my sweet, young mind."

"Right." Amused by him as always, Sam drew out the single word for effect. "You were easily led." She approached the paramedics who were hovering over Lonergan. "We'd like a word with Mr. Lonergan," she said to the one who seemed to be in charge.

He used a hand motion to tell his team to allow her and Freddie in. The witness wore a tank top, running shorts and high-tech running shoes. Sam put him at midthirties.

"Mr. Lonergan, I'm Lieutenant Holland—"

"I know who you are." His shoulders were wrapped in one of those foil thingies that runners used to keep from dehydrating or overheating or something like that. What did she know about such things? She got most of her exercise having wild sex with her husband. Except for recently, thus her foul mood.

Lonergan's dark blond hair was wet with perspiration. His brown eyes were big and haunted as he looked up at them.

"Can you tell us what you saw?" Ever since she'd taken down a killer at the inaugural parade, she was recognized everywhere she went. She hated that and yearned for the days when no one recognized her. But that ship had sailed the minute her sexy young husband became the nation's vice president late last year. Her blown cover was entirely his fault, and she liked to remind him of that every chance she got.

"I was running on the trail like I do every day, and when I came around that bend there, I saw something in the water." He took a drink from a bottle of water, and Sam took note of the slight tremble in his hand. "At first I thought it was a garbage bag, but when I looked closer, I saw a hand." He shuddered. "That's when I called 911."

"How far out was it?" Sam asked.

"About twenty feet from the bank of the river."

"Was there anything else you could tell us about the body?"

"I think it's a woman."

"Why do you say that?" Freddie asked.

"There was hair." Lonergan took another drink of water. "Once I realized what I was looking at, I could see long hair fanned out around the head." He looked up at them. "Do you think it's that student who went missing?"

Sam made sure her expression gave nothing away. "We'd have no way to know that at this point." The entire Metro PD had been searching for nineteen-year-old Ruby Denton for more than two weeks. She'd come to the District to take summer classes at Capitol University and hadn't been seen since her first night on campus. The story had garnered national attention thanks in large part to the efforts of her family in Kentucky.

"I bet it's her," Lonergan said.

"Do me a favor and keep that thought to yourself

for now. No sense upsetting the family before we know anything for certain."

"That's true."

Sam handed him her card. "If you think of anything else, let me know."

"I will." After a pause, he said, "I was out here yesterday, and she wasn't there. I would've noticed if she'd been there."

"That's good to know. Thanks for your help."

"It's sad, you know? For someone to end up like that."

"Yes, it is." She stepped away from him to confer with the paramedic in charge. "Is he okay?"

"Yeah, he's in shock. He'll be fine. You think it's Ruby Denton?"

"I'll tell you the same thing I just told him—we have no way to know until Dr. McNamara gets the body back to the lab. Until then, we'd be speculating, and that sort of thing only makes a hellish situation worse for a family looking for their daughter. Ask your people to keep their mouths shut."

"Yes, ma'am. No one will hear anything from my team."

"Thank you."

"What's going on over there?" Freddie asked, drawing Sam's attention to the tapeline, where Beckett was arguing with a bunch of suits.

"Let's go find out."

They walked back the way they'd come, along the trail to where Beckett held his own against four men in suits with reflective glasses and attitudes that immediately identified them as federal agents.

"What's the problem, gentlemen?" Sam asked.

"There she is," one of them said in a low growl that immediately raised Sam's hackles.

"Let us in," another one said. "Right now."

"I'm not letting you in until you tell me what you want," Beckett said. "This is a potential crime scene—"

"We need to speak to Mrs. Cappuano." The one who seemed to be in charge of the Fed squad took another step forward. "It's urgent."

Sam's heart dropped to her belly and for a brief, horrifying second she feared her legs would give out under her. *Nick...* Why would federal agents have tracked her down at a crime scene in the middle of her workday unless something had happened to him?

Please no.

Sam immediately began bargaining with a higher power she didn't believe in. She'd give up anything, anything in this world except Scotty, if it would keep the man in front of her from saying words that could never be unsaid or unheard.

Only Freddie's arm around her shoulders kept her from buckling in the few seconds it took for Sam to recover herself enough to speak. "What do you want with me?"

"We need you to come with us, ma'am."

"That's not happening until you tell us who you are and what you want," Freddie said.

In unison they flashed four federal badges.

"United States Secret Service," the one in charge said. "We need you to come with us, ma'am."

Sam didn't recognize any of them. Why would she? Nick's detail was in Iran, and Scotty's was with him. "I... I'm working here. I can't..." Bile burned her throat as her lunch threatened to reappear. With her heart beating so hard she could hear the echo of it strumming in her ears, she somehow managed to choke back the nausea. Later she'd be thankful she hadn't puked on the agents' shoes. Right now, however, she couldn't think about anything other than Nick. "Has something happened to my husband?"

Freddie tightened his grip on her shoulder, letting her know his thoughts mirrored hers. That didn't do much to comfort her.

Looking down at her with a stone-faced glare, the agent said, "We're under orders to bring you in. We're not at liberty to discuss the particulars with you at this time."

"What the hell does that mean?" Freddie asked. "You can't just take her. She's not under Secret Service protection, and she's working."

"I'm afraid we *can* take her, and we will, by force if necessary."

"What the fuck?" Beckett spoke for all of them. At some point he'd moved to the other side of her.

Like someone flipped a switch, they moved with military precision, busting through the tapeline, grabbing hold of her arms and quickly extracting her before her stunned colleagues could react. Sam fought them, but she was no match for four huge, muscled, well-dressed men who whisked her away with frightening efficiency.

In the background, she could hear Freddie and Beckett screaming, swearing—at least Beckett was—and giving chase, but they, too, were no match for this group. Before she knew what hit her, she was inside the cool darkness of one in the Secret Service's endless fleet of black SUVs, the doors locking with a sound that echoed like a shotgun blast.

"Move," the agent in charge ordered.

The car lurched forward just as Freddie and Beckett reached it. Freddie pounded once against the side window with a closed fist before the car pulled out of his reach.

Sam watched the scene unfold around her with a detached feeling of shock and fear. Something awful must've happened. That was the only possible reason for this dramatic scene. She was far too afraid for Nick to work up the fury she'd normally feel at being kidnapped by federal agents. Her hands were shaking, and her entire body was covered in cold chills.

If Nick had been harmed in some way or if he was... *No, no, no, not going there.* If he was hurt, what did it matter if Secret Service agents had grabbed her? What would anything matter?

She bit back the overwhelming fear and forced herself to focus. "Would someone please tell me what's going on here?"

Don't miss the explosive new book in
New York Times *bestselling author*
Marie Force's FATAL *series*

FATAL THREAT

Available August 2017 wherever
Harlequin HQN titles are sold.

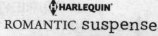

SPECIAL EXCERPT FROM

HARLEQUIN®

ROMANTIC suspense

*After befriending Mandy Wright in a snowstorm,
Brody Booth is certain they'll stay "just friends." That
is, until a killer forces Brody into a protector role that
brings all his worst fears about himself to bear.*

Read on for a sneak preview of
SHELTERED BY THE COWBOY
by New York Times *bestselling author* Carla Cassidy,
the next thrilling installment of
THE COWBOYS OF HOLIDAY RANCH.

Most people gave him a wide berth, but not Mandy. He
shoved those thoughts away. She was nothing more to
him than a woman in trouble, and he just happened to be
in a position to help her. It was nothing more than that
and nothing less.

He left the bathroom and blinked in surprise. All the
lights were off except a nightstand lamp next to Mandy's
bed and the glow of two lit candles on the same stand.
The room now smelled of apples and cinnamon.

"I hope you don't mind the candles. I always light a
couple before I go to sleep."

"I don't mind," he replied. Hell yes, he minded the
candles that painted her face in beautiful shadows and
light. Hell yes, he minded the candles that made the room
feel so much smaller and much more intimate.

He walked over to the sofa and found a bed pillow and
a soft, hot pink blanket. He placed his gun on the coffee
table, unfolded the blanket and then stretched out.

"All settled?" she asked.

"I'm good," he replied.

She turned off the lamp, leaving only the candlelight radiance to create a small illumination. Too much illumination. From his vantage point he could see her snuggled beneath the covers. He closed his eyes.

"Brody?"

"Yeah?" he answered without opening his eyes.

"Somehow, some way I'll make all this up to you."

Visions instantly exploded in his head, erotic visions of the two of them making love. He jerked his head to halt them. "You don't have to make anything up to me," he said gruffly. "Now let's get some sleep."

"Okay. Good night, Brody."

"Good night," he replied.

Seconds ticked by and then minutes. When he finally opened his eyes again she appeared to be sleeping. Candlelight danced across her features, highlighting her brows, her cheekbones and her lips.

He couldn't be her friend. She was too much of a temptation and he couldn't be friends with a woman he wanted. He didn't want to be friends with anyone.

He'd see her through this threat, and then he had to walk away from her and never look back.

Don't miss
SHELTERED BY THE COWBOY by Carla Cassidy,
available September 2017 wherever
Harlequin® Romantic Suspense books
and ebooks are sold.

www.Harlequin.com

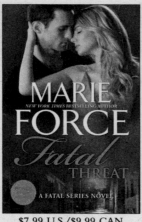
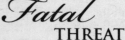

THE WORLD IS BETTER WITH

Romance

Harlequin has everything from contemporary, passionate and heartwarming to suspenseful and inspirational stories.

Whatever your mood, we have a romance just for you!

Connect with us to find your next great read, special offers and more.

f /HarlequinBooks

🐦 @HarlequinBooks

www.HarlequinBlog.com

www.Harlequin.com/Newsletters

HARLEQUIN®

A *Romance* FOR EVERY MOOD™

www.Harlequin.com